The Empress: A Promise of Rain

VAL TOBIN

ISBN: 978-1-988609-23-2

DEDICATION

To Bob, Jenn, Mark, Chanelle, Savannah, Jack, Ian,
and Scully.

ACKNOWLEDGMENTS

Thank you to Alis B. Kennedy, PhD; Wendy Quirion; Val Cseh; John Erwin; Michelle Legere; and Diane King of The Hedge Witch (www.thehedgewitch.com) for beta reading, professional advice, and suggestions.
Developmental editing by Tahlia Newland tahlianewland.com. Thank you, Tahlia.
Thank you to Kelly Hartigan (XterraWeb) editing.xterraweb.com for her superb line editing and proofreading.
Thanks to Sharon Brownlie of Aspire Book Covers (www.aspirebookcovers.com) for the amazing cover.

CHAPTER 1

A faerie servant girl bustled around Dakota Lawson, adjusting the bridal gown and veil the young dhampir woman wore. To the untrained eye, she appeared human, and in Autumnland, species identification pins weren't required. On the Earth plane, she'd worn the pin identifying her as a half-vampire. But the faerie didn't need to see a pin. Everyone in the kingdom knew who and what her mistress was.

"You're beautiful, my lady," the servant girl, three years younger than Dakota's nineteen, said with a warm smile.

"Thank you, Lysandra." Dakota returned the smile with one of her own, though hers held more tentativeness than warmth. Even after a year-long engagement, she still found it difficult to believe that she and faerie prince Culain Shiels would wed.

She called up his handsome face in her mind's eye. Using visions of his sandy-blond hair and emerald eyes, she anchored herself to reality and strove to forget the

1

man she'd once loved and had foolishly expected to marry. Someday, she'd look back on the relationship with fondness. Her scribbles of *Mrs. Dakota Davis* and *Mr. and Mrs. Josh Davis* in notebooks that would turn to dust over the years would elicit nostalgia rather than pain. Would it take decades to heal? Centuries? Either way, Josh, as a human, would be dead, and she and her prince would continue living out their long lives— hopefully happily. *Because I love Culain.*

She honestly did. But loving him, marrying him, came with a price that made her heart ache to pay it. It would also, however, bring her closer to her ultimate goal: revenge. When she held power—genuine power she could wield as a ruler of the fae—she'd ensure those who'd robbed her of her previous life paid.

Breath held, she turned and faced the mirror. Her golden hair cascaded down her back in loose curls, and her skin was pale and flawless. She wore a stunning emerald gown made from the finest silk and adorned with intricate lace and sparkling jewels. It'd surprised her to learn they expected her to wear green, a color that symbolized fertility, life, and abundance. No virgin white for the fae—though they'd demanded she remain a virgin until her wedding. Symbols of fertility, growth, and prosperity meant more to them than those of chastity for the woman who'd become their queen.

The breath escaped in a rush. She skimmed her fingers over the pearl necklace nestled against her throat with hesitant fingertips: seven large pearls centered within a string of tiny ones. She'd resisted when Culain presented her with the bauble and asked her to wear it at the wedding.

"Pearls represent tears," she'd said. "They're for funerals."

She didn't consider herself superstitious, but her mother had raised her on this belief.

"You're among the faeries now, my darling," he'd replied. "For us, they symbolize love and represent Aphrodite."

With a blush, he'd added that they also symbolized purity and innocence, so they hadn't excluded the virginity piece of the transaction.

She'd accepted the necklace as well as the myrtle wreath—another symbol of love, fertility, and chastity—for her hair, to which Lysandra had attached a lacy white veil.

At her servant's insistence, they applied minimal makeup. The maid had the right of it. A touch of blush on the bride's cheeks, a hint of gloss on her lips, and one press with the eyelash curler made her look fresh and dewy. Anything else would've overpowered her delicate features.

Dakota turned to the faerie girl, who fussed with the wedding dress's bustle. Her voice shook with nerves as she said, "You've done an amazing job."

Lysandra smiled and curtsied. "'Twas my pleasure, Your Highness."

A knock at the door sent the servant girl scurrying to open it. Muffled voices floated in from the hallway, and then Lysandra replied, "Two minutes."

She shut the door without another word, so the guards must've simply wanted to fetch the bride for the ceremony.

Heart fluttering, Dakota stepped forward, only to pause and scan the room. "My shoes. Where are my shoes?"

"Don't fret, my lady. I know exactly where they are." The maid rushed around the bed and bent down.

"Right here, by the vanity."

When she stood up again, she held low-heeled emerald sandals adorned with bright white flowers and pearls to match Dakota's necklace and wreath.

Lysandra carried the shoes to her mistress and helped her put them on. She then handed her long, emerald gloves. The soft, cool silk against Dakota's skin triggered a sensation that her human half felt intensely. A vampire would've noticed the touch but wouldn't have appreciated the texture. Softness, for them, was but a memory.

"Perfect, Your Highness," the faerie girl said as she stepped back to admire the view. "If you're ready, they're waiting for you in the garden."

Lysandra picked up a bouquet from the table in the sitting area. She carried it to her mistress, who buried her nose in lavender, roses, and carnations in varying shades of purple and white. A white ribbon tied everything together, but a fall of eucalyptus leaves obscured most of it. Dakota sucked in another breath and slowly released it. She savored the floral scents that were, again, more noticeable to her human side—as were the nerves she experienced at the prospect of her upcoming nuptials. The butterflies flitting in her stomach settled after another deep inhale, and she smiled, this time with genuine warmth.

Culain.

Her pulse pounded. Tonight, they'd have their wedding night. Their first time together as husband and wife. Her first time—ever. That thought had her stomach fluttering again but with excitement rather than fear. She'd yearned to make love with Culain for so long, but the fae court was positively medieval in its customs and traditions. Not even Culain dared break

4

them, and faerie society afforded men far more leniency in the sex-before-marriage arena. Why, he behaved more prudishly than she did, but she questioned how much of that was an act. Sometimes, she wondered if he'd slept with someone else before they'd met, but she never asked him. She was positive he'd remained faithful to her once she'd entered his life, not only because custom demanded it but because he truly wanted to.

This'll be one hell of a wedding night. Her smile, this time, was mischievous.

Lysandra led Dakota from the room and handed her off to two official guards dressed in their finest livery of reds and golds. They each carried a spear, point up, that was taller than all of them. Dakota, at five-foot-ten, towered over most humans, including many men, but among the fae, she was of average height for a woman. The men were even taller than that. Culain hit six-one.

The guards walked her through halls decked out in ribbons and finery. The entire palace was decorated for the royal wedding, and it'd taken three weeks to get everything just right. She hadn't had to do any of the work herself, and part of her regretted it. They'd at least allowed her to make some of the decisions that affected her personally, such as choosing her wedding gown's style, if not the color. "They" meant Culain's family, since Dakota's family had no part to play in the wedding. King Killian had banned her father from the faerie realm, and her mother wanted nothing more to do with her. She had no one else on her side. Culain's brother, Colin, would escort her down the aisle and give her away.

Give me away. An ironic term, considering they bought me

from my mother. She'd never learned how much cash her mother had received in the transaction.

The guards' bootsteps echoed down the deserted hallway, drowning out the muted patter of Dakota's sandals. The empty corridors seemed eerie. Though typically bustling with activity, the halls had emptied as the minutes to the ceremony ticked down, the guests gathering in the massive garden. Those working behind the scenes also left the bedchambers' corridors, relocating to the kitchens, gardens, and banquet hall. Even outside the palace, those without an invitation or who weren't members of the well-to-do gathered to celebrate. A fair was set up on the fields beyond the castle's drawbridge, and the celebrations would carry on for the entire week.

The archway leading into the garden loomed ahead, and Dakota's steps involuntarily slowed. In consideration of her vampire half, the gardens and the paths that led to them had extra shade created with plants, trees, and strategically placed umbrellas and canopies. The half-vampire in her shunned direct sunlight, but her human half could tolerate it. Sunlight didn't burn her, but it prickled any exposed skin uncomfortably.

One guard gently placed a hand on her elbow, and she allowed him to guide her outside into the courtyard and onto the path that led to the ceremony. Bushes obscured the seating area, but rustling and soft murmurs betrayed the presence of the crowd awaiting her.

She didn't know her three bridesmaids well, but a young fae woman who'd befriended Dakota was her maid of honor. Alina Lawrimore smiled encouragement. She looked beautiful in the cream, strapless maid-of-honor dress the two friends had selected. Her bouquet of dried lavender, baby's breath flowers, and eucalyptus, their stems wrapped in burlap with lace detail, added color. Each bridesmaid wore a similar dress and carried a smaller, though similarly adorned, bouquet. Three groomsmen and Culain's best man paired up with the women. The men wore traditional fae garb with doublets and breeches rather than tuxedos, and each carried a ceremonial sword at his side.

A rustling in the leaves beside Dakota pulled her attention off the flowers. A hand touched her arm, and she stared into green eyes so like Culain's they startled her. But it wasn't her betrothed; it was his brother, here to walk her down the aisle.

Give me away.

Colin's lips quirked up. "You're not nervous, are you?"

The amusement in his voice placated her. He always found the humor in every situation. Culain was always so serious, but Colin made her laugh despite herself and her circumstances.

"As a long-tailed cat in a room full of rocking chairs." She grinned. "But I feel much better now you're here. How's Culain?" Was he as nervous and excited as she was? A temptation to peek around the foliage and get a glimpse of him overcame her. But she didn't want anyone to see her until she rounded the corner and walked to join him, so she suppressed the urge.

"He's happy." Colin's expression smoothed to almost serious. "I've never seen him so happy." He looked her up and down. "When he sees you, he'll be delirious."

Embarrassingly, she blushed, a drawback of her dhampir physiology. A true vampire didn't have the ability.

She dipped her head, acknowledging the compliment. "Thank you."

"After today, you'll be like a sister to me." He smiled again. "Which means I can tease you the way I do Culain."

She stifled a laugh. "I don't think so. You wouldn't be that merciless."

"Perhaps not. Perhaps sister isn't quite right." He winked as he offered her his arm, and she slipped her hand through the crook, wondering what that last remark meant.

The guard stepped from behind the bushes onto the pathway, the signal to start the ceremony. A row of musicians blanketed the garden with acoustic music. It had a sweet but moving melody and sounded Celtic, but she knew such tunes originated from the fae to the Celts. She let the melodies from lutes, violins, cellos, and a harp wash over her.

The bridesmaids and groomsmen went next.

Salton Hoxworth, the best man, sidled up to Alina, who took the arm the swarthy faerie from Southern Realm offered her.

Alina whispered, "I'm off," and the pair vanished around the corner.

Colin waited a few seconds before he stepped forward, Dakota matching his pace. His solidity kept any panic at bay. He really would make a wonderful brother-in-law. The Shiels boys—men—would also make outstanding leaders, and Culain, one day, would be king. That, she reminded herself, was why, in the end, she'd agreed to be sold into marriage like a slave.

CHAPTER 2

Culain wasn't wearing a tuxedo. While some faerie grooms these days wore clothing fashionable in the human world, the fae prince adhered to tradition and wore his ceremonial garb— mostly to please his father but also because Culain enjoyed following tradition. Instead of a tuxedo jacket, he wore a red and green doublet that brushed his hips. Gold-plated, intricately carved buttons adorned it. Underneath this were loose-fitting linen breeches held up by a jeweled belt. Soft brown calfskin boots covered his hose. A ceremonial sword, with jeweled hilt and scabbard, hung at his side. He'd avoided wearing a headdress of any kind, preferring to leave his shoulder-length sandy-blond hair uncovered. The last thing he wanted on his wedding night was hat head, and he refused to wear a crown. He wasn't king yet and considered crowns the height of pomposity for anyone other than the ruler.

As soon as the music started, his gaze flew to the entrance where, under the vine-covered arch, stood the guards who'd escorted Dakota, *my bride*, to the ceremony. The guards stepped aside, and the bridesmaids and accompanying groomsmen traipsed down the path. Alina followed with Salton at her side. Slowly, they strode down the stone aisle, Alina's gaze fixed on the front of the room.

For a moment, Culain's eyes locked with hers. She'd become friends with Dakota over the months, but he suspected Alina had never revealed to the dhampir girl her past relationship with the two Shiels brothers. Culain had considered revealing all to his fiancée, but in the end, he'd left it alone.

The past, as they say, is the past.

Why bring up an innocent childhood friendship that evolved into harmless teenage hormone-fueled games and introduced the three of them to sex play? They'd never quite crossed that final line, so Alina's virtue remained intact, but both brothers had explored her erotic offerings on multiple occasions.

While Culain hadn't minded sharing Alina with Colin, he had no intention of doing so with Dakota. Not that his brother had broached the subject. They were men now, each expected to marry and settle down. The older prince's betrothal had taken priority, but as second in line to the throne until Culain produced an heir, Colin, too, was obligated to wed.

Neither brother had been permitted to marry Alina.

While that had been fine with Culain, Colin resented it. He cared for her in more than a girl-who's-a-friend way, but her family's lack of prominence or wealth made her an unsuitable mate for a prince. The irony didn't escape them that Dakota's mother, from whom they'd purchased the dhampir girl, had been dirt-poor. Genes, in this case, mattered more than family wealth and prestige. Her vampire father was wealthy, but that also had no bearing on the match. Dakota was a perfect biological specimen for Culain, and dhampirs were more fertile than faerie women. She'd give him a half-fae half-dhampir child who'd survive to adulthood.

While Culain's mother had been purebred fae, as was his father, they hadn't had problems conceiving, but of the eight pregnancies she'd had, only Culain and Colin had survived to full-term. The king didn't want to take chances with his sons' offspring. He demanded they marry dhampir.

Culain spotted Colin next; then his gaze traveled to his brother's side to take in Dakota in all her splendor. He might've even gasped when he saw her.

She's radiant. She'd never been more beautiful. Of course, all brides glowed, much as all expectant mothers did, but his bride ... a knot formed in his throat.

How hokey. I'm not tearing up. Ridiculous. His chest swelled with pride.

The guests had risen from their seats when the music started, and all eyes now focused on his woman.

Culain shot a glance at his father, King Killian Shiels. He stood on the stone dais next to the high priest and also had his gaze riveted on the bride. The king's neutral expression betrayed nothing of what he was feeling. Were his father's thoughts on his own long-ago wedding day?

As he had so often since his mother's death, Culain wished she'd lived. The unfairness of losing her had never left him. Faeries were long-lived but mortal. They didn't die of old age or disease, but weapons or poisons could kill them, and his mother had been brutally slain.

The wedding party members arrived at their places in the enormous garden. The groomsmen stood to Culain's left while the bridesmaids formed a mirror-image line opposite them. Alina and Salton parted and joined their respective groups.

Dakota and Colin drew close, Culain's brother wearing a too serious expression.

He's trying not to laugh, the bugger. If he loses it, so will I. At least Colin was keeping it under control. So far.

Culain avoided meeting his brother's gaze. It wouldn't do for the princes to burst into guffaws during this solemn moment.

All thoughts of Colin and unbridled mirth flew from Culain's mind when his gaze landed on Dakota and reminded him of the point of the whole day. His bride. The beautiful dhampir woman he'd gotten to know over the last year of their engagement. She'd already held his hopes when he'd chosen her from a catalog of women, but she'd thoroughly captured his heart when he met her.

The mischief fled from Colin's eyes as the couple reached Culain.

Gently, Colin placed Dakota's hand in Culain's and said, "I give you this woman to be your bride, my brother. I place her in your trust and care."

Her eyes narrowed at the words, but her expression changed to warmth and affection when their hands met and she stared into his eyes.

"Thank you, brother. I accept the gift you offer and welcome her to my home and hearth." Culain held his breath, waiting for her response. He understood her reticence, her opposition to subjugating herself to her husband. The faerie ways seemed antiquated to a dhampir woman from the modern world, but she'd promised him she'd play along, for his sake, for love of him.

After what felt like an eternity, her lips parted, and she spoke. "Thank you, my prince. I surrender to your care."

Grateful she sounded as if she meant it, he led her to the place on the dais where the king and the high priest waited.

CHAPTER 3

The ceremony passed in a flurry of vows, prayers, readings, the exchange of the rings, and a jump over a broom. The newlyweds also added their names to a large book that contained only a small number of signatures. Dakota assumed the book was for royalty only, and the rest of the faerie population entered their marriages into a different one. Or maybe only royalty or upper-class faeries married here. *Then why bother to marry at all? For legal reasons? To please the gods?* Wouldn't it displease the gods that the prince married outside of his species? She still had so much to learn about the culture she'd embraced.

The high priest stood tall and, projecting to the far corners of the garden, he said, "I present to you Your Royal Highnesses Prince Culain and Princess Dakota Shiels."

Princess Dakota Shiels. She was a princess. She was a wife. The ceremony had ended, and her new life would begin in earnest. How quickly it had all happened, and time seemed to speed up even more the moment those words were spoken.

Before she knew it, her new husband was whisking her back down the path amid cheers and livelier Celtic music. Irish uilleann pipes had replaced the more delicate instruments. Her lips still tingled from Culain's kiss. For a blessed moment, for the length of that kiss, she'd shut out the crowds and her new father-in-law and the high priest and lost herself in her husband's embrace. It didn't last long, though, and she swept along the current of excitement with him toward the banquet hall.

The guards fell in around them as they left the garden courtyard and strode into the castle's side entrance.

Thankful she wore low-heeled shoes, she squeezed Culain's hand and gave him a sideways glance. He smiled as though to himself, and affection flooded her at the sight.

"A penny for your thoughts, husband." She loved the sound of the word. Husband. Her husband. *I'm a married woman!* It didn't seem real.

"A penny? My thoughts are worth more than that, wife, and we don't use human currency here." His smile broadened into a grin, and hers answered.

"What would you have me pay then?"

His brows rose suggestively. "You'll see when we retire to our bedchamber, which I hope will be sooner than later but fear will be very late."

Her body practically vibrated with anticipation. If they could outrun the guests and lose the guards, she'd gladly escape with him to his bedroom this second.

"Tell me now, and I'll pay you later." She waggled her brows in what she hoped was a beguiling manner, but he signaled her failure with a mirth-filled sputter.

"All right—and I'll hold you to it. I was thinking how badly I'd like to peer under that dress."

Her breath caught, and she choked on the retort she'd planned to make. His scent, so spicy and male, made her head swim. His suggestive banter made her ache for him more than ever.

She moaned. "You're torturing me, my prince."

"It'll be a long night," he responded, "but I promise you the wait will be worth it." He paused at the banquet hall's main entrance doors, which stood propped open. The couple were to lead the guests inside and take their places on the dais at the head table, which overlooked the hall.

This was the main banquet hall, where the kingdom held all major feasts and celebrations. Large mullioned windows let in bright sunlight. If Dakota were a full vampire, she'd have needed to cover up despite the glass the light traveled through—the parts not covered in stained-glass pictures. As it was, she preferred to stand in the shadows and looked forward to the freedom of movement nightfall would bring.

She kept her eyes averted from the walls that displayed exquisite tapestries depicting gorgeous fae in various historical settings. The grimmest scenes illustrated events from the Earth plane's species wars, when the fae had first unmasked and tried to integrate into the human world. They'd made the mistake then of allowing crossing between the worlds, and that had cost them the life of their queen, Culain's mother. Dakota always avoided staring at the scene showing the queen pinned to a tree with a huge spear through her chest and blood staining her white gown. She'd asked Culain once why they'd want that displayed in the banquet hall. He told her it was to remind them to never mix with anyone in the Earth plane and to trust no one outside their own kind.

"But you ... marry dhampirs." She'd almost said kidnap but stopped herself in time. She didn't want the discussion to digress into something unpleasant. This topic skirted the line.

"Those dhampirs integrate into our society," he replied. "We don't stray out into the mortal world. Well, not often," he added, referring to the fae custom of Running Loose, extended to faeries once they turned eighteen. They were given leave to venture into the physical plane to test the experience. Most returned, vowing never to leave the faerie realm again.

"Not a mortal world anymore," she said, thinking about the other magickal creatures that had unveiled. No one knew what had triggered the great unmasquing, but somehow, it had happened simultaneously worldwide.

"Even so," he'd said, "we keep to ourselves and shun what isn't like us. Dhampirs are the exception. It used to be humans we'd take. I'm grateful for the unmasquing. It created you, and now you'll be mine."

His explanation hadn't satisfied her, but she'd accepted it. Yet that meant every time she entered the hall, she kept her gaze away from the tapestries. Instead, she focused on the thick oak benches and tables in the dining area. Place settings organized the seating, but none of the tables had numbers, and none held seating lists or place cards. Most people sat at their usual places, and if someone strayed, no one minded.

An enormous fireplace, carved into the middle of one long wall, crackled with wood-burning flames, a throwback to before the unmasquing. But the castle wasn't completely medieval. Giant chandeliers, electrically powered, hung from the high, ornate ceiling.

A wide area in front of the rows of tables served as the dance floor. Tables along the side of the dancing space held urns for coffee, hot water for tea, and all the associated condiments. Baskets of dinner rolls already sat on the tables along with small dishes holding pats of sweet butter.

Culain escorted Dakota down the middle aisle and up the steps to their table. King Killian Shiels would take the center seat, Colin would sit on his left, Culain on his right, and Dakota would sit next to Culain. This was their typical arrangement. Their marriage hadn't changed the hierarchy yet. How would Culain inherit the crown if faeries didn't get old and die? She suspected King Killian planned to retire, but she couldn't guess how or when. He looked as spry as a thirty-year-old.

Culain waved away the guard who wanted to pull Dakota's chair out for her and did it himself. She smiled her appreciation, sat down, and scanned the room.

The wedding party all took seats at the large table, Alina sitting between Colin and Salton.

She must be in her glory. Alina had a long-standing crush on Colin, but she also had an attraction to Salton. Cattily, Dakota wondered who Alina didn't have a crush on. The fae woman kept her virtue—so to speak. She was no prude and admitted to having had trysts with Culain when they were younger. Dakota never let on that she knew his secret. She'd hoped Alina could reveal all the women in his past, especially if he'd slept with them, but as far as Alina knew, she'd been the only one he'd experimented with.

"He takes his royal responsibilities seriously," she'd told Dakota over glasses of wine one night during a sleepover in the dhampir woman's bedchamber. "A prince isn't supposed to risk fathering bastards."

"Are you sorry you two never slept together?" She knew she risked an emotional upheaval asking, but she had to know. What if Alina still pined for him?

"Not at all." Alina sighed. "I liked Culain, of course, and I'm not stupid. If he'd courted me, if he'd been allowed to court me, I'd have married him in an instant. But my heart favored Colin. He's the one that got away."

Dakota had masked her relief with sympathy for Alina's situation and a promise to help her friend find the man of her dreams who would make her forget Colin and royal dictates.

Culain prodded Dakota from her reminiscences. "A penny for your thoughts, wife."

Not about to tell him anything of her thoughts, she said, "I thought you didn't use human currency." She grinned and then leaned over and kissed him firmly on the mouth. Public displays of affection were not only accepted at the wedding feast, they were encouraged. The distraction worked. Amid cheers and whistles from the guests, he kissed her back with toe-curling passion, and the question remained unanswered.

CHAPTER 4

Late into the night, a crowd of wedding guests followed Dakota and Culain from the banquet hall to their bedchamber. It was tradition to escort the royal bride and groom to their room. From this night forward, his bedroom would belong to them both. While Dakota welcomed joining her new husband to live in his quarters, she'd grown to love her private rooms. Curling up on the couch in the sitting area before a roaring fire, a cup of tea or cocoa—or bottle of blood—on the table beside her, had become one of her favorite pastimes. Culain's room had a similar setup, but how often would she find herself alone in their bedroom?

Probably more than I think. What's my problem? Was it a problem? Nerves, she told herself. Wedding-night jitters were finally catching up to her, and she was creating problems that stoked anxiety.

Culain opened the door and ushered his bride inside. He turned on no lights, but since Dakota could see in the dark, she didn't care. Besides, he'd had the servants build a fire in the enormous stone fireplace. The soft orange glow provided enough illumination for what the couple had planned, and the shadows and gentle flickering gave the room a romantic ambience she loved.

She kept her back to the door as he bid everyone a bawdy goodnight, and they all responded with cheers, leers, and lusty jeers. Rarely did they get to jest so with their prince, which explained the crowd's size. Even women had joined in though not as loudly as their men and in far fewer numbers. Most of the women's faces were bright red with embarrassment. Dakota had noted Alina's presence and her lack of red-tinged cheeks.

The door thudded closed, and the lock snicked into place. Dakota turned around then; only her husband watched her now.

In silence, they stared at one another. Culain swiped at his damp brow.

So he's just as nervous.

He licked his lips, but it was another sign of nerves rather than a demonstration of lasciviousness. Her vampire half discerned the difference.

The dhampir part of her wanted to launch herself at him and bite, an urge that slowly grew until it almost overpowered her. She refused to start their marriage with her vampire side controlling her, so she wrestled it down until she could speak without growling.

"I'm a woman of my word, husband." She smiled coyly at him and placed a hand on the bodice of her dress. "Time to pay the toll for your thoughts." Only one problem existed: her dress fastened in the back. She wanted to tease him as she slowly undid her dress, but her attempt rapidly grew awkward. Giddy, she

21

giggled and turned her back to him again.

"You'll have to help me." She peered at him over her shoulder.

His breath shallowed, and her dhampir sense caught the quickening of his heart and the scent of his arousal. It stimulated her own lust, and her fangs pushed their way through. She hadn't bitten him before. They'd agreed to save this for the wedding night too.

"Dakota." He choked the word out through emotion-laden breath.

In response, she managed a hiss through gritted teeth. "I want you. I need to bite you, but I want to savor the moment."

"Have you ...?"

She knew what he asked. Something he'd never had the nerve to ask her before. Now that she was his wife, he dared ask her anything.

"... bitten anyone else?" he finished.

She rotated on her heel and faced him. Her gaze locked on his eyes, holding him, drawing him in.

"No, never." *Not even Josh.* They'd kissed, caressed, fondled, but she'd feared unleashing her demon vampire half. If she'd sampled his blood, things would've escalated, and Culain's family wouldn't have found her a virgin. Would they have rejected her then? Demanded their money back and let her keep her life in the mortal world? She shoved that from her mind. Time enough after to ponder those questions. It surprised her that she'd never wondered this before— but then, of course, she'd never come close to letting her inner vampire off its leash before—not with a person; animals weren't the same—they were strictly food.

He approached her slowly but without hesitation.

When he reached her, she turned her back on him again.

"My lord." The words came out like a caress. She backed close enough into his personal space that his energy radiated onto her body. "Undo my dress. Slip it off."

She ripped off the wreath and veil, mussing her hair and scattering pins, and dropped them on the floor.

His hands gripped her shoulders and then slid to where the lacings started at the top. He swept her hair out of the way and started to unlace her bodice. His breath brushed her nape, and then his lips pressed against the curve where neck met shoulder. She let out a gasp but held still, letting him trace kisses down her skin until his lips met cloth.

He groaned in frustration as he finished unlacing the bodice but found a zipper underneath. "God in Heaven, woman." The bodice fell away, revealing the dress underneath. He yanked the zipper down fiercely only to find a slip beneath the dress. "How many layers are you wearing? Are women's garments deliberately designed to stymie a man?"

Delighted at his frustration, she peered over her shoulder at him and winked. "Probably. No doubt one of your faerie women designed it. What will you do if you find me wearing a chastity belt?"

He shoved the dress off her body, leaving it to pool at her feet. The slip quickly followed, and she caught the slight sizzle of cloth tearing as he ripped it from her. Wearing only a bra and panties, she turned to face him.

"Now you know," she said.

He frowned in puzzlement. "Know?"

"You said my payment was to show you what's

under my dress. Now you know." She twirled around and then posed. "A bra and panties. A thong, of course." She turned her back on him to prove it. "I do enjoy wearing human fashions." Many fae women did, but only the rich could afford to buy them. Having access to money, to whatever she wanted, still felt surreal to her, but she refused to become accustomed to it. What if it corrupted her? She pushed those thoughts aside as well and focused on her husband. Time enough to overthink her entire life in the morning. Tonight, they would enjoy each other.

Dakota faced him again. The panties and bra she could easily remove without help. She unhooked the bra and let it drop.

CHAPTER 5

Her milky skin shimmered in the glow of the fire crackling on the stone hearth. Culain held his breath as Dakota's fingers flicked to the waistband of her thong. A red thong, more transparent lace than solid cloth. He gulped. Swallowed around a lump in his throat. His breeches felt suddenly tight. He wanted to tear them off but feared to move lest he break the moment's spell.

She held still after the panties joined the rest of her garments on the floor, and he reveled in her nakedness, in her soft curves and female perfection. He'd wanted this for so long, had dreamed of it for months. He could have her now. The thought was almost unbearable.

"Your turn," she whispered. Her eyes sparkled and reflected flame, hypnotizing him.

He'd removed half his clothes before he realized he'd done as she'd asked. Part of him wrestled to take back control, but another part of him wanted to surrender completely and do whatever she desired.

Which would be more fun? He'd have the rest of their lives to experiment and find out.

Culain continued to strip, his fingers trembling with anticipation. He wanted to drop everything and leap on her, but she'd done what he wanted without losing control; he owed her the same. At last, he stood naked before her. Ready.

Her gaze roved over his body. Her lips parted. Fangs appeared.

The sight of them didn't frighten him. He wanted her to sink her teeth into his soft flesh. Where would she start? His skin tingled. Would she start at his neck? An arm, perhaps.

He grew painfully hard.

She stepped forward and put her soft, cold hand on him.

He almost fell to his knees.

Then she kneeled before him, and everything became delicious pleasure. She started at his thigh.

***

Dakota sighed contentedly and rolled over so the front of her body lined up with Culain's. Sheets tangled around her legs, but nothing separated their naked torsos. The bed was huge, and they'd made use of every square inch of it throughout the night. She'd expected to love sex with him, and he hadn't disappointed her. And, oh, his blood! She licked her lips, thinking about his taste. His flavor. How he'd moaned and panted as she feasted on him. Faerie blood tasted different from the donated human plasma she usually drank. Definitely, it tasted better than the animal blood she'd gorged on the few times she'd hunted. It held sweetness and made her quiver with delight.

"Penny for your thoughts," she said, smiling, when he opened his eyes and met her gaze.

Lust flickered across his face. "You want to do it again?"

"I'll always want to do it again." She frowned as a thought crossed her mind. "Do you think I got pregnant?" Her hand slid between them and pressed onto her belly.

He touched a hand to her cheek and stroked it. "Would you like that?"

She considered. "I would. Maybe not right away." She grinned suggestively. "I like the idea of having to work at it." She stretched and then pulled him to her. "Practice makes perfect."

As he rolled his body onto hers, she lost herself in him and welcomed the oblivion.

***

The castle was quiet. Too quiet. Josh Davis strolled the grounds, scouting out the area before entering the main building. He'd heard a wedding feast was in progress, and it made him uneasy. Could it be Dakota's wedding? Was he too late?

He came across the courtyard where they'd obviously held the ceremony. Chairs filled the main area. A dais, decorated with vases and bouquets of flowers, stood in the center. He stepped up onto it and sniffed.

Dakota. When he caught her scent, his fangs threatened to break free. With effort, he kept them hidden. *She's married. I'm too late.* How could he have gotten it so wrong? He was positive he'd calculated the time correctly and that he'd catch her before she wed the prince whose family had stolen her away.

His inner vampire exerting itself despite his efforts to control it, he growled low in his throat. He quickly scanned the area, verifying no one was around, no one who could've heard him. While he'd disguised himself as a half-fae half-dhampir upper-class citizen, he preferred to keep attention away from the vampire half. Some might want to question him about it. So few dhampirs lived among the fae that any who did were curiosities. He could've disguised himself as all fae, but that would've required more effort to maintain. If they caught him intruding on fae territory, he risked not only his life but his mother's and vampire father's as well.

What now? If Dakota and Culain were indeed married, what the hell was Josh to do? His plan had been to reveal himself as a vampire to her before her wedding and convince her to run away with him. They would fake her death so no one would search for her, and they'd disappear together. Time in the faerie realm ran differently than time on the Earth plane. He'd thought he'd mastered the calculations, but he'd obviously screwed up, and he'd arrived too late. He'd have to change the plan.

But not all of it. He'd reveal himself to her anyway and let her make her choice. Together, they could figure something out. At least he knew where her private rooms were, but if they'd married the day before, she wouldn't be in them. He tried not to think of where she'd spent the previous night.

When he arrived at the door to her room, he listened with his vampire senses. He detected no heartbeat, no sound of breathing or movement. He picked the lock with ease and slipped inside, shutting and locking the door behind him.

As expected, the rooms were empty. The bed was made, and everything was neat and clean. He saw no sign of the preparations from the previous day, but her scent lingered in the room. She'd stood there, beside the bed, just yesterday. He ached with longing. Would she return, or was she done with this room?

He took a good look around.

Her books remained on the shelves—and she had a lot. Were they hers to take with her? Whoever had stocked this place for her, whoever had decorated it and made it comfortable for her, surely intended to gift her everything. He opened her closets and searched through her dressers, wardrobe, and vanity. All her possessions remained as he'd seen them every time he'd broken in here and snooped.

Her dhampir senses weren't as acute as his vampire ones, but they'd detect an intruder even after he'd left. However, the room was filled with the scent of servants. He'd shown himself to her while in his servant disguise so she'd grow familiar with his scent. Anytime he visited her rooms when she wasn't there, she'd assume he'd come in to perform servantly duties. He never took anything on those visits, except once when he'd taken a hairpin—a minor trinket she'd never miss. When he came here, he simply sat and reveled in her scent, basking in her aura and touching the things she touched. This time, though, he had no intention of letting her mistake him for anything other than who he was.

She'll be back. He removed a book from the shelf and sat down to read while he waited.

CHAPTER 6

"It's getting late." Dakota stretched, arms above her head, toes pointed. The sigh she gave emphasized her contentment and satisfaction. She squeezed her eyes tight. "Ah, but I don't want to get out of bed."

Facing her, Culain propped himself on an elbow. "I'm more exhausted now than before we came to bed," he said, but his alert eyes and peppy tone belied his words. "I'm surprised the servants have left us alone. I was certain my father would've ordered them to roust us before this."

"Maybe he's hoping we're in here making a little Culain."

"That's my guess." He smiled. "Or a little Dakota," he added. He tilted his head. "Do you feel different this morning?"

She raised her brows. *What a strange question.* "Different how?"

"Than you did before our marriage."

She still didn't understand. "Different how? Why?

Do you feel different?"

He lay down on his back and stared at the ceiling.

She did the same but clasped his hand.

"I think I love you even more than I did before." He closed his eyes, his voice growing dreamier as he talked. "I want to care for you. To have children with you."

"You didn't before?"

"Well, yes, but it was all ... theoretical before."

She started to laugh but stopped when she realized she felt the same way. "I get it. It's more real. Us. Together." She sat up and kissed his cheek. "I can move all my things in." She scanned the room. "Where will all my books go?" The books were important to her. Whenever she was down or needed escape or consoling, she turned to her books.

I can turn to Culain now, too. Over the months, she'd found herself drawing comfort from his presence, from talking with him, laughing with him. She still held some things back from him, but she trusted him enough to relax around him and confide in him. Little things only, sure, but they'd grown closer than she'd ever been with anyone else—even Josh, and she'd trusted him with her life.

Culain opened his eyes, and she gazed into the deep, calming green of them.

"You can keep your quarters if you like. Bring your clothes here, of course, and your toiletries and cosmetics, but keep the books and use the rooms as a personal space," he said.

"You mean that?" She held her breath.

"Of course. I know how much your privacy means to you. How often you escape there to read and relax. Besides, where else would you and Alina have your sleepovers?"

She released the breath and giggled. "You make it sound like we're schoolgirls."

His expression sobered, and it pained her to see him flinch at her words. "I intended no offense."

"Neither did I. My jest was in poor taste." She kissed him again, this time full on the lips. When she pulled back, she said, "You understand me, and I'm grateful. I love you."

They made love again, because of course they did, and then they got up to shower and dress when the servants finally arrived. Someone had left an appropriate change of clothes for her so she wouldn't have to put her wedding attire back on. Lysandra did Dakota's hair first, sweeping it back on two sides and fastening it with a white rose behind her head. The maid then placed a circlet on Dakota's forehead and a ribbon with tiny white flowers along the side of her head. She then helped her out of her dressing gown and into her garments. The butler helped Culain. Dakota had never seen the young prince dress in the morning before. Watching him prepare for the functions they'd have to attend felt surreal, but she figured she'd get used to it eventually.

She met his gaze over the heads of the servants, who fussed over them and ensured they looked presentable, regal.

The wedding feasts would continue for another six days, and the newlyweds would attend all the evening ones. Breakfast, however, they were permitted to take in private. A servant wheeled a cart in and set everything up for them in the sitting area. Lunches they'd attend in the dining room with family and close friends only.

In the main banquet hall, guests would come and go, and food and drink would constantly flow. Wedding gifts already accumulated in a corner of the hall, a pair of guards watching over the stack. Dakota was curious to see what they'd get. They had everything they needed, and a sense of guilt tempered the excitement at the prospect of opening dozens, maybe hundreds, of presents.

"We could donate some of our gifts to the needy," she said.

Culain stared at her. "Where'd that come from?"

She shrugged as Lysandra zipped up the back of Dakota's flowing, off-the-shoulder gown, which was ivory with gold trim decorated with gold and silver gems. "We have so much. We should share it with those who don't."

He smiled. "It's a generous thought, but we risk offending those who gave them to us."

"We have to keep everything?"

He contemplated a moment. "For a while. Perhaps, in time, we could donate those items we don't use or need."

"Doesn't it bother you to live so decadently?"

"Not at all. We're rulers. The gods put me here—us here. My family and I might've chosen you, but the gods put you in our path. Together, you and I must rule, and we must also accept the perks that come with the position."

"The gods put me in your path." Even she heard the smirk in her voice.

"Did you think you came here accidentally?"

She strode to his side and watched the butler finish buttoning Culain's vest. "No, I thought my greedy, grasping mother sold me for money."

"Consider all that had to fall into place for you to end up here. Doesn't that indicate a divine hand intervened?"

"No. I think my mother, my father, however unwittingly, and Frank Evans and his organization had a hand in it. I think your family had a hand in it. You had a hand in it. But the gods?" She shook her head. "If they exist, they don't care what we do. Why should they? I certainly had no hand in it."

He waved the butler away and swept her into his arms. "You had a choice, if you recall."

"A forced choice isn't really a choice, Culain." When he looked stricken, she added, "I don't regret it. You know I've grown to love you. I never expected to, and were we both free, I'd choose you again. Gods had nothing to do with our marriage, though."

"You don't believe in the gods?" His glance shifted from Dakota to the two servants, and he lightened his tone. "We should eat." He met her gaze again and squeezed her hands.

She smiled reassuringly at him. "Of course."

He could talk all he wanted to about divine intervention. Most people considered vampires cursed, soulless. Was the hatred directed at them an act of the gods? Of the humans' one God? If He, or they, existed, she had no respect for any of them.

Culain dismissed the maid and butler and, holding Dakota's hand, towed her to the table. He pulled a chair out for her, and when she settled into it, he strolled to the opposite side and sat.

"Our first breakfast together, Princess Shiels."

She grinned at him. "Yes, my prince."

The thrill of the wedding and their first night together as husband and wife not only hadn't worn off but had increased. She wanted to revel in it and delighted in their time together. It almost made up for the fact that they'd have no traditional honeymoon. The fae didn't take trips to exotic locales. The newly wedded couple was expected to tour the kingdom and meet their people—under heavy guard, of course. Not that they expected trouble, but tradition demanded it. This tradition had evolved after the species wars. The fae considered infiltration from outside a genuine threat, but she doubted anyone would willingly visit faerie country. Most who did ended up trapped here— at least most humans did. The faeries had a complicated history with humans. They both feared and envied them. Since the unmasquing, though, and with dhampirs replacing humans in the faeries' demand for fresh blood to keep their species alive, almost no humans visited faerie anymore. Dakota's mother had gotten pregnant with her to fill that demand. If the demand hadn't existed, neither would Dakota. For that, she'd resent her mother forever.

CHAPTER 7

Breakfast ended, and while Culain attended a meeting in the king's chambers, Dakota returned to her old bedchamber. Hiding out with a good book and a cup of mulled cider sounded like the perfect break before diving in to the day's obligations.

Culain walked her to the room—two guards escorting them, naturally. He kissed her goodbye with such passion she almost hauled him into the room with her so they could christen her bed as well. She would have if his appointment hadn't been with the king. No one kept the king waiting, not even his sons, and Dakota refused to cause trouble for her husband on their first full day of marriage. Despite that, when he released her, she let him walk away reluctantly.

"Return quickly, husband," she called after him, suggestion in every word.

He froze, making the guard accompanying him halt, and spun back to face her. "You have my promise I'll be out of there as soon as possible."

Dakota giggled as she unlocked her bedroom door. Leaving the remaining guard outside her door, she slipped into the room, still laughing. She closed the door behind her but left it unlocked.

She'd barely taken two steps inside when a hand clasped tightly against her mouth, and a familiar voice whispered into her ear. "Don't cry out. I just want to talk to you."

Her fangs sprang out, but she retracted them as soon as she recognized him.

"You promise not to call out?"

She nodded.

"I'm risking my life coming here. My mother's life. Your father's life." His hold on her loosened, and she yanked away from his grasp and spun around.

His sandy-brown hair was black, his ears were pointed and his skin darkened, and the all-black outfit he wore made him look like some kind of Goth dhampir-fae, but it was him all right.

"Josh." She whispered the name and backed away from him. "Have you lost your mind? You'll get us both killed—and that's if they're feeling compassionate."

"I'll leave, I swear—if you want me to after I've told you what I have to say. But I had to see you. I have to know."

"Know what?" Was this another attempt to convince her to turn her back on the fae? To break her promise to them, to Culain. *Culain.* How long before he returned? She rushed to the door, intending to lock it, but he grabbed her hand as she reached for the lock.

"Please. Hear me out."

She pressed a finger to her lips and shook his hand off her wrist. After silently sliding the deadbolt in place, she waved a hand in the sitting area's direction. "Over there," she whispered, leading him to the sofa.

He followed her, but when she sat, he remained standing. "I have to move fast if someone comes to the door."

"No one will bust in on us. They'll knock first, and few have a key. Sit down." His scent finally penetrated her senses. *Vampire.* She gasped. "How?"

"I disguised myself as you see me." He dropped the glamour and revealed his real features—excepting those that he'd used makeup and putty to cover.

"How are you a vampire?" She answered her own question before he could respond. "My father turned you." Rage welled in her heart. *How dare he?* She imagined Josh convincing Philip to turn him, imagined them going through all the paperwork. For what? To convince her to return to her old boyfriend? Her anger at her father shifted onto Josh. "You made him turn you?"

His brows drew together, and his lips curled into a sneer. "You assume much—all of it false."

She calmed herself with an indrawn breath that eased more tension on the exhale. "Tell me." She glanced toward the door. "But be quick. No one can catch you here."

"They held my mother captive in her store, and one of Evans's men shot me to prove a point to your father and my mother." He paced, keeping to the side of the coffee table farthest from her. "Philip gave the choice to my mother."

"Kelsey told him to turn you?"

"When the options came down to turn me or let me die, she ordered him to make me a vampire. He acted in that split second and did as she wished."

"No paperwork." She shuddered, horrified at what that implied. "That's the death penalty for him and imprisonment for her. Why would he even offer her the choice?"

"Dakota, we don't have much time. Listen. Things are different. I'm a vampire. I'll outlive you. Your reason for giving up on our relationship no longer exists. Come away with me."

She jumped to her feet and thrust her fists on her hips. "Are you insane? I have more reasons now to stay here."

"Your marriage?"

"Yes." She hissed on the sibilant consonant. "I gave my word. More than that, I love him."

He winced. "You love him?" All his dejection poured into the question.

"I do." She strode to Josh's side, interrupting his pacing. "I married him because I love him. Please, you have to leave. If we're caught together, it'll end badly for all of us." She studied him. "I recognize your disguise." Her voice held wonder. "Oh my god, you've been visiting here. Interacting with us. Attended ..." She choked on the words, but after swallowing around the lump in her throat, she continued, "... attended our banquets. I danced with you! You *are* crazy. Why would you risk everything to come here?"

"I had to make sure. At first, I wanted to verify you were happy with him. Then I thought, well, maybe you were here only because I'd die in fifty or sixty years anyway. You didn't want the heartache of outliving your husband by untold centuries. I could understand that. But that's no longer the case. I wanted you to make your choice knowing all the facts." He punched the air with his fist. "I wanted to get here sooner, but I miscalculated, and now you're married to that kidnapper."

"Yes, I'm married to Culain, but he's no kidnapper." Dakota put a hand on Josh's shoulder. "I love him. You have to understand that. If I were free to choose, I'd pick him because I love him."

Josh scowled and shrugged her hand from his shoulder. "Fine. I believe you." His fangs slid free, but he reeled them back in. "I should've known. They've got you bewitched. Some kind of faerie spell."

"Oh, please. They couldn't if they tried. Go live your life. Forget about me."

He stared at her for so long she wondered if he planned to attack her. She could fight him, scream for the guards, or let him pummel her until he wore himself out, but none of those options suited her. She forced herself to remain still and simply returned his stare.

At last, he said, "You'd think I'd have learned from the other two times you rejected me to my face. I thought it was because I was human, but clearly, it's not. It wouldn't have mattered if I'd been a vampire then, would it?"

"It's not that simple."

"It is. You want him. You don't want me. It can't get any simpler."

She averted her eyes, and her gaze traveled to the window across the room. Through the panes, she glimpsed tree branches covered in orange and red leaves and the blue sky beyond. A robin perched on a branch, and as she watched, it burst out with loud chirps. When it stopped, it spread its wings and flew away.

"He's my husband," she said, keeping her gaze on

the window. "I love him. I want him. You and me, that's in the past. I loved you then." She faced him again, meeting his eyes with her sorrow-filled ones. "Loved. We were kids. We didn't know what love was. I'm sorry my father turned you without your permission. He never should've done that."

"I'm fine with it."

"Good." But the word was a lie. Her father had ruined Josh's life, but retaliation for it wasn't her call to make. She couldn't predict the future, but she was certain her ex wouldn't have an easy life as a vampire. Since he was here, though, she might as well ask him for news. Hesitantly, she asked, "How is my father?"

"Just fine. Has my mother." The grin he gave her sent a chill through her. "I turned her."

Dakota gasped. "Why? How?"

He laughed. "How do you think?"

She gave her head a violent shake and furrowed her brows. "I know how the process works. That's not what I'm asking."

He shrugged. "Evans's men attacked us. She fell through ice into a lake and drowned. I turned her so she wouldn't die."

Suddenly, understanding changed irritation to sorrow. "Oh, no. To get revenge on her for turning you?"

"Not entirely." He crossed his arms. "Mostly because he loves her. They looked happy together. Well, when they weren't arguing. Even then, I could tell they loved each other but refused to admit it. Now they can be together."

Not wanting to point out the issues with that—too late now to change what he'd done—she nodded silently while absorbing everything he'd said. When the silence grew too uncomfortable, she broke it. "What about my mother?"

"What about her?"

"Have you heard anything about her?" She couldn't have explained why she asked. Did she care, or was she hoping he'd say Annabelle was suffering from guilt over selling her daughter?

"I don't know. She's not on my radar."

Dakota sighed with relief. "Probably better that way. She's a horrible person."

"If you want, I can check for you."

"No. Stay away. If you haven't heard any news of her, it's better you don't seek it out." She regretted asking. Her mother was the last person she wanted anyone she liked involved with.

A knock at the door interrupted the discussion. She threw a glance at the door and took a step toward it. When she turned back to tell Josh to hide, he was already gone. The window across the room yawned open, the tree's branches still swaying from his passing.

CHAPTER 8

C hurches always had a distinctive smell. This one was no different, but it was the church Kelsey had attended when she was human, so the familiarity wasn't surprising. It was one of the older churches, built before the species wars. By some miracle—*yeah, right, as if miracles, or even God, exist*—it'd survived unscathed though the neighborhood's other buildings had been destroyed. The main doors stood propped open, and members of the congregation filed in.

Kelsey stood on the sidewalk across the street from the walkway leading up to the church: St. Michael's, named for the archangel of strength and protection. She'd heard someone refer to him as "the bouncer" once and thought the term bordered on disrespectful, but now she understood how apt it was. Archangel Michael would likely bounce Kelsey out of the area if their paths crossed right now. Vampires weren't welcome here. They were soulless. Everyone knew that.

Hypocrites. What happened to love one another as I have loved you? The stream of churchgoers had dwindled to a trickle until the flow finally stopped and the doors swung closed.

Kelsey fisted her hands. She'd visited this church at the start of the mid-morning service every Sunday for the past two months, but she'd never mustered up the courage to set foot inside. She wasn't afraid for her safety—vampires bursting into flames when setting foot onto holy grounds was a myth from books and movies—but she wasn't ready to face rejection by the priests she'd respected and the community she'd once been a part of.

As she'd done every Sunday since her return, she walked away. Instead of spending the morning in church, she went to the shooting range—another habit she'd developed recently.

If she couldn't get divine protection, she'd make sure she had physical protection. Evans had given them each a gun in case they needed it in the line of duty, but she'd never told him she didn't know how to use it. For her own sake, and for Josh's and Philip's, she'd vowed to learn how. The sight of Philip getting shot as they tried to escape a vampire tracker the winter before had seared permanently into her memory. The longer she worked for Evans, the more certain she grew that, sooner or later, she'd need to fire that weapon.

She only hoped it would be much, much later.

***

Behind a row of shops on Dundas Street in downtown Tkaronto, Philip Belanger awaited his prey. He carried no weapon other than his fangs and his vampire ability to mesmerize, but he needed nothing else. The one he waited for was a human, and humans made easy targets. The early afternoon sun hung high in the sky, but shadows drenched the alley, which was bordered on each of two sides by a brick wall and ended in an impenetrable eight-foot wooden fence.

The stink from puddles of oil, grease, urine, vomit, and the garbage bin Philip hid behind threatened to overwhelm him. He slipped the bandanna he wore around his neck over his face, hoping to filter out at least some of the stench.

All day as he'd conducted his business, he'd felt watched, but his senses picked up nothing and no one suspicious. Because he couldn't shake it, his nerves had wound tighter the longer he spent slinking through alleys and meeting up with the degenerates and addicts who owed the mob money.

Hurry up! If the guy didn't show up soon, he'd leave, Frank Evans and his orders be damned. Except Philip knew he wouldn't walk away. Even if it took all day, he'd stand here waiting for the target. He owed the human his life and his family's life, and whatever the crime boss demanded, Philip would do. No questions. No arguments.

Frustration had his fangs popping out. He forced them to retract.

Something stirred at the alley's mouth.

About damn time. He braced himself, ready to spring out the moment the man, expecting to meet with a drug dealer, stepped fully into the alley's seclusion.

The scent of human wafted into the alley, and Philip caught the thump of the man's heartbeat. It was normal, fear, for the moment, absent. The man was anxious, of course, because he craved the drugs he intended to buy.

Come closer.

As if he'd heard the command, the man shuffled three more steps into the alley. He stopped, still too near the sidewalk, and glanced around.

Come closer.

This time, the man stayed put.

Philip would have to reveal himself. The vampire stepped from behind the dumpster.

"You lookin' for me?" He'd squelched the slight French accent he usually sported. When he wanted to, he could sound like he came from English Skanadario rather than French Kébec where his family originated.

"Who's askin', eh?" The man wiped his brow with one hand. The other remained stuffed in his trench coat pocket, which must've made him hot because the day was warm for May.

"Want me to leave?" Philip bluffed, but he wanted the target to believe he risked losing his next fix.

"No. You have ... it?"

"You have payment?" This was the man's final chance to set things right with Evans. If he had the money—all the money he owed, not just what would cover today's rations—he'd get his fix and walk away. If not, he'd still leave the alley, but not under his own power.

This was what Philip had been reduced to: low-level thug for a criminal who reveled in ordering him around and seeing how high he'd jump on command. So far, Evans hadn't forced him to kill anyone, but the vampire had broken numerous kneecaps over the last three months of service.

"Yes." The word tumbled out, trembling and

uncertain.

"All of it?"

The man gulped. "For this. I swear, I'm good for the rest."

Philip reached into his jacket pocket and retrieved a small packet wrapped in plain brown paper. "Come and get it. I ain't comin' to you."

From outside the alley came a low growl. If he didn't know better, he'd have sworn it sounded like a grizzly. All his senses went on alert, but the only heartbeat and breathing he detected belonged to his target.

Now I'm hearing things. Great.

"Move it," Philip said with a snarl.

The man hesitated, and his heart rate sped up, but he walked forward, his hand free of his pocket and clutching a wad of sweaty bills. When he reached Philip, he held the paltry stack out to him like an offering.

The vampire stared at it with disdain. "That's not enough. Deal was you pay it all. Today."

The man gulped. "I had a bad run. I can have the rest tomorrow. Honest."

In a flash, Philip pocketed the drugs and splayed the man onto the ground, legs broken at the knees. After a gut-twisting scream, the man whimpered in overwhelming agony that even the drugs wouldn't diminish.

Philip snatched up the money. "This'll go toward your debt. Next time, have it all, or we won't be so forgiving." He vanished from the alley with a leap over the fence, landing in a small copse of trees in a townhouse complex's courtyard.

The homes here belonged to government-subsidized housing. Anyone nearby would refuse to get involved. Most of them worked in one capacity or another for Frank Evans's crew. Even so, Philip used his vampire abilities to escape the area in a blur of speed that would've made him invisible to cameras though this poverty-stricken neighborhood had none.

With the bills stuffed into his jacket pocket, he headed for home.

When he arrived at the condo unit—the penthouse—he shared with Kelsey and Josh, Philip found no one home. Just as well. He didn't want to talk about his work with either of his vampire family members. Neither would care enough to ask, but he preferred they didn't mark his activity. What they didn't know, they couldn't discuss.

He hid the money he'd taken from the drug addict in a safe located in the walk-in closet in the master bedroom he and Kelsey shared. She too had a safe there, and if she used it to store similar illicit cash or goods, he never asked.

The entry door slamming had him speeding from the closet into the hallway. Before he reached the living room, he recognized the newcomer's scent as Kelsey's.

When he appeared, she froze. "What are you doing home?"

He shrugged. "Just got back."

"Working for Evans?"

He nodded but didn't elaborate. She didn't ask. She never asked.

"Done for today?"

He nodded.

"Josh?"

He shrugged. "Not here."

She walked to the balcony's sliding doors at the far

end of the living room and gazed outside. "He's been gone a while."

"Probably at the lake." The boy spent most of his time in or near Lake Skanadario. For some reason, he enjoyed being underwater, something Philip couldn't relate to.

"Maybe." She sounded dubious.

"What?" Since when did Kelsey care about or notice their comings and goings? That was the nice thing about her change from human to vampire: she no longer stuck her nose into anyone's business. At times, he missed her interest, but he never missed the grillings she used to give him.

She turned and faced him. "I've rented my apartment out to Chase and Jaycie."

Interesting. He'd assumed she'd want to return to it to live in herself—he'd braced himself to argue against it.

Keeping his expression impartial, he said, "Convenient for him when he needs to work." Chase worked in the bookstore and café part-time while he attended mage school.

"Yes. He jumped on it when I suggested it."

"Makes sense for you. Gets you some income and an employee on the premises twenty-four-seven."

"Close to school for them, too, and the hospital when Jaycie has the baby."

"You've really thought this through." A good sign. If Kelsey was thinking of others to the point where she wanted to help them, her humanity must be returning. Baby vamps typically had no conscience. Their sires had to teach them not to act like sociopaths—which, at first change, they were. Kelsey, though not recently turned and disciplined enough to be able to go among humans unsupervised, still had to recover her conscience. She didn't do the right thing because it was the right thing to do; she did it because, if she didn't, she'd get the death penalty. The law wasn't lenient with vampires who gave free rein to their baser instincts.

"Someone needs to look after the place, and renting it brings in extra income."

Okay, her primary reasons remained selfish, but he still considered it a good sign she'd at least given thought to how it helped the young mage couple. They'd struggled through a lot recently and were expecting their first child. Providing them a place to themselves, getting them out of the apartment they shared with two other students, helped them.

"I haven't told Blair."

Philip's ears pricked up. She hadn't mentioned her ex since they'd returned from exile, but the vampire was aware the couple talked and had met up at least once. Blair had lived in Kelsey's apartment above her store while she was in hiding, something that bothered Philip.

Did he go through her personal things? Sleep holding one of her panties?

"Not really his business," he said.

Her expression grew pensive. "In a way, it is. He was nice enough to look after things for me while we were ... away."

Again, her consideration for another reassured him. When he answered her, he kept his tone as neutral as his body language, but the battle was hard won. He preferred to deny his true feelings for her, but when she mentioned dealings with her ex, Philip couldn't help the twinge of jealousy.

"How is he?"

Her eyes refocused, and she met his gaze, her brows rising and lips pursing. "Why would you care?"

"I don't. Unless it affects you—or us. All of us. He's Josh's father. Your ex. Whatever he does affects me if it affects you." Was that rambling? Had he revealed too much of his true feelings by overexplaining? Damn, why'd she have to have such a death grip on his heart? He'd prefer feeling nothing for her, but here he was stuck loving her when she had no feelings for him—other than sexual. They still screwed like rabbits regularly. He wasn't complaining—he'd take whatever she offered of herself and he'd take it guilt free—but he'd prefer it if she had real feelings for him.

What a sap. He resented how weak that made him feel.

She shrugged, but her next words made him perk up. "I don't know how much what he does affects any of us anymore. He let me go. Last time we met, he said goodbye and told me to contact him only if Josh needed him. We're done."

CHAPTER 9

For Dakota, the week of wedding celebrations and feasting both flew by and dragged. Time raced whenever she was with Culain or in her private quarters, but it crept along when she had to go among the fae out of duty. At last, a morning dawned when the celebrations were done. Culain's family wouldn't expect the couple to have lunch with them, and King Killian's subjects wouldn't require her presence in the banquet hall that night.

Her subjects, too, since the wedding, but she still felt like an outsider and self-conscious whenever she mingled with them. Besides Culain, Alina was the only one who made Dakota feel normal and able to relax and be herself. Unfortunately, she got little time alone with her friend, and after that upsetting visit with Josh, she craved someone to talk to other than her husband. She didn't want to keep secrets from him, but in this instance, she felt justified. How would it help anything to tell the man she'd married that her first love, now a vampire, had infiltrated the faerie realm? Culain would either have to turn Josh over to security or to Evans. Neither option would end well for Dakota and her family. Most of the time, she suppressed thoughts about the visit so she wouldn't drive herself crazy, but flashbacks of it intruded at the most inconvenient moments. Sometimes, when the stress became unbearable, she wished she hadn't forbidden Josh from visiting again. She'd have liked another opportunity to throttle him.

Dakota always awoke before her husband, and this morning was no exception. She stayed in bed a few minutes longer, taking in his beautiful, peaceful face as he slept. The sun had yet to breach the horizon, but enough soft light filtered through the curtains that he was visible even without her enhanced dhampir sight.

An urge to snuggle back down into the blankets and wake him with morning sex tempted her, but she reluctantly shoved it aside. Today was the first day her princess training would begin in earnest. They'd already coached her before the wedding in their traditions and the etiquette of dealing with servants. Now they'd teach her the responsibilities of a princess who'd eventually become queen. She'd technically be queen consort since she was a dhampir, but the duties and obligations were the same as for any fae woman who married the future king.

At least before things got too serious, they'd get to open their wedding gifts. She looked forward to that with the excitement and eagerness she assumed all brides possessed. Servants had relocated all the gifts from the banquet hall into the family's great room. King Killian, Colin, and a few other close friends and family, Alina included, were to meet there after breakfast to watch. Little of what she and Culain did, it seemed, would be private between them.

Thank the gods they let us have sex alone. Since that sounded more cynical than she liked, Dakota rose from bed and asked a guard to request servants bring breakfast up. Time to get the day started.

***

In early May, Lake Skanadario's waters were still cold. Snow had disappeared in the southern part of the state, but the large lake's waters hadn't warmed yet. Skanadario was once the province of Ontario, but borders and many location names changed after the species wars. All the North American countries had merged, making North America one realm with a ruling board composed of various species. Humans no longer controlled all the land.

Josh Davis considered all that ancient history. It didn't bother him at all—especially now that he was a vampire and benefited from the rights drafted into the new North American constitution. He didn't care who owned what as long as he could have his share someday and retain unrestricted access to all waterways.

Low temperatures didn't deter him from entering Lake Skanadario's frigid depths and remaining under for hours at a time, and that's where he was that afternoon.

Ever since Dakota had rejected him, he spent most of his time in the water. His mother gave him a few questioning glances but kept her thoughts to herself. What a drastic change from the old Kelsey, who'd constantly wanted updates on his whereabouts and activities. If any part of him missed that version of his mother, he ignored it. The autonomy he wanted and deserved meant more to him than having her micromanage his every move even if it showed she didn't care about him.

She cares, he told himself. Sort of. If something happened to him, she'd turn vengeful, that much he knew for certain.

He explored the murky depths for over four hours before turning back to shore. As he made his way toward the shallows, Josh ignored everything around him and enjoyed the flow of water through his long hair. The icy water refreshed him, energized him. He kept his lips pressed into a tight line to avoid taking in any of the water. Pollution wouldn't hurt him, and the lake was cleaner than it had been before the species wars, but he had no desire to taste it.

Lake Skanadario proved far more interesting than the small lakes he'd explored while they were on the lam. As he walked along the bottom, his rubber shoes kicked up silt and sand. He saw not only large fish, rocks, and bits of garbage but also, most fascinatingly, old shipwrecks and plane wrecks. He'd at first explored them, but the frequency of each find and the number of skeletons he found depressed him so he stopped. One small ship had held the staked remains of vampires, verifying for him that they didn't turn to dust or burst apart when killed; he'd already witnessed that once before when he'd killed one of Evans's vampires in a fight to the death. Obviously, the vessel had gone down during the wars. Josh deduced the crew had been all vampires, but other creatures had seized the boat, killed the vamps on board, and scuttled it.

He avoided dwelling on what could've taken down a ship with an all-vampire crew. Perhaps one among them had turned traitor. That was common during the

Great Species War. He'd learned in school that those wanting to prevent the species from mingling had turned against their own kind. No one was safe, and you could trust no one. Fortunately, it was over before he was born.

He reached shore in a secluded section of beach, away from marinas, parking lots, and industrial or commercial sites. When embarking on these excursions, he always verified witnesses were few or nonexistent. While humans knew vampires could submerge for hours, he didn't want to flaunt or advertise his abilities. Some humans still resented vamps and their superior capabilities. Josh always avoided drawing attention to himself from that quarter. The less involvement he had with humans, the better, which made working for Frank Evans's human-dominated organization grating. Most of the assigned tasks involved direct contact with humans. It was as if Evans identified what each of them detested and forced it on them.

To make matters worse, the crime boss hadn't requested Josh for a job in over a week. While he enjoyed the respite, he dreaded the next call to duty. A distasteful assignment always followed a long stretch of time between tasks. So far, it'd stopped short of murder, but he held little hope that Evans wouldn't one day force Josh to cross that line.

He put thoughts of what his next job might entail aside and strode through the sand to his car. He'd left it parked off the road in a secluded spot most vehicles couldn't access. With the money he made from working for the mob, he'd purchased a brand-new car with the latest technology. It ran on distilled water and could fly when traffic got too bad. He'd eagerly leaped on the option as soon as the government had approved the air cars. Working for Evans had its unpleasant side, but it had its perks, too, and if forced to work for the mob boss, Josh intended to enjoy the benefits.

He scanned the area with all his senses. No humans around. The only heartbeats he picked up belonged to small animals and birds. Seagulls whirled low in the sky in the futile hope he'd drop food for them. Driftwood and seaweed covered the sand near the shore, and he sniffed something decaying amid the detritus. It overpowered the odor of rotting vegetation and the peaty smell of algae. He recognized it as an animal, probably a raccoon or rabbit, so no need for concern.

He popped the car's trunk and removed dry clothing. Wet clothes didn't bother him, but he didn't want to soil or dampen the expensive synthetic suede upholstery in his car. He changed, keeping alert for any movement in the vicinity. When dressed, he bagged his wet stuff and left it in the trunk. He got into the car and opened his glove box. When he checked his phone, a burner that Evans paid for, he saw a message from Kelsey and, to his dismay, one from Frank Evans.

He listened to his mother's message first: "You could at least check in. Call me."

All right. He'd just finished thinking she'd stopped butting into his business, and here she was doing it again. He'd call her after he listened to Evans's message. If he had to return a call, the mob boss took precedence.

"Got a job for you. Meet Digits at Crossroads Café at eight o'clock tonight."

Great. Josh's brief vacation was definitely over. Max "Digits" Malone would pass along an unsavory task for sure. The goon was one of organization's main men.

He'd acquired the nickname Digits when he'd first crossed Evans back when Josh was still a toddler and knew nothing about mob bosses or vampires. Evans's thugs had relieved Max Malone of two of his fingers on each hand after he'd double-crossed the gang in a drug deal. Grateful they hadn't killed him, he'd worked for them ever since, making his way up the ranks until he held a position near the top. If Digits was giving him the assignment, Josh could be sure he didn't want it. Like it or not, he'd do it, though. No one denied Frank Evans, not even a vampire.

Time to call Mom.

CHAPTER 10

From her place next to Culain on the loveseat, Dakota accepted the gift Alina handed her from the slowly dwindling pile beside the chair where the faerie woman sat. The package was heavy, the wrapping colorful and tied with ribbon. Dakota set it on her knees and removed the attached envelope. She handed it to Culain, who slit it open with a penknife and removed the card. Their fingers brushed as he passed it to her, and she returned his affectionate gaze with a wink and a smile. She'd never felt happier than she did in this moment.

They'd opened over half their gifts, most of them beautiful and items she wanted to keep. They'd even received books from the mortal world—first editions she couldn't wait to add to her collection. Culain, too, liked to read, but Dakota was the collector. She appreciated that the fae knew it and had troubled to hunt down books she didn't already own. They'd also received more traditional gifts: towels, bed linens, a tea service, a coffeemaker, but the more personal gifts touched her.

She opened the card, and when her gaze landed on the signature at the bottom, she sucked in a startled breath, and her stomach churned with revulsion.

Best wishes, Frank Evans and family.

How dare he? She reread the words, but, unable to bear touching a card the mob boss might've handled, she shoved it at Culain with a trembling hand.

His wide-eyed stare indicated he'd noticed her reaction. He glanced at the writing on the open card, snapping his gaze back to her when understanding dawned. "It's okay. Hand me the package. I'll open this one."

Before she could move, King Killian said, "What's the problem, son?" He leaned forward in the richly upholstered red armchair in which he sat.

"Nothing. Someone we didn't expect a gift from."

"Well, read the card."

Culain, with an apologetic glance at Dakota, did as ordered.

"Excellent," Killian said. "He and his family couldn't attend, naturally, but it was nice of them to send a gift."

Culain cleared his throat. "You invited him?"

"Of course. We do business together. Something you'll have to get used to."

Culain didn't reply, but he wasn't done with the conversation. His heart rate had sped up, and his lips pressed into a thin line.

Dakota surreptitiously scanned the faces of the friends and family sitting in the room with them. None of them appeared concerned, including Colin.

Had they all known Evans had received an invitation? Why hadn't anyone told her? Why had they kept it from Culain? Based on his reaction, it'd surprised him as well. Were they worried he'd let it slip to his wife and cause her to, what? Back out of the wedding? She and Culain had had minimal input into the guest list, but she hadn't known any humans were on it—especially the one who'd almost destroyed her life. That she was happy with the end result didn't make what the mob boss had done okay. An urge to fight Evans and his gang flared up, but she forced it down. It wasn't the time for revenge or activism. Plenty of time for that later.

To distract herself, she peeled the ribbon from the package and tore off the wrapping. She removed the lid from the thick blue box and peered inside. Again, she gasped, this time in wonder. The porcelain sculpture, nestled among silk padding, depicted the prince and princess strolling hand in hand. The Dakota figure's free hand was raised, and a butterfly rested on one of the fingers. The figurine's expression was one of delight, and the Culain figure gazed adoringly at his wife.

She gulped. It was exquisite. Had they received the gift from anyone else, she'd have adored it. As it was, she wanted to rip it from the box and smash it at their feet. The box quivered on her lap as she shuddered from her visceral reaction. Culain gently took it from her and lifted the item from the box so everyone could see it.

He looked up and met his father's gaze. "It's a lovely gift and must be worth a fortune. Perhaps it should go on display in the art museum."

Dakota stared down at her empty lap. Giving it to the museum would allow their subjects to view it, would send the message to Evans that his gift was well received, and it would also get it out of their living quarters. She would never have to see it again if she wished.

"Very well," Killian said. He signaled for the family butler to take possession of it and ensure the gift made it to the museum in Central Realm.

Dakota sighed with relief and turned grateful eyes on her husband.

***

I don't care where you go or what you do, but when you're working, tell us. Kelsey's words echoed in Josh's brain. When he'd returned her call, she'd sounded almost like her human self again. Josh sat at a table for two in Crossroads Books & Café, waiting for that weasel Digits to show. He'd picked an out-of-the-way spot, putting his back to the wall and his face to the entrance. He didn't expect anyone to enter the place guns blazing, but he'd learned to watch for it. Philip had trained him in survival strategies. His vampire father hadn't revealed much about his previous life tied to the local mob but had shared tips and tricks to stay alive.

Behind the counter, one of the part-time staff— Chase Spenser, since it was a weeknight—served customers. The young man worked most weeknights even though he attended mage school every weekday. He had weekends off to catch up on his schoolwork and spend time with his pregnant girlfriend. The pair rented the apartment above the store, since Kelsey and Josh no longer needed it.

Kid works hard.

Josh respected that. Before becoming a vampire, he'd attended college. He'd wanted to go into archaeology, his main area of study the history of the species wars and the time period before it. Human history fascinated him, and he wanted to understand what had led to the unmasquing. He'd imagined himself figuring out what had triggered the world-changing event. His dreams, though, had vanished along with his humanity, and now his life revolved around surviving another day of keeping a crime lord happy.

The café did a brisk business while he watched and waited. He checked the time on his phone every minute or so, impatient to finish the meeting.

At last, Digits entered. He walked in alone, which meant the man had grown to trust Josh. Anytime they'd met previously, Digits had brought backup.

The human waved when he spotted the vampire lad but detoured to the counter. He pantomimed drinking from a cup, but Josh shook his head and pointed to the mug in front of him. It was empty. He'd only ordered it so he wouldn't attract attention taking up space without supporting the business. That the place belonged to his mother didn't matter. The demonstration targeted the customers, not the staff.

Digits, a heavyset though not obese man with thinning hair and a thickening black beard flecked with gray, set a takeout cup of coffee on the table. He removed a packet of disinfectant wipes and cleaned off his half of the table and the chair he intended to use.

Right. The guy was a germaphobe.

"Not planning to stay long?" Josh wagged his chin at the takeout cup. He didn't really care. He was just making small talk until they got down to business.

"I always get to-go cups in these places." Digits tapped a finger on the table, three beats. It drew attention to the two missing digits: the pinkie and the middle finger. "Don't trust the dishwashers."

Josh, a bland expression on his face, simply nodded. The insult wasn't personal; it was a comment on food places in general.

Digits wasted no time getting to the point. "Boss wants a favor."

"Of course." What choice did he have? Evans had saved their lives in exchange for their services. Each time, Josh completed the job quickly and then put it from his mind.

"Could be fun or ... not."

Josh sat up straight and stared at Digits, who averted his eyes, probably afraid to risk getting mesmerized.

"I'm listening," the young vampire said.

"Get a woman pregnant."

I knew I'd hate the next task. Not that he didn't enjoy women, but he detested the prospect of sex with a stranger. A strange vampire? That could be exhilarating. Some strange woman who expected him to knock her up? Not so much.

Shocked into silence, he continued to stare, but the thug kept his gaze fixed on his coffee cup.

The silence stretched too long, so Josh broke it. "You want to expand on that?"

"Simple. Dhampirs are in demand, and we don't have a large enough supply. We're recruiting you to help fill the orders."

"You want me to have sex with a human and get her pregnant." His tone betrayed contempt, but he kept his expression neutral. Didn't matter. Digits never looked up from his coffee.

"Not necessarily. It can be done the artificial way if

you prefer."

Philip had gotten Dakota's mother pregnant. Had that happened under orders from Frank Evans?

Josh's lips parted as his fangs thrust out. A low growl escaped him before he could squelch it. Digits did look up then, his eyes widening, his heart rate picking up speed.

"What does that mean?" Josh forced the fangs to retract.

Digits exhaled, and his heart rate eased. "Through a lab. We'll set it up. All you have to do is donate."

Is that what my father did? Josh didn't think so. From what Dakota had told him, Philip and Annabelle, her mother, had slept together. Had actually dated. He'd sent child support payments.

"Why me?"

Digits sipped from his coffee before answering. "You're young. A vampire. Unencumbered. Working for us. It's a perfect setup. You don't have to worry about a relationship or child support. The women participating get paid to carry to term, and our organization collects the kid whenever the mother wants to give it up. The women get a final payment on delivery."

"Don't you have orders to fill? What if the mother changes her mind?"

"She can. She'd have to pay us back any money we've given her, and we'll never work with her again."

Josh doubted the mothers got off that easily, but he couldn't exactly call the man on it. "You selling kids to pedophiles?"

"Evans doesn't allow it."

Frank Evans has a line he won't cross? The mob boss had kids of his own; perhaps that gave him a bit of a conscience.

Donating sperm had advantages over what Philip and Annabelle had done, so why hadn't she gone the in vitro route? Based on everything Dakota had said, her mother had tricked Philip into a relationship.

Since Josh had no choice, and because it meant he'd avoid any romantic entanglements, he said, "Fine. Where do I get this done?"

CHAPTER 11

"You invited the man whose organization sold us Dakota." Culain paced between his father's desk and the coffee table in the sitting area in his father's office. The door was closed and locked. Four guards stood outside in the hall as a matter of course, two for each royal. King Killian sat behind the desk, his elbows on the chair, his fingers steepled in front of him.

"Didn't we cover this already? Of course we invited the Evans family. Frank Evans is a business associate. They wouldn't have come. They can't join us in a feast—they'd lose time on the other side."

Culain scowled. "I know that," he said, snapping out the words. "That's not the point. The point is, you invited them. It's a slap in the face to my wife." His speed increased, and his arms waved as he spoke, his hands gesticulating. "So much for avoiding human politics. We want nothing to do with their world until we do, right?"

The king sighed and, lips pinched, shook his head.

"You know how it works, son. We've always had to rely on the human world to boost our numbers. We still must. We can't source dhampirs without them." He indicated one of the chairs in front of the desk. "Sit down. You're wearing me out."

"Sorry. I wouldn't want my new wife's hurt feelings to distress you." The sarcasm in Culain's voice had Killian dropping his hands and leaning forward with a frown of displeasure. Even though he wanted to remain on his feet, Culain dropped into the chair.

"She's a woman and your property. Her feelings don't matter."

Culain sneered. "I beg to differ."

"I'm tired of reminding you how our society works. You marry. You beget children. Her job is to give you those children and perform the duties expected of a princess and then a queen: administrative tasks, public appearances, and charity work. That's it."

Culain leaped to his feet and resumed pacing. "She wouldn't see it that way."

"Make her see it that way. She lives here now. Pledged herself to you." Killian leaned back in his chair. "I suppose I can expand her functions somewhat. She seems clever enough."

"Swell. So we can agree she's not just a broodmare." Culain strode to the row of bookcases beside the door. They covered the entire wall. Across the room, a cheery fire burned in the stone fireplace. He recalled spending more than a few afternoons as a child playing with Colin on the colorful braided area rug in front of the fire while his father worked. Killian hadn't allowed them the pleasure of his company often, but after their mother was murdered, he had the nanny bring them to the office more frequently. Had guilt motivated their father to spend more time with them or had he worried someone might want to kill the boys too?

He spun around to face his father. "How did Mother die?"

Killian's face paled. His whiskers bobbed as his mouth opened and closed while he sputtered unintelligible words.

Culain held still while his father composed himself.

His face regaining its color, Killian said, "You know the story. It's depicted in the tapestry in the banquet hall—a reminder to all of our great loss, the fragility of even so-called immortal lives, and the reason we refuse to live among those on the Earth plane."

"Of course I know what the tapestry shows. That's my mother impaled on a tree with a spear rammed through her heart. But it doesn't show her killer, and no one has ever told me who's responsible."

His father's confused stare had Culain adding, "I asked." *Everyone but you.*

Father or not, Killian was the king and grief-stricken. At first, Culain hadn't asked because he hated to see the pain in his father's eyes anytime someone mentioned the queen. As time passed, though, he kept the question to himself because he feared the answer. Everyone he questioned refused to tell him. He assumed it was because of his youth. Eventually, he stopped bugging them, and they dropped it, probably relieved he'd forgotten about it. But he hadn't.

"I'm not a child anymore. I deserve to know."

Killian rose and moved to the nearby window. He peered into the courtyard below. Keeping his gaze fixed outside, he said, "An assassin targeted her."

Culain remained silent. The news didn't surprise him. He had a vague recollection of a silver teapot his mother had received. She'd called him over and showed him, explaining the so-called gift was an attempt to kill her. The teapot was pure silver, inside and out. If she drank tea steeped in it, she'd die. Anyone of faerie blood would. Silver burned them. Drinking something steeped in silver would burn them internally and would likely be fatal.

"She told me someone wanted her dead."

Killian turned from the window and faced his son. "You were just a boy when she died. She told you that?"

"Yes. She warned me to always guard against traitors. She said something beautiful can still kill you, and the closest ally can betray you. Even family." It struck him then how many layers and innuendos that warning contained. "Who, Father?"

The king nodded, his eyes distant. "She was wise—and cautious—but it wasn't enough to save her. Humans and mages lured us from the faerie realm. They made promises they had no business making, and when the species wars started, they turned on us when we refused to fight in them." He sighed as he dragged a hand through his thick mane of pale hair. "We backed away from that world, but they brought the war to us. Gave us no choice but to fight them. Luckily—or more from skill and ability—we purged our land of all others except the dhampir. They'd become ... necessary."

"Who gave the order to kill her?" Culain asked in a whisper.

"I can't tell you because he didn't do it himself. He sent an assassin," Killian replied. "I know only that they desired our family's demise to secure the throne for another. Someone they could control and manipulate. Any species outside our own is as bad as humans. All they want is wealth and power. They wanted to rule all the worlds, and it pained them they couldn't take over this one."

"Is the one who ordered it still alive?" Surprising that the fae hadn't sought retribution.

"I'd assume as much. Why do you think we have no position on the governing board? All others have a seat, share in leading the various empires. We don't."

Culain thought he understood. "They stay out of our affairs as long as we stay out of theirs. We give no power; we get no power."

"Correct." Killian returned to the seat at his desk. "We keep to ourselves for good reason, the only exception that blasted Running Loose tradition. I never liked it, but our subjects demand it. It's a wonder they permit us entry, but then, they probably still hope to conquer someday, perhaps from within. All who return from Running Loose are subject to scrutiny and must earn our trust before they're embraced once more into our communities." He shook his head. "The unmasquing helped some species, I suppose. At least, they probably think so. It harmed us, for the most part. I wanted nothing to do with non-faeries."

"Except the dhampir." Culain resumed his seat. "Without dhampir blood, we'd slowly go extinct."

"We'd have continued to use humans if the dhampir hadn't revealed themselves."

"How'd it all happen?" History books never specified what triggered the unmasquing. Culain had searched all the reference books about that and the species wars, but not one explained why it'd happened.

Killian shrugged. "Why do you think I'd know?"

"You know more than you let on, Father, and you lived it. History may reflect the views of the victors, but you were there when it all happened. Despite what our books say, what the humans' books say"—he'd requisitioned books from the human world and studied them without success—"you saw what actually happened. Perhaps it's time you shared it with me."

A knock at the door interrupted them. Culain rose and opened it.

Killian's butler stood there, a tea cart at his side. "His Majesty's afternoon tea, sir."

Culain waved him in. "Thank you."

"We'll continue this discussion another time," King Killian said as the butler poured tea into a dainty china cup.

"But—"

"Not now. I have work to do, and you'd best get to your duties. Don't you have a honeymoon tour to prepare for?"

He did, but it'd been so pleasant chatting with his father. He couldn't remember a time when his father had given him so much attention or treated him as an equal.

Reluctantly, he said goodbye and departed.

CHAPTER 12

A wooden trunk stood open on the floor in front of Dakota, and she picked through the clothes strewn across the bed in the room she shared with Culain.

"Three weeks is a long time to gallivant around the realm," Alina said from where she reclined on the bed. She'd kicked her shoes off and puffed up the pillows behind her so she could watch her friend pack.

"I agree, which is why I'm glad Culain let me invite you along." Dakota held a gown out to Lysandra, who was helping her pack. "This?"

"Yes, ma'am. You'll need at least ten gowns. Almost every day we're away, after you attend the feast, you'll have a formal ball in either a castle or a wealthy homeowner's mansion." The young servant girl carried the gown to a tall trunk that yawned open on the floor next to the walk-in closet.

"I don't know what I'd do without you, Lys. All these clothes, all this touring. I wish I could have a normal honeymoon." Dakota tried to picture strolling with Culain down the sidewalk next to the falls in Niagara Falls and chuckled softly. Niagara Falls was highly commercial—even more than before the species wars.

I wonder if the wax museums have Culain's mother's death on display the way the fae have it in their tapestry. She shuddered at the thought, but it wouldn't surprise her.

On the physical plane, they taught that piece of history in schools. Books never mentioned who'd killed her, but the famous scene of her impaled on a tree was ubiquitous in the history books. Journalist Mitzi Rainier had taken a photo with her phone's camera, and it became an indelible mark on history's landscape. The journalist was long dead, but her photo and name lived on.

"If you could go anywhere, where would you go?" Alina asked as Lysandra gave a shy smile to acknowledge her mistress's compliment.

Dakota considered, pausing in her quest to find enough stockings for a three-week trip. At least she wouldn't have to do the laundry herself. Those days were long gone.

The more she thought about it, the more she realized she had nowhere she wanted to visit so badly she'd leave the faerie realm.

At last, she said, "Here." Her expression reflected the stunned tone of her voice when she answered Alina's question. "I don't want to leave the faerie realm." She felt safe here. "I guess I've lived with the fae so long I no longer wish to return. It's beautiful here, and I have nothing over there I want." *Anymore.* Not her mother, that was certain. Not even Josh. Her romantic love for him had vanished, replaced by a hope that he'd find a way to be happy.

Alina sat up and folded her arms around her shins, resting her chin on her knees. "I've never visited the other side. My family wouldn't allow women to cross through the portal. My brothers went, and my father and his brothers as well."

"It's much safer on this side, trust me," Dakota replied. "Are any faerie women allowed across?"

"Oh, yes. I know a few who did, but they returned pretty quickly. I've heard tales of one who never returned, but I don't know her fate. They say she vanished, but when you're talking about faerie history, it can get distorted to suit what they want you to believe."

"What did your brothers think of the other side?"

After Running Loose, Fae youth could choose to stay on the other side or return to the fae realm, but once they decided, the choice became permanent. Culain had said he'd never heard of a faerie man staying on the Earth plane. They'd all returned, which echoed Alina's claims.

Dakota found that difficult to believe. Adults might feed this story to fae youth to manipulate them into returning. Even so, the tale might be true. Given the choice between the world that sold her and the world that bought her, she decided she'd take the latter.

"My brothers all came back. They didn't talk about it much. Said they explored different cities. Mingled with humans. Did you ever meet a faerie on their Running Loose?"

"Only once. I didn't talk to him. He walked into the coffee shop where I was sitting with my friends. He didn't do anything interesting. Didn't pay us any attention. He browsed through the books, bought something, and left." Dakota laughed. "Not exactly what I'd call making the most of your freedom."

Alina frowned. "I've heard some go wild. Go to bars." Her voice dropped to a whisper, as though she feared someone might overhear. "Have sex with humans—or other creatures. I heard of one fae boy who slept with a mermaid while she was in her fish form."

Dakota couldn't help smiling at that. "I don't think that's possible."

In biology, they'd studied mer physiology. Mers had to change into their human shapes to perform certain biological functions, and procreation was one of them.

"I never entered a bar before I came here." Some of the resentment she thought gone forever welled up then. "Too young."

She hadn't had a chance to live much beyond her childhood. Had barely dated. That brought Josh to mind again. Where was he? Was he okay? Had he given up on her? She hoped so, but it made her sad to think she'd never see him again. She handed the stockings she held to Lysandra and opened another drawer to retrieve her undergarments.

***

All their bags and trunks were loaded onto the carriage and secured in place. Three other carriages, transporting servants and more of the royal couple's belongings, completed the caravan.

Alina Lawrimore and Salton Hoxworth also joined them on this trip. As maid of honor and best man, the pair shared the coach directly behind Culain and Dakota's carriage. Colin stayed behind to perform Culain's duties in his absence.

Offering Dakota his hand, Culain helped her climb inside and take her seat.

While horse-drawn, there ended any resemblance the carriage had to medieval times. The body had electric windows, temperature control, and hydraulic stabilizers. The frame was gold, the body black. A royal coat of arms for the faerie realm adorned the doors and the back panel.

The coachman and footman climbed into their places as Culain took his seat next to his wife. Across from the royal couple, two guards took positions in the rear-facing seats.

One guard closed the door and signaled for the driver to start the journey.

Crowds had gathered to see them off, and amid cheers and best wishes, the carriage, heading toward the drawbridge spanning the castle's moat, rumbled down the castle drive.

Culain lowered the windows so he and Dakota could wave at their subjects.

Dakota's lessons in royal etiquette had started the day after she'd signed the agreement promising herself to him. She'd learned to do the delicate hand twist characteristic of the royal wave like a pro. She also had the smile down pat—no teeth, just a gentle curve of the lips. His actions and demeanor mirrored hers, and they kept it up for as long as the crowds lasted.

After what felt like forever but was actually ten minutes, according to his watch, they entered the forest, leaving the crowds behind. The trees formed a shady, green arch over their path, and with the breeze soft and cool, they kept the windows down.

"Highwaymen won't waylay us, will they?" Dakota asked. The smile she gave him was mischievous yet uncertain.

Culain returned it with a reassuring grin. "No. Patrols keep such folk off the roads, and over the last few days, the number of security teams sent out doubled. My father doesn't want us to run into any trouble. You don't see them, but we've got watchers along the way throughout our journey. Four armed riders will accompany us, and Godric Wagar, our captain of the guards, is personally coordinating everything and riding along as well."

He didn't mention the two guards sitting across from them, but he gave each man an appreciative nod.

Both soldiers returned the acknowledgment of their service with a polite nod of their own, their expressions remaining respectfully somber.

Dakota relaxed back into her seat, clasping his hand as she did. The motion was so unconscious his affection for her swelled. When they'd first brought her to him, she'd rebelled at the thought of an arranged marriage.

Be honest. She objected to being sold by her mother—to the fae buying her as if she were chattel. In her position, he'd have done the same.

That she'd not only given him a chance but had also fallen in love with him was nothing short of miraculous.

Not miraculous, he corrected himself.

Fae scientists had examined her DNA and had judged her perfect for him in every way. He was grateful that, after she'd learned that, she still gave him a chance. Perhaps she felt sorry for him because he also had little choice in the arrangement, but he'd at least had some say in who they brought him. He'd literally picked her out of a brochure, and then Evans's men kidnapped her and brought her to him. However, he'd had no choice in the picking. He'd had to choose someone from the photos even if he believed it unethical and immoral.

For now, his heart was full, and he gave thanks for whatever forces had brought this smart, beautiful woman into his life. She might not believe in fate, but he did. They were meant to be, and if she gave him a son soon, their lives would be complete.

CHAPTER 13

Downtown Tkaronto's major artery, Yonge Street, held commercial buildings, offices, and condos. The condo Josh shared with Kelsey and Philip stood on the corner of Yonge and Dundas. The original building had collapsed during the species wars. The current building claimed that location for the last fifty years. While young in vampire years, for a building it was old enough to render it outdated. However, the structure that housed their unit had been updated within the last five years. It contained all the desired amenities, met building codes, and looked almost brand-new. A holding company owned it, and Frank Evans owned the holding company—which made him their landlord.

Josh entered the foyer two days after meeting with Digits and greeted the security guard on duty at the front desk. The guard, a vampire, since this was primarily a vampire-tenanted building, returned the greeting. Josh strode to the elevators and pushed the up button. When the doors opened, a human female stepped out. She had fang marks on her neck and smelled of blood and sex.

His fangs threatened to protract, and he quickly brushed past her and hit the penthouse button. The doors closed before he lost control.

I win. He considered self-control a game he competed in with himself. It was all he could think of to keep himself in line. The baby vamp in him had receded, but it still threatened to leap out at inopportune moments. He could've snatched that woman back into the elevator and snacked on her, then hypnotized her so she wouldn't recall the incident, but he hadn't for various reasons. One, it was risky for him. Feeding off a human required written consent. Without that, he'd be breaking the law. The elevator had cameras. If the wrong person viewed the footage and identified him, he could wind up with a hefty fine or jail time. Two, it was risky for the woman. Someone had already fed from her—recently, from the looks of it. If he drained more from her without knowing how much she'd already given, she could slip into a coma or even die. And, three, he dreaded the prospect of losing control. He'd experienced it often when he'd first turned, and that period of his life was a haze of an overwhelming drive to violence overpowered by the frustration and fury over Philip forcing him to heel. Josh didn't want to return to the days when he needed a babysitter. Self-control meant freedom. He refused to backslide.

The hallway was empty when the elevator doors opened. He made his way quickly to their unit's door. Instead of entering, he paused to sniff and listen.

All seemed quiet until he detected the scent and sound of Kelsey and Philip. Josh hesitated. Did he want to see them right now? He was fresh from his first donation to the sperm bank Digits had directed him to. He'd told neither Kelsey nor Philip of Evans's latest assignment, and Josh wanted to keep it that way. He could lie well enough and maintain the requisite poker face if they questioned him, but he preferred to avoid the questions altogether.

"What're you hovering for, Josh?" Kelsey's shout from within the apartment decided for him.

He unlocked the door and entered the unit.

His mother reclined on the sofa, her head in Philip's lap. The older vampire stroked her hair, but she ignored his demonstration of tenderness as she always did. Sometimes, Josh pitied Philip the unrequited love he so obviously had for her. She slept with him, spent time with him, and acted very much the part of girlfriend for him, but she didn't love him. They all knew it. Still outgrowing her baby vamp phase, Kelsey had achieved the self-control required to go out in public unsupervised, but she hadn't manifested the capacity to love. It didn't appear to bother her, either. Josh related because he'd lost the capacity to love as well after turning—until his feelings for Dakota returned with such force they bordered on obsessive.

His last visit with her hadn't gone as hoped, but it'd gone as expected, so he didn't dwell on it. He simply added it to his self-control personal challenge to-do list.

With his thoughts still on Dakota and his recent visit to the lab—also owned by Frank Evans's holding company—to donate his sperm, Josh couldn't help but wonder about Philip and Annabelle's situation.

"Nice to see you home." Kelsey's tone was noncommittal.

Probably just making conversation.

Josh humored her. "Nice to see you, too." He strode to the loveseat, set at a ninety-degree angle from the couch.

Philip continued to stroke Kelsey's hair. She continued to seem oblivious to it.

At least she's not swatting his hand away. She'd done so in the past.

Josh cleared his throat, which brought Philip's gaze from staring at Kelsey's face to staring at her son with puzzlement.

"I need to ask you something," he said.

Philip's brows rose, but he said nothing.

Josh assumed that meant he should continue. "Annabelle. Why'd she go through the trouble of trapping you when she could've avoided that hassle and gone to a lab?"

Kelsey sat up and angled her body so she also stared at Philip. From where he sat, Josh couldn't see her expression, but now he regretted raising the subject in front of her.

"Why do you ask?" Philip said, his voice calm and controlled.

"Did you know about the labs?" Had Philip actually colluded with Annabelle and lied about Dakota's origins?

"Yes, which is why I believed her when she told me she loved me."

"Why would you get involved in a romantic relationship with a human?"

Philip rose and moved to the balcony doors. He gazed out into the city.

Josh followed, unable to drop the subject. The responsibility for everything Dakota had endured at

Annabelle's hands included Philip because he'd fathered the dhampir girl.

"I didn't want to," he said, opening the sliding doors and stepping outside.

Josh pattered along behind. His father behaved as though trying to run away from the conversation.

Kelsey rose from the couch and joined them.

Taking a seat at the patio table, Philip propped his elbows on it and buried his head in his hands.

"I fell in love with her." It came out a rasp of frustration. He lifted his face and glanced from one vampire to the other, settling on Kelsey. "I told you she made me think she loved me. I didn't want to get involved, but she scammed me. She led me to believe she needed my protection. That only I could keep her safe." He scowled. "She had that damsel-in-distress act down to an art, and I fell for it. What was worse, my business partner was in on it. He steered me right into her arms."

Josh sat down beside his vampire father. "But why go to all that trouble? Why not go through the lab? She could've avoided trapping anyone. She'd still get paid. Evans pays the women who carry dhampir babies to sell."

Pain wracked Philip's face. "She wanted my DNA. Some vampires' DNA carries a premium. I'm one of those." He rose again, went to the railing, and looked down. "She also wanted child support. I didn't know Evans was paying her. I took responsibility and sent her money every month for the child."

Traffic sounds and the bustle of life below wafted up along with the slight smell of oil and exhaust. The sun had started its climb back toward the horizon, and long shadows protected the three vampires from direct sunlight.

"Why you?"

Philip snarled. "What's with the third degree? You'd better not mess with the fae again."

"No. Of course not." He joined his father at the railing.

Traffic had slowed to a crawl, the streets jammed with vehicles, the sidewalks with pedestrians.

"I want the truth of what happened. Why you? Why'd we have to endure all that shit? Dakota. Me. You. My mother." He glanced back at Kelsey.

She'd taken a seat at the table and observed the two men, her expression unreadable.

"She had a choice. Didn't she?" he asked.

Philip contemplated. "She had a choice, but I'm not sure she knew it."

"Oh, please. She knew." Josh was certain Annabelle had known what her options were. She chose to take the longer way and hook Philip. "She didn't want you to marry her?"

"I wouldn't have married her. She understood that."

"Because she's human?"

"What other reason would I have? Why do you think your mother and I didn't want you and Dakota to date?"

"What right did you have to keep us apart?"

Philip put a hand on Josh's shoulder, but he shrugged it off.

"Don't touch me." A hiss escaped him.

"What do you want from me?" Philip spread his arms, palms out. "Tell me what you want, why we're really having this conversation."

"Dakota's married. Did you know that? Did you send a gift, perhaps? Did they *invite* you?" Rage over everything that had transpired since he'd last seen Dakota suddenly spilled out. He hadn't realized how much resentment he harbored over it. "She's out of my reach now. For good."

Philip grabbed Josh's arm. "What do you mean 'now'? She was out of your reach long before now. Did you go back after I ordered you not to?"

Horrified at the turn the conversation had taken, Josh tried to pull away, but the older vampire's hold was too great. "Not since you guys went to the spa last year." As soon as the words were out, he wanted to retract them. He'd forgotten Kelsey didn't know about that visit.

She leaped to her feet, her chair crashing to the cement floor of the balcony. "What are you saying? You went to the fae without telling me?" She whirled on Philip, fangs out. "You tricked me. You lied to me. How lovely. I thought you were so sweet taking me to a spa to relax. It was all a ploy to distract me so my son could sneak away to visit your daughter. You risked our lives." She growled and turned her fury back onto her son. "You!" She pointed an accusing finger at him. "You're why we got caught. Evans found us because you couldn't stop seeing that goddamn dhampir girl."

Josh tried to step away from the onslaught but bumped up against the railing. One glance told him his father thought he was lying about visiting the fae. He'd have to face them both.

CHAPTER 14

Philip stepped between Kelsey and Josh, his back to the boy. The elder vampire's arms rose in a placating gesture. "Hold on a minute. Josh didn't expose us. He entered and exited the faerie realm with no one the wiser." He spared a glance over his shoulder. "Right?"

"No one saw me." But the words sounded dubious. "I think." Less certain.

Philip raked a hand across his hair, his palm settling on his ponytail. When he realized he was fiddling with it, he released it, dropping his hand to his side.

"I was careful," Josh said. "I did exactly what you said, Father. No one realized I wasn't a fae citizen. They all thought I was a servant in the castle."

"When did you drop the glamour?"

Kelsey drew closer to the two men, and Philip placed a hand on her shoulder. "Let the boy speak." He kept her in his periphery while he watched Josh's expression.

"I ..." The young vampire's face fell.

"Not until you left the forest, correct?" Philip prodded.

"The fae forest."

"Be specific. Outside or inside the mushroom circle?"

The kid gulped. His lips parted. "Inside."

"Did you search for cameras?"

Josh's wide-eyed, guilty stare told them everything.

Kelsey snarled. "Perfect. You two colluded behind my back to spy on the fae and exposed us. That's why we're here." She waved her arm around the balcony, the gesture encompassing the condo's interior. "I'm a vampire because you couldn't control your obsession with that girl."

Philip pulled her into his arms. "I'm as much to blame as he is. I wanted to verify she was okay without causing you to worry. You needed to get away."

"So you took me to a spa and let him do whatever he pleased." She shrugged him off. "I never should've trusted you."

The regret and contempt in her voice tore at him, but more pressing issues existed. He fixed Josh with his gaze. Vampires couldn't mesmerize each other, but as the boy's sire, Philip could exert some control with his stare. "You went back, didn't you?"

"Yes."

"How many times?" He should've considered that if the first visit succeeded, the kid would risk more. How stupid not to realize how deeply Josh cared about Dakota.

"I'm a vampire now," Josh said. "She needed to know."

Philip growled low in his throat, and his fangs flicked out. The effort to retract them was almost too much, but he managed it. It wouldn't do to lose control or threaten violence in front of baby vamps. They struggled with it themselves, and he had to lead by example. But oh, how he wished he could leap onto Josh and give him a sound thrashing.

Forcing calm into his voice, Philip repeated the question. "How many times?"

"Four?"

"Are you asking me?"

Josh hung his head. "Four."

"When? Tell me everything about every visit."

Kelsey stepped forward, but Philip cut her off before she could interfere. "He'll tell us both, and we'll listen to everything he has to say. I'm assuming Evans doesn't know about these other visits or we'd have heard."

Josh strode to the chair Kelsey had knocked over and set it back in its place. "You might as well sit down. This'll take a while."

A scowl marring her features, Kelsey nevertheless sat without a word. She glared at her son, hostility oozing from her like sludge from a treatment plant.

To distract her, Philip said, "Grab us some bottles of blood from the fridge."

She bared her fangs but just as quickly retracted them. She rose and went inside.

He slid the patio door shut behind her so she wouldn't hear him and said, "If she loses control, you get inside and I'll deal with her."

"She's my child."

"Irrelevant. You defer to me. Clear?"

Josh nodded.

"Say it. Are we clear?"

"Yes, we're clear." He grimaced.

Kelsey returned, carrying three bottles of synthetic blood. She passed them around, and briefly, the three vampires drank together as though this were a normal evening around the patio table.

From the street came the distant sound of traffic. Overhead, a plane flew toward the Tkaronto airport. A movement in Philip's periphery had him glancing over to spot a shadow moving across the building. He rubbed his eyes, and it was gone.

Now I'm seeing things. He could've sworn the shadow had resembled a bear rearing up on its hind legs. *I need a vacation.*

He set his empty bottle on the table's glass top and opened the discussion. "Does anyone in Evans's organization know you recently visited the fae?"

"I thought they were oblivious to the first visit." Josh squinted, his brows lowering. His posture grew rigid. He set his unfinished bottle down and crossed his arms. "You're assuming I gave us away."

"You dropped the disguise while still at the portal. That was reckless."

"I made a mistake, okay? I was so relieved I got out that I dropped the disguise as soon as I crossed. I haven't done that again, and I changed my disguise. No one would know it's the same person." He shrugged. "Besides, I race through the portal. Any cameras would capture nothing or just a blur." He leveled his gaze at Philip, held it for a beat, and then confronted Kelsey. His words, when he spoke again, were defensive and defiant. "I learned from my mistake." He scrubbed a hand across his face and then placed it on his breastbone. "I'm sorry I wasn't more careful. You warned me." He faced his father again. "I did my best, and then I got reckless right when I should've used more caution. Easy to see that now, in retrospect. Armchair quarterbacking." His voice rose again, and his stance grew more defiant. "But I learned."

Philip stared out into the distance, but at this angle, other condos and office buildings blocked his view—not that this location afforded them much of a view unless you liked cement, steel, glass, and cars.

Ignoring, temporarily, that Josh never should've returned to the fae realm even if he'd learned from his mistakes, Philip said, "Tell us about your visits."

Josh relayed everything then—at least, Philip hoped they got the whole story. He wanted to believe the boy, but he'd been conning them for months. He'd have to work hard to regain their trust after this, especially since the kid had not only mingled with the fae while he'd infiltrated their home—the king's home—he'd also danced with Dakota at a major feast. On his last visit, he'd revealed himself to her. That put them all at risk again. They'd have to trust her to keep the visit to herself. No telling how immersed in the faerie culture she'd become. What if she felt obligated to reveal the visit to her husband? Philip said a silent prayer to whatever god might be listening that Dakota never spoke about Josh to anyone. At least he'd promised to never return to the fae realm.

CHAPTER 15

The first days of their honeymoon tour sped by in a blur of celebration and happiness for Dakota. The royal carriage stopped at every town the road passed through. Considering the crowds attending each feast, held on the evening of their arrival, folk from every neighboring town converged for the event. So far, they'd spent the night in three different villages. She'd grown accustomed to the routine after the second stop.

The carriages always pulled into a field provided for their use by the landowner. Culain explained that, rather than staying on the property of the wealthiest citizen, they paid rent to a struggling farmer. Culain and his father had chosen all the farms where they'd stay two weeks prior but had kept the route a secret from all but a few members of the royal security detail and the farmers themselves, who'd received messages ahead of time. The towns provided provisions for the feasts, but they were well compensated. The trip's goal was to not only show off the newly married couple to their future subjects but also to contribute to the towns and the citizens financially. It demonstrated the generosity and caring of the royal family. Ultimately, it illustrated how valuable and necessary the monarchy was to all the realms.

After Culain had expressed that, en route to the first town, Dakota asked, "Was the monarchy's existence ever questioned?"

He immediately said, "Never. This tradition plays a major role in that."

She believed him.

Everywhere they went, crowds greeted them with frenzied cheers and warm welcomes.

The setup for the nightly feasts fascinated and awed her. The fae erected enormous tents in the chosen farmer's field. Long tables and benches were hauled in. Servants prepared food in firepits and outdoor brick ovens. Kegs were tapped; wine and mead flowed generously. She'd expected a buffet-style setup, but considering even the largest feasts at the palace were served family style, she should've known these would be set up the same way. The royal company hired wait staff from the town, paying them more than they typically made as servers. All of those who'd waited on them treated the royal couple like beloved celebrities.

The first night, Dakota and Culain had sat outside on the porch of the farmer's house, watching the preparations. The nights following, though, she preferred to spend quiet time with him in the room the family assigned them—always the master bedroom.

On the night of the third feast, held in the town of Àird Nam Murchan within Eastern Realm, her guilt finally made her speak out about it.

"Must we always take the biggest room? We're

throwing a husband and wife from their bedroom. It bothers me." She stood, brushing her hair, in front of a dresser with an oval mirror on the wall above it. Lysandra had already helped her get dressed in her gown for the banquet and would return soon to help put up Dakota's long hair. Dakota used the time to, for once, brush it herself.

In the mirror, Culain's reflection smiled indulgently at her. "I'm sure you know the answer to that."

She sighed. "Yes. Why must we shove it in people's faces that we're ... their superiors? We're not, you know."

"My darling wife"—he grinned with delight at the word wife—"we have a role to play, and we must play it for the good of the realm."

"Who decided a class system is the best one? The realm has enough wealth to elevate every destitute person from poverty. Why doesn't the king do that?" Greed? Tradition?

"It's no different from the way countries run in your previous world. Did you have any issues with that?"

She shook her head. "I didn't realize the injustice of it all then. I didn't have servants when I lived there. No one dressed me, combed my hair, and applied my makeup for me. Every day! I've stopped trying to dress myself. It's stopped feeling strange when someone else puts my clothes on for me and does my hair. I'm surprised we feed ourselves and wipe our own asses." She set the brush on the dresser and turned to face him.

Culain guffawed at that last bit. "Your brashness never fails to astound and amuse me," he said between sputters. "I've never met a woman who told me exactly what she thinks."

He sat in an armchair with faded upholstery. The

room reflected the rest of the house: neat, clean, but old and shabby. The couple who owned it had worked hard to make their royal guests comfortable. They and their two children considered it an honor the prince and princess had chosen their home in which to spend the night. The money they'd get for it would help them run the farm and buy food or whatever else they needed. But this was merely one family in a town of roughly three hundred other households who could've used the extra money.

She almost made a comment about fae women, but they'd debated the subject before. He knew her thoughts about it. In the time since she'd first blurted out that fae women needed lessons in assertiveness, she'd mellowed in her judgment of them.

Judge not, lest ye be judged. She wasn't a big reader of the Bible, but she'd latched on to that tidbit as something worth remembering.

"This home we're in ... I'm happy we can help this family, but what about other families?"

"What about them?" He rubbed his chin. "I understand you feel sorry for their situations, but you can't take responsibility for every person in this realm."

"Isn't that what a good ruler does?" If they insisted on putting her in a position of power, they were damn well going to accept her input. *First the fae realm, then the world.* Her lips twitched as she smothered a grin. What nonsense that was. They hadn't given her any real power, nor would they. Culain would become king. She'd be the trophy at his side.

No. If they force this on me, I'll use it to help people.

As had happened many times in the past, her thoughts returned to the mermaid girl Dakota had encountered when Frank Evans's men had first kidnapped her. What had happened to the poor girl?

"Do faeries ever marry mermaids?"

Culain's mouth fell open for a second, but he recovered from his surprise at the abrupt change in subject and said, "No. Humans or dhampir. They suit us best. Mermaid-faerie—or merman-faerie, for that matter—matings wouldn't work. Can't reproduce."

"I see." Then who'd they kidnap the mermaid girl for? Why kidnap a mermaid? The possibilities that came immediately to mind made her sick inside.

Culain must've noticed her distress because he leaned forward, concern on his face and in his voice. "What's wrong?"

"Just ... I met someone once. A mermaid. I sometimes wonder what happened to her." Should she confide in him? Tell him where and how she'd met the girl? What could he do? What would he do? He'd probably tell her to forget they'd ever met.

"You know you can trust me. If something worries you, tell me. I'll do everything in my power to ease your burden. What's happening in that clever, beautiful head of yours?"

Overcome with love, she strode to his side and sat in his lap. She buried her face in his neck. "Thank you."

He ran a hand gently through her hair. "For what?"

"For letting me know you care." She sat up straight and stroked his soft, sweet face with the back of her hand. "I'm fine. A little overwhelmed with this whole excursion, I suppose."

A knock at the door had them both turning toward it.

"Come!" Culain said.

The door cracked open, and Lysandra stuck her head into the room. "My lady, might I come in? It's time to do your hair."

"Of course." Dakota gave Culain a peck on the cheek and hopped off his lap. She met his gaze and gave him a reassuring smile. "I'm fine. We'll talk more later, if Your Highness will allow me the pleasure of a private audience in the bedchamber tonight."

He chuckled. "If we have a private audience in the bedchamber tonight, we won't be doing much talking."

She giggled as she moved away to take a seat on the chair Lysandra had positioned facing the mirror. Once again, Culain had allayed her fears and squelched her doubts. Perhaps she should tell him her secrets. He was, after all, her husband. They shouldn't have secrets from one another. Josh popped into her mind then. Could she tell him about the vampire's visit? Somehow, she didn't think she was ready to go that far. *Yet.*

CHAPTER 16

Their journey's fourth feast was going as well as all the others had. Culain took pride in watching Dakota interact with his people. *Our people*. She was their princess. Everyone who met her in person loved and accepted her. He'd never questioned they would. The fae were used to embracing both humans and dhampir into their society. They had to or they'd grow extinct. Over thousands of years, sure, but without the infusion of blood from another species, they'd have probably already died out.

Culain, seated at the head table and finishing the last bite of his dessert, had to refrain from following Dakota. She had a guard for that.

She'd expressed a desire to circulate on her own, to talk to people without her husband the prince around. The young dhampir insisted it would allow people to open up to her.

He'd reluctantly agreed despite the uneasiness that plagued him whenever she left his side. He loved how independent she was, but that didn't mean he remained detached when she struck out on her own—even if that striking out was within his line of sight.

Does that make me a stalker? Controlling? He trusted her to make a good impression and say the appropriate things but feared for her safety.

His mother had been similarly outgoing and assertive. Is that why he'd fallen so hard for Dakota right from the beginning? Her looks had drawn him initially, of course, since a photo of her was the first thing his father had shown him. Then Culain had read the specs that went with the photo, and he'd fallen harder.

When he'd met her, the attraction became infatuation and then love after they spent weeks and months together. Now, he didn't think he could live without her—which spiked his unease again.

He rose.

If you can't beat 'em, join 'em, he thought as he wandered out among the guests' tables, his bodyguard trailing behind him.

Keeping Dakota in his periphery, he distracted himself by shaking hands and kissing babies. Before he knew it, he caught himself enjoying the socializing.

He moved to the next table, where a young faerie woman holding a half-dhampir half-fae toddler on her knee greeted him. When she tried to stand, he waved her down.

"Please, sit. The lad looks heavy. Growing like a weed, is he? And how old might he be?" He gently stroked the boy's hair but dropped his hand when the kid tilted a drool-soaked face into it. Culain unobtrusively wiped it off on his robe.

"He's two, just, my lord. We welcome you to our humble town and thank you for stopping here." Her grin revealed a missing molar on the top left side of her mouth.

He frowned. "Good woman, if I might ask, what happened to your tooth?" He gestured toward the left side of his mouth.

She quickly lost her grin and covered her mouth with one hand. "Nothing, Your Highness," she mumbled.

He glanced around, and when he saw a crowd watching them, he pulled out the chair next to her and leaned in close. "We fae rarely get cavities. Might I ask how you lost the tooth? I promise, if you answer me truthfully, I'll pay for you to have it repaired."

She dropped her hand and goggled at him. "Now, my lord, you know that's not possible. The tooth is gone."

He patted her hand. "You can get implants. We've learned a thing or two from the unmasqued world, and not just how to fight dirty."

The woman, who looked pretty in her own way whenever she kept the gap in her teeth covered, averted her gaze. "I went on the Running Loose, my lord."

Stunned, Culain replied, "Many do, and no shame in that, but they don't return with missing teeth."

A tear ran down her cheek. "I ran afoul of another creature. He pulled it to hear me scream, sir."

His heart beat madly, and his hands clenched into fists. "Who'd do such a thing?"

"Humans. They wanted me to do things with them. To them. I refused. They pulled my tooth, laughing while I screamed. Said it was a trophy they'd keep." She dipped her head, her face flushing with shame.

"They let you go after that?" He wanted to punch

something—or someone. Wanted to kick tables over and smash dishes. He held it in.

She shook her head. "Not until I did what they demanded anyway, and with a dhampir man." She stared at her child's head. "They said we do it to them, you see, and they'd make me pay." She met his eyes with a defiant gaze. "Jokes on them, my lord. I love my child what come of it."

"What's your name, lady?" he asked.

"Melanie Avril, my lord." She averted her gaze, ashamed once more.

"You have a mate?"

She nodded and met his gaze again. "They wanted to make me stay. Told me ... told me I could sell my child to them and then they'd let me go. They knew I'd get with child, you see. But I escaped and came right home. I'm raising my boy. My man, he always loved me. We were childhood sweethearts, but I needed to see what was outside."

She waved a hand as though the outside world were within hailing distance and continued. "He said he always wanted to have a half-dhampir half-fae child, and I was giving him his wish." She swiped at the tears. "I'm sorry, my lord. I didn't want to tell you, but you insisted."

He patted her hand. "That I did, and I'll keep my promise. You'll get that tooth replaced."

He waved over his assistant and instructed the man to ensure Melanie Avril received the dental care she needed.

Inside, Culain steamed. He didn't know who thought Running Loose was a good idea, but when he became king, he'd ensure no fae ventured into the other world again. He'd see the law changed even sooner if he could convince his father to pass a bill outlawing it. Surely, if their subjects knew of the real dangers on the other side, they would allow their rulers to outlaw it.

Culain bid farewell to Melanie, who cried from joy now rather than shame, and continued his tour of the feast tent. His mission had changed though. He'd come to socialize; now, he searched for information. How many faeries ventured into the unmasqued world only to return damaged and traumatized?

CHAPTER 17

On the following Sunday, Kelsey approached a church again, but this time, it wasn't the large and prosperous St. Michael's. She'd chosen one in a small town north of the city where no one would recognize her. St. George's hadn't existed before the unmasquing, and Kelsey had never set foot in it as a human. None of the members, including the priests, knew her. Even so, she lingered across the street and watched as the members filed in.

She'd dressed for the occasion, determined to attend the service. Since the morning was mild and sunny, she wore a long-sleeved white blouse and navy dress pants to protect her arms and legs. A wide-brimmed formal hat covered her head and shielded her face from the sun. She'd applied sunscreen and wore white cotton gloves. A kerchief draped around her neck, and she pulled it up over her nose and mouth whenever she stepped into direct sun. At the moment, trees shaded the sidewalk where she strolled, and she'd pulled the kerchief down.

The church was quaint, old-fashioned. Many churches built after the species wars had a lot of steel and sharp edges. This one was brick, and the many windows were stained glass. It made her feel at home and drew her to it.

She took a few hesitant steps onto the road.

A car swerved around her, the driver honking and giving her the finger. He startled when she bared her fangs at him but kept control of the vehicle and drove out of sight.

She pulled the kerchief over her nose and mouth, hurried across the street, and trotted up the cement steps to the propped-open double doors. A greeter stood at each side of the entrance, and both smiled at her. Acting as though she belonged there, she swept past the one on the left, accepting the paper he offered her as she did. She glanced at it to note the service schedule and agenda.

The smell of incense and candles burning mixed with lemony wood polish overwhelmed her. The roar of blood whooshing through veins and arteries throbbed in her ears. Her nose caught the tang of it over the other scents. A gentle murmur rose from the congregants, then a baby's cry, quickly silenced as its mother put it to the breast. When the organ burst into a loud melody, she almost walked out.

No, I'm doing this. She walked to the nearest pew— last row, left side. She slipped into the aisle seat. The church wasn't packed. A couple sat on the other end of the pew, but the bench was long enough that they were at least six feet away from her.

She tugged the kerchief off her face, letting it settle around her throat, and smoothed nonexistent wrinkles from her pants. Her hands, still clutching the piece of paper, she folded in her lap, the sheet of paper sticking up like a boat's sail.

The mass passed more quickly and less irritatingly than she'd expected. She remembered all the prayers, hymns, and motions required to participate. The priest droned on about sin and God and how everyone needed to follow Jesus to get into Heaven, of course, but her ears pricked up when he talked about redemption. He told the parable of the prodigal son— a parable she'd heard countless times when she'd attended church as a human—but now it resonated with her. One couldn't get more prodigal than by becoming a vampire.

Can a vampire return to the fold, though? Even if I worship God, what difference does it make?

Her hand wandered to the species identification pin on her lapel. So far, no one had looked askance at her. No one had made her feel unwelcome, but she assumed that was because they hadn't looked at her closely enough to notice her vampire status. Would they scream and point if they did? Would they chase her out? Her thoughts brought with them rage at the sense of injustice as she envisioned herself treated with contempt, and her fangs snicked out. Startled, she forced them to retract. No one had threatened her. The two greeters at the door had surely noticed her pin, and they'd simply smiled. Perhaps other vampires worshipped here. She scanned the church with all her senses but detected no other vampires in the building. A shame. She'd want to question them. Ask them how they reconciled their soullessness and connection to the demonic with the desire to worship God and enter His kingdom upon death.

It crossed her mind that most vampires wouldn't

care about that. Only a few months ago, neither had she. She'd gleefully sucked blood from living creatures—still hunted animals for a change of diet and for the thrill of taking them down.

She kept her seat as everyone else stood to take communion. The last time she'd gone to confession, she was a human and living in the apartment above her bookstore café with her son. *Simpler times.* She missed them. Philip had shattered their peace, but she refused to believe he was responsible for destroying their lives. If she believed in God—and she'd done so all her life—she could lay some of the blame at His great feet. After all, didn't everything happen for a reason? Wasn't it God's will that she became a vampire?

Kelsey closed her eyes and listened to the organ play, struggling to retrieve a semblance of peace from her God and her religion.

Why in the world does God want a Catholic vampire?

CHAPTER 18

Not that Josh gave a rat's ass where his mother was, but it puzzled him that she disappeared every Sunday morning without a word about where she went. It nagged him enough he questioned Philip about it even at the risk of opening himself up to his vampire father's probing.

"Where's Kelsey?" Might as well get to the point.

Philip muted the television from his seat on the couch, sat up straight, and met his son's gaze. "What are you doing up?"

Josh strode across the living room and sat on the loveseat. He rested one ankle across the thigh of the other leg. "Where'd my mother go?"

"Out."

"No shit. She gone again without telling you where? Something for Evans, maybe?"

Philip shrugged. "Didn't say." He scowled, demonstrating he, too, resented the secrets she kept.

"Why don't you ask her?"

"Why don't you?" Philip responded. "Why are you

up? Couldn't sleep?"

The mistrust between them was so palpable Josh's fangs slid out. He dropped his leg and sprang to his feet. Before his father could stir, Josh was in the kitchen with the fridge door open.

"Drink?" he asked, holding up a bottle of donated blood.

"Grab me a synth," Philip replied. "I already drank my quota of donated for the day."

Josh sneered. "We could afford all donated with the money Evans pays us."

"Just bring me a synth."

He grabbed a bottle of synthetic stuff and carried it to Philip, who accepted it with a nod of thanks.

"To answer your question," Josh said, twisting the cap off his bottle, "I sensed you both up, and I couldn't sleep."

"Sorry."

"Not your fault. I know you wake up when she does, and she always rises early on Sunday mornings." Realization dawned and Josh's jaw dropped. "Damn. It can't be."

"What's that?" Philip popped the cap on his bottle and took a long pull.

"She's going to church."

Philip pressed a hand to his mouth to contain the blood in it and swallowed with visible effort. He set his bottle on the coffee table. He said nothing for a minute or two and just stared incredulously.

Finally, he said, "Church? You're serious?"

Josh nodded. "That must be it. She used to go every Sunday. Before." No need to elaborate on what before meant. Philip understood because he averted his gaze as though self-conscious.

Good.

"But why? She's a vampire." Philip's tone reflected his puzzled expression.

Josh almost laughed. "She's still my mother."

"Who is a baby vamp. She shouldn't care about that."

Josh shrugged. "I don't, but it used to mean something to her. She believed. Maybe it's ..." He didn't quite know how to say it. Finally, he came up with "... muscle memory."

Philip smiled. "I doubt that, but I understand what you mean. She always did carry more than her fair share of angst."

"Should we stop her?"

"What for?"

Josh drained his bottle before replying. "In case it attracts attention. What'll the priest think? What'll the congregation think?" He recalled some of the holier-than-thou judgmental humans they'd met and frowned. Would they even allow her through the doors?

"Are you worried?" Philip finished his drink and stood.

"No. Yes. A little."

Pointing to Josh's empty bottle, Philip said, "You done?" When the boy nodded, the older vampire grabbed both empties and carried them into the kitchen. His voice floated out over the water running in the sink. "Want to go with her?"

Josh sputtered and then laughed out loud. "Are you kidding? Me? Step into a church? I didn't want to go when I was human."

Philip poked his head out from the kitchen. "I'll go then."

Josh stared. *That won't go over well.* He didn't voice the opinion. What he wanted was to make sure his mother didn't wreck their lives with another one of her stupid decisions. The irony of that didn't escape him. His stupid decision had brought Evans down on them. *Maybe.* Well, he'd never return to the faerie realms, so that point was moot, but it reminded him he wanted to discuss one more item with his father while they had the apartment to themselves. He broached the subject before he changed his mind.

"Have you ever donated sperm?"

Philip hurried from the kitchen and sat on the couch again. "Why?"

"For money."

"You're not considering it, are you?"

He tried to keep his tone and expression neutral. "What if I am?" What if he'd already done it? What if he'd had no choice?

"Are you okay with the idea of having your offspring out there somewhere without knowing where?"

No. "Sure."

"Look what happened between me and Dakota. Me and Annabelle. You don't want that."

"Which is why donating sperm works best."

"Why would you consider it? We make good money already."

"Just wanted your take on it."

Philip's gaze held steady. "My take is don't do it, but if you insist, I won't stop you."

"Any danger in it?" What concerned him most was having his DNA out there or the possibility of blackmail or another catastrophe he hadn't thought of.

"Everything carries risk, especially something like

that. I suppose it wouldn't hurt you personally. It puts your DNA in circulation. We work in a dangerous, risky business."

"Everyone's DNA is out there. The government collects it at birth. Took more when we registered my transition to vampire."

"Let's put it this way," Philip said. "Other than money, I don't see an upside."

That, Josh thought, was what bothered him.

CHAPTER 19

Kelsey strolled from the church, raising her scarf over her mouth and adjusting the hat on her head to protect herself from the sun as she did. Mass had calmed her nerves, as it had when she'd been human, but the feeling quickly vanished as she headed to her next destination. She had a list of businesses to visit. Evans had her collecting protection money from them once per month, much as his men had from her business before she turned vampire. Now she collected it from herself—one more thing to add to the litany of resentments building in her against Evans and his organization.

The row of shops she visited ranged along Yonge Street, south of Bloor Street, far from the vicinity of the Crossroads, where her small café still operated. Evans had at least spared her the humiliation of extorting her neighbors.

She visited five stores each Sunday, a different set each week, on a monthly cycle. No one spoke to her during these visits unless she spoke to them first. The business owners treated her as she'd once treated the two goons who took her protection payments: with grudging politeness and suppressed rage.

The first store she entered sold high-fashion clothing. Kelsey rarely shopped here. She cared nothing for the designer attire they sold. In the months since she'd started working for Evans, though, she'd found two occasions where she needed a fancy dress, and both were events to which the mob boss demanded her and Philip's presence in formal attire.

Jewel, the store's owner, glanced up when Kelsey entered, the opening door sounding a chime to alert employees to a potential customer's arrival.

The two women nodded to one another, and Jewel immediately strode to the cash register.

Kelsey worked alone. She had no reason to fear the store owners. Not only were all of them human, but they also distrusted vampires and, more specifically, Evans. They'd learned long before Kelsey started her rounds that they needed to pay up or lose their livelihoods if not their lives.

Even so, most of her intimidation tactics consisted of smoke and mirrors with the help of her vampire abilities and strength. So far, she hadn't needed more than that. Her visits always went smoothly. She recalled the two men who'd visited her store in the days before Philip had crashed her life. Two big, burly guys, and they'd had to pair up to pry protection money from a single mom? *Laughable.*

Jewel returned with an envelope. Kelsey accepted it with another nod and stuffed it into her jacket's inside pocket. She left the store and immediately entered the coffee shop next door.

A bottle of donated blood awaited her when she

entered the restaurant, and she carried it to a table near the front windows. She took her time sipping it while she watched the owner serve customers or spot clean when the foot traffic dwindled.

The owner, Kent, was an older man, salt-and-pepper hair on his head and in his beard, whose wife had recently passed. He'd insisted on offering Kelsey the drink whenever she came in, and she'd ceased protesting that she didn't want it.

Perhaps he needed to do it, but she couldn't figure out why. Did he think she'd cut him a break on the payments? Intervene on his behalf to Evans? Would he poison the blood one day, adding colloidal silver to it to burn her internally? Or perhaps he wanted to build goodwill. Maybe he was. She'd grown fond of him over the months. He'd tried to engage her in conversation despite her making it clear he shouldn't. Every so often, though, she indulged him and let him talk. He was the one who'd informed her when his wife had passed. She hadn't felt sorry for him, but later that day, she'd purchased a sympathy card from the variety store down the street. She'd signed it and stuck it in her purse. It was still there.

Whenever the urge to give it to him overcame her, she squelched it. Evans had warned her not to get involved with any of their "clients." So far, she hadn't. He'd told her not to bother learning their names, but that she couldn't help. They all insisted on it, probably afraid that if she didn't know their names, she'd view them much as a farmer viewed his cattle.

They had a point.

She drained the bottle and walked the empty back to the counter. She exchanged it for the envelope of money, and with a nod, she left the coffee shop. Kent's place was always the one that slowed her down. One of these days, she'd ask him about it or give him that damn card, but so far, she hadn't broken down.

The next three store visits went more quickly than the coffee shop, but she spent extra time at the last one—an antique store. She couldn't help herself. She got a gift for Philip, much to her surprise. For the first time since her turning, she thought about making him happy, putting a smile on his face. Not understanding why, she picked up trinkets that harkened back to the 1980s, a time before the unmasquing and the species wars. Maybe even before he'd turned.

He'd never told her much about that time—he'd certainly never shared the identity of his maker—but sometimes he waxed nostalgic about the good old days. What she'd bought him wasn't much—a case containing buttons with different rock group logos or designs on them. The square buttons had mirrors with band names or logos on the front. Each had a safety pin glued onto the back. The bands originated in the 1960s and 1970s. Philip insisted no one made music like that anymore. He'd probably enjoy seeing the badges from his youth. She couldn't wait to take it home and give it to him.

She adjusted the scarf covering her nose and mouth when it started to slide down but then realized she walked on the shadowed side of the street. She yanked it down so it puddled around her neck. A glance at the time on her cell phone showed it was almost three. She needed to deliver the money to Evans's second-in-command before she could clock out for the day.

A nearby shortcut led directly to her destination, but it meant going through an alley. She hesitated but not for long. Kelsey patted the gun in the holster under her jacket and zipped into the alley at vampire speed.

When she paused to scale the fence bordering the parking lot she wanted to cross, a hand on her shoulder hauled her back to the ground.

"Not so fast," someone hissed. A powerful hand spun her around.

Before her stood two vampires. One of them had a gun pointed at her breast.

"The money," Gun Vamp said, his long dark hair falling across his face in wisps.

Each would-be mugger wore a wide-brimmed hat, and a bandanna over his face that covered nose and mouth. Both stood tall and lean.

"Now," Gun Vamp said. "The bullets are wooden."

Kelsey considered leaping at him and attempting to wrestle the gun from his hands, but she had no idea how. She glanced at his partner, a blond with piercing gray eyes.

He shook his head. "Wouldn't turn out well for you."

"You're crossing Frank Evans," she said. She couldn't overpower them, but perhaps Evans's reputation would prevent them from taking the money or killing her.

"Yeah. We have a message for him you can pass along," Blondie said.

"What's that?" She shifted from one foot to the other. Set her bag from the antique shop on the ground beside her.

"This is our territory now." Blondie followed up the words with a fist to her face.

After that, everything blurred, and when the beating ended, Kelsey lay on the ground at their feet.

Blondie crouched beside her and leaned in so he

could speak into her ear. "Tell him the Chief says hello."

Before they left her, bruised and bleeding on the pavement, they stole her gift to Philip.

This is why it's better to have a partner, she thought and slipped into unconsciousness.

***

Josh had been about to dive into the depths of Lake Skanadario when Kelsey's terror and rage pierced his psychic veil. Immediately, he homed in on her, but he arrived too late to catch the culprits in the act.

He kneeled and touched her shoulder. She stirred and took a weak swing at him before recognition dawned in her eyes.

"Sorry," she rasped.

"What happened?" Though he could guess. He drew her into his arms, cradling her against his chest.

"They took Evans's money."

He ignored that for the moment as he examined her injuries.

"Take my blood." He opened his wrist before she could protest. He insisted she suckle and assumed they'd beaten her severely when she didn't protest.

Her superficial wounds healed quickly, but the black eyes and any internal injuries would need more time. Her pride would take even longer.

"I couldn't hold them off. Didn't get in one decent shot." Her fangs snicked out, and she didn't attempt to retract them. "I won't let that happen again. Teach me how to box."

He raised his brows. "I don't think I can. You need to learn from someone who can teach, not just fight."

She scowled. "Evans will blame this on me."

He shook his head. "Two against one, and they ambushed you."

Her head drooped, and for a moment, he feared she'd passed out again. Then he realized she hung her head in shame.

"Don't tell Philip what happened."

He put a finger under her chin and raised her head so their gazes met. "I won't, but I will come with you to face Evans."

"Josh …"

"Not up for debate, Mom."

His use of Mom had the desired effect, and her gaze softened. "Then we'd better go. Looks as if there's a new boss in town, and he flexed his muscles at my expense." Her lips pressed into a thin line, and her eyes hardened. "I'm not letting him get away with it."

He helped her to her feet as he rose to standing. "Then we'd better go see Evans immediately." Whoever had dared cross the mob boss was either extremely powerful or extremely stupid. Josh didn't want to waste any time telling Evans. Let him focus his wrath on some unknown entity and not on Kelsey.

CHAPTER 20

The sun set on another feast. Dakota could barely keep track of the towns they'd spent nights in, but she had no trouble remembering the name of the town where Culain's mood had taken a downturn: Eastern Realm's Àird Nam Murchan. He didn't want to talk about it, which irritated her. He actually tried to pretend everything was fine. At first, she'd wondered if she'd done something to offend him, but when she pressed him on it, he insisted he loved her and nothing bothered him—especially as far as she was concerned.

And yet.

And yet he frowned more often. Danced less. Smiled less. His appetite suffered.

At the moment, they sat on the front porch of another farmhouse they'd commandeered for their own use.

Not commandeered. The family had a choice, and we paid for the rooms. Those facts helped ease her conscience, but they didn't completely assuage her guilt.

Dakota sipped from the mug of creamy hot chocolate she held. She usually drank tea in the evening, but the townsfolk had proudly presented her and Culain with a personal supply of the highly prized and scarce chocolate. The royal couple felt obligated to crack into the stash and share it with the farmer, his family, and the servants. Lysandra had gushed with gratitude at their generosity, as had the farmer's children, who'd never tasted chocolate before.

Culain hadn't touched his drink and, as was the case since they'd left Àird Nam Murchan, spoke little as they sat together watching the deepening darkness. Out in the yard, solar lights flicked on, throwing a soft glow onto spots around the property.

Dakota tried to bring him out of whatever funk held him captive. "This drink is delicious. I love it. The people in these towns are so kind and generous. They call us that, but we can afford to be generous. Those who have nothing and still give—they're the generous ones."

Her husband nodded. He stared out into the cornfields surrounding the house's main property.

The front yard had flowers and bushes and neatly manicured grass with a small pond near the road. Dakota's sensitive nose picked up the sweet smell of various night-blooming flowers and somewhere in the distance the aroma of skunk. The chorus of peepers dominated the evening sounds from the yard and the water from which bulrushes grew tall.

"They've made a beautiful home for themselves on very little money." She peeked at him from the corner of her eye.

Culain continued to stare into the distance. His eyes refocused as he realized she'd spoken to him. He turned and smiled at her.

"Yes. This family struggles less than others we've stayed with. This town struggles less than others we've spent time in."

"We have one more week of travel. Are you looking forward to returning to the castle?" Maybe the length of their trip and enforced absence from his life at court disrupted his normally cheerful self.

He nodded.

They fell silent, Culain back into his shell and Dakota lapsing into frustration at her inability to draw him out. Should she confront him on it? She'd tried to treat him gently, hoping tact would help him relax enough to confide in her, but she was his wife. He should confide in her for that reason alone.

Unable to sit quietly any longer, she said through clenched teeth, "Tell me what's bothering you. I've tried to give you space, but something's clearly upsetting you ever since we left Àird Nam Murchan. What happened to make you so sullen?"

When he didn't respond at first, she almost jumped to her feet and walked out on him in frustration, but she forced herself to wait.

"I'm sorry." He turned away from the sunset and met her gaze. "I didn't intend to shut you out. Honest. I didn't want to burden you with what is my problem. The realm's problem."

She sipped from her cocoa to give herself time to calm down.

He's acting the man. Don't take it personally. Yet she couldn't help feeling hurt. Wasn't she at his side for a reason?

She kept her voice even and said, "Tell me. What happened?"

THE EMPRESS: A PROMISE OF RAIN

He scanned the area and squinted through the screen door into the house to verify no one was around. Their two guards, always on duty in twelve-hour shifts, stood out of earshot at attention on the grass. Both were fae and so didn't have a vampire's hearing.

Culain lowered his voice when he spoke. "I met a woman who'd visited the human world. She was ... mistreated there. Harmed. Nothing was done about it when she returned. No retaliation for what they'd done to her."

"Who did this?"

"Humans—and a dhampir. She didn't know who controlled them, but someone did."

With a sinking feeling, Dakota suspected she knew. Frank Evans held much of the territory outside the nearest portal into the Earth plane. If this young woman had run afoul of a human gang, Evans, or someone working for him, likely gave the orders. Feeling a bit hypocritical, she kept that to herself. *At least until I know what he intends.*

"You want to do something about it?"

"Yes."

Hot chocolate churning in her stomach, she said, "What?"

He sipped from his drink then, a good sign, but now she'd grown anxious and couldn't choke down another drop. She'd dreaded the thought of him wasting expensive chocolate. At least she no longer had to worry about that. Why it should bother her so much, she didn't know.

Because it's wasteful. When she'd lived with her mother, they'd endured long and frequent periods of poverty. *Until she started selling herself for money, and she must've made a nice chunk of cash from selling me to the fae.* The stab to her heart that brought with it distracted her from the current conversation, but Culain abruptly brought her back.

"I want to ban our citizens from visiting the Earth plane. No one should risk going there."

Dakota placed her mug on the porch's wooden boards and buried her face in her hands. That wasn't the answer she'd hoped for, but it was the response she'd feared. How would he react when she disagreed with him?

Unable to stop herself from speaking out, she said, "No one will want that. I don't think you should pursue that course of action." In an attempt to soften the verbal blow, she added, "My lord."

The flush of fury creeping up his face told her she'd chosen her words rashly.

CHAPTER 21

When Josh and Kelsey arrived at the Evans home, they were refused entry.

"I'm sorry, but Mr. Evans says you must make an appointment," the woman in the maid's uniform who opened the front door told the pair. "He also says you should've announced yourselves at the front gate."

"We're sorry," Kelsey replied, a distinct note of sarcasm in her tone, "but when Mr. Evans hears our news, he'll be grateful we came. We didn't have to take time out of our day for this visit."

The woman, about twenty and youthfully pretty, frowned and shook her head, her dark curls bouncing atop her shoulders. "He said he didn't want to be disturbed and you should schedule an appointment."

"I'm fed up with this nonsense," Josh said. Grabbing her around the waist, he lifted her up and set her, struggling and with tears in her eyes, aside. "No need to show us to the office. We know the way." He barged into the large foyer.

Without caring what she did after that, he charged down the hall, Kelsey following in his wake.

The maid's protests chased them, but she didn't try anything more to stop them.

"He won't like this," Kelsey hissed.

"I don't give a shit. Someone has to tell him."

"I mean he won't like you pushing your way inside. He might make an example of us over it." She hated working for the man, but so far, he'd given them money and jobs that weren't dangerous—if you ignored the fact that she'd just been beaten and mugged. Every job had its risks. She could've gotten mugged walking home from the grocery store. If Evans wanted to, he could make their lives a living hell.

They strode past the living room, a powder room, and a kitchen before they arrived at the closed door they recognized as the entrance to Frank Evans's office.

She raised her hand to knock, but Josh shoved it aside.

"He knows we're here." He slammed the door open, bouncing it off the inside wall with a bang. He caught it on its return and ushered her inside with a flourish of his hand.

Evans had risen from his desk, his face purple with rage. The patch over his left eye wrinkled as his good eye squinted at them. "What do you two think you're doing?"

She checked his hands and verified he held no weapon. She was also relieved to see they'd caught him alone. If he had guards on the premises, they were nowhere in sight.

"Give me one reason not to have you thrown out of here."

They stepped inside, but before Josh could close the door, a thuggish-looking vampire stopped its progress with an outthrust arm.

"You think one vamp can do that?" Josh said.

Evans did a double-take as his gaze slid over Kelsey. "What the hell happened to you?"

She pressed a hand to her eye. It still felt tender but had already healed substantially. What he saw was nowhere near the damage she'd initially sustained not so long ago.

"That's why we're here."

"Step outside and shut the door, but stay close," he said to Vampire Thug, who obeyed immediately.

When the door thudded shut, the crime boss moved from behind the desk and approached mother and son. "All right. What happened?"

"Two vampires mugged me after I did my collections this morning."

Evans's face, which had returned to its usual olive white, darkened again. "They took all the money? Beat you up?"

"That's the definition of a mugging," she replied. She glared at him, daring him to tell her to replace the day's take out of her own pockets. Wisely, he didn't, but she couldn't decide if it was out of fear of her reaction or because it was unfair.

"Going forward, have a partner accompany you," he said.

"Sure." She side-eyed Josh, but he wasn't looking in her direction. Either he or Philip would have to accompany her on her rounds, and she'd prefer her son. He scowled suddenly, which meant he'd probably drawn the same conclusion.

"They knew I work for you," she said. "They want

me to give you a message." She averted her eyes. The whole situation seemed ludicrous. Like a bad movie or gangster show.

"Well?"

She shrugged and met his gaze. For an older man—she guessed he was almost sixty—he remained ruggedly handsome even with the few extra pounds he carried. "They said that territory is theirs and to tell you the Chief says hi."

"Who the fuck is the Chief?" He spun away and stalked to his desk as though not expecting a response.

"Someone with a death wish," Josh said.

Evans dropped into his chair and brushed a hand through his wavy salt-and-pepper hair. His gaze met Kelsey's, and he gave a loud sigh. "Learn to fight, and then find those guys and teach them a lesson. Two vampires shouldn't have gotten the jump on you."

So that was her punishment for losing the money. She wouldn't have to repay the stolen cash, but she'd have to get her hands dirty. Kelsey suspected that once she successfully got violent for him, she'd never return to simple collection jobs again.

The image of the muggers pummeling her and stealing Philip's gift flashed into her mind. She smiled. "Whatever you say, boss."

***

"I don't want to tell Philip what happened," Kelsey said as soon as she and Josh left Evans's house and the door shut and locked behind them.

"We have to." He followed her down the front steps and to the walkway.

"No, we don't." She strode forward, barreling

ahead.

He caught up and kept pace easily. "Of course we do. You were mugged. Beaten. He'll not only want to know two vamps jumped you, but we have to tell him someone's trying to horn in on Evans's territory. Plus, we can't avoid telling him about your new assignment."

She stopped walking and talking as they arrived at the closed gate. She glared at it, and whoever manned the camera noticed because it slid open. The pair strode through the opening.

Kelsey led the way home along the side of the road, but they'd have to hit vampire speeds eventually to arrive that day.

"We keep our assignments to ourselves," she said. "We always have. I'm not about to change that. Just because you know about it doesn't mean I have to tell Philip."

"He still loves you."

"That's his problem." Because that sounded cold even to her ears, she added, "I sympathize with him— I really do—but I can't change my ability, or inability, to love." She hoped that would satisfy him.

It must have because he didn't comment further on the subject of Philip and love, but Josh maintained his insistence that they needed to reveal to their leader what had happened.

"I'll tell him there's a new boss in town," she said at last, suggesting the compromise to get the kid off her back.

"He's at the bar," Josh said.

"You want to tell him now?"

"He needs to know, Mom. If they hit you, they might be after him, too."

Shock made her halt and face him. It'd never

occurred to her they'd want to attack Philip. *Or Josh. Maybe I'm just the first one they found.* But she'd given Evans the message. Surely, the Chief, whoever he was, would consider the job done.

Even so. "You watch your back, too, Josh. They might decide Evans isn't taking it seriously enough." Suddenly, she wanted more than anything to verify Philip was okay.

"Let's go," she said and hurtled away at vampire speed toward Blood Shots.

CHAPTER 22

At this time on a Monday afternoon, Blood Shots, the bar Philip had owned that now belonged to Frank Evans, was silent and empty. Philip strode through the bar area but stopped short when he noticed an unfamiliar painting on the wall. A metaphorical chill raced up his spine.

It showed a grizzly rearing up on its hind legs, a full moon beaming down on it. The bear stood next to a tree, and behind it flowed a stream from which a salmon jumped.

He zipped over to the painting and studied it. A slight film of dust coated the top of the frame, telling him this wasn't a recent addition. Why hadn't he noticed it before? Why had he noticed it now?

Because I've had grizzly on the brain. It was nothing. Meant nothing.

His First Nations grandmother would've begged to differ, but she was long dead. He shrugged it off as a coincidence.

As if mocking his denial, a shadow moved across

the wall, too swift to identify but as huge as a bear. He spun around but saw nothing and no one.

Before entering his office, and after he'd toured the bar area to make sure everything appeared in order, he visited the back rooms. They were used for private activities, including consensual sex between patrons—for a fee, of course. All legal, as far as the police were concerned. As long as no money between participants changed hands, they could do whatever they wanted. They need only sign waivers and ensure no one got hurt. As usual at this time of day, the rooms were empty, neat, and clean. Cleaning staff had refilled condom dispensers and restocked the complimentary toiletries. Fresh towels filled wicker baskets next to a small sink and vanity. No trace of anything messy or sordid remained in evidence—as long as you ignored the fact that a bed was the focal point of each chamber and a mirror graced every ceiling.

He checked the bathrooms, which were also scrubbed clean and made ready for the business day to begin.

A sound and scent alerted him to someone's presence on the loading docks out back, but he recognized one of the regular employees. He took only a cursory peek to verify they'd received the proper shipments for the night and continued on his way.

He entered the back where the offices were located. Evans had used insurance money to rebuild and redecorate the entire building, giving it a more modern look and a more spacious feel. The arson case remained open because Philip, who'd burned down the bar in a fit of rage and vengeance, remained free. He assumed no evidence tying him to the crime existed. He hadn't worried about getting arrested in months, but he remained uneasy that, one day, Evans would learn the truth.

Not as long as Dwayne Rathburn remains missing. Dwayne might be able to turn the investigation's spotlight back onto Philip. Philip, after his return, had refused to admit to anything when the cops—and Evans—questioned him. As far as they were concerned, Philip, Kelsey, and Josh had all been hiding in Algonquin at the time the bar burned down. Both mother and son had backed the story up, and without solid evidence, Philip remained a free vampire.

As much as he was capable of doing, he pushed the anxiety aside and entered his office. The new room held none of the personal touches he'd had in the old one, but he preferred it that way. This was his workplace. Business only. Whenever he came in, he did whatever he needed to do and left. The office was sparsely furnished, the desk fake wood, cold steel, and sharp edges. The chair was ergonomic, imitation leather, and the room's nicest piece of furniture. He no longer had a private wet bar. He didn't even bother to keep a bottle of whiskey and some glasses handy. Anyone he wanted to meet for business would join him at a table in the bar. If they wanted privacy, he'd meet them in his office and have a server bring them drinks. It was his way of silently and, if he was honest, passive-aggressively, protesting his situation. Every visit to Blood Shots was another reminder of what he'd lost. Evans ordering Philip to manage the bar stolen from him chafed, and the mob boss meant it to.

One of these days, Philip would get his revenge and reclaim it, but no strategy to accomplish that came to mind. So he arrived at work each day, ran the bar, and made it profitable.

He strode to his desk. The message light blinked at him. He entered his code and listened to the three messages awaiting his attention.

The first was a supplier confirming an order. The second voice belonged to a woman asking for a job. The third had his fangs popping out and a snarl escaping his lips.

Annabelle.

He held his nonexistent breath as he listened to what she had to say, which wasn't much.

"Call me. I have a proposal for you I think you'll want to hear." She'd left a number and disconnected.

Tempted to not only ignore the call but also erase the message, Philip hovered his hand over the delete button but changed his mind and pressed the save option. He could just imagine what kind of proposal she had for him.

The bitch is relentless. And crazy. Why would she think he'd want anything else to do with her? Ever since she'd sold Dakota to the fae, he had no reason to speak to her. They no longer shared a child together. He owed her nothing. If anything, she owed him though what, exactly, he couldn't say—a moral obligation, perhaps. Or an apology he'd never receive.

He finally decided returning her call was the best choice. If he didn't find out what she wanted, it might end up causing him problems. She clearly had some scheme in mind and expected to drag him into it.

As he punched in her number, he remembered to retract his fangs and calm himself. When she answered the phone with a cheery hello, he sounded reasonable and simply curious rather than enraged.

"I got your message." *Or I wouldn't have called.* His fangs threatened to bust out again, but he controlled them, and the urge passed.

"Well, Philip Belanger. I didn't expect you to call me back so soon. How are you?"

"Fine." He scowled, but naturally, she didn't see it. He kept the animosity out of his voice when he added, "What's the proposal?"

"It's too important to discuss over the phone. I want to meet with you."

His temper got the better of him. "We're done, Annabelle. Tell me what you want so I can turn you down and never speak to you again."

"Don't be like that."

Did she really think that wheedling tone would sway him? "Out with it."

She sighed. "I want to get pregnant again. I'd like you to be the father."

Silence filled the air between them as he hunted for a word to settle on that would convey how insane he thought her. "I said I want nothing to do with you."

"I'm upfront about it this time. We don't even have to sleep together. We can do it through in vitro. You donate it and sign it over to me." The timbre of her voice changed to contain a sexy lilt that disgusted him. "Unless you want to do it the old-fashioned way. We had a good time together. I know you enjoyed it. I'd make sure you came away satisfied."

"Listen carefully so I won't have to repeat myself. No. Never. Get out of my life. I want nothing to do with you." In case she'd missed his point, he asked, "Do you understand?"

All he heard in response was shallow breathing. He waited. Just as he was about to repeat the question, she said, her tone dejected, "I understand." Neither spoke for a long moment; then, her voice perky once more, she said, "If you change your mind, call me."

"Sure." Not caring if she caught the sarcasm in his tone, he hung up without saying goodbye. Satisfied he'd heard the last from her, he went on to the next item of business and returned the job-hunting woman's call. As he listened to the phone ring at the other end, he recalled his conversation with Josh about donating sperm. Two people he knew were messing with reproduction for pay. He almost didn't hear the woman's hello as it hit him that Evans must've orchestrated both situations.

Suddenly, he'd lost his desire to talk to anyone.

"Sorry," he said to the woman. "Wrong number."

He'd no sooner hung up than someone tapped on the door and opened it before he responded with an invitation to enter.

His face pinched in irritation until he recognized Josh and Kelsey. Both looked agitated; both barely concealed their anxiety.

"What's up?" He hurried to greet them.

"We need to talk. Some new mob boss is trying to take over Evans's territory," Kelsey said. She strolled past him and took one of the two chairs in front of the desk.

Her tone was all business, which irritated Philip.

The two men exchanged glances, but neither spoke until they'd followed her to the desk. Josh sat beside his mother, and Philip moved around to the other side and took his seat.

He folded his hands on the desktop and tried to keep his expression neutral.

"What happened?" Something had or they wouldn't have shown up at his office. They could've phoned to tell him there was a new boss in town.

"Two vamps mugged Mom."

Snarling, Kelsey shot her son a withering look, but he continued, unperturbed. "They jumped her and stole her money. Gave her a message for Evans."

Philip studied Kelsey. Based on her reaction, she hadn't wanted Josh to tell him this. He ignored the fear that had settled in his chest. They'd mugged her but hadn't killed her. She looked unharmed, but that didn't mean they hadn't hurt her. Depending on when it'd happened, she could've healed from anything minor relatively quickly. That reassured him. They'd wanted to send a message, but not one that triggered a war between the two organizations.

"What was the message?"

"The Chief says hi."

"That's it?"

"That and they stole all the money I'd collected. Roughed me up so I still had black eyes and obvious bruises when we visited Evans." She scowled.

Philip turned to Josh. "I assume you sensed her in trouble and raced to help her?"

"Yeah, but they'd disappeared by the time I arrived—and it didn't take me long to show up." He leaned back in his chair. "They expected me and left before I caught them in the act."

"How'd Evans take it?" Philip turned his gaze back to Kelsey. "Is he expecting you to pay him the money they stole?"

"Yes."

Josh's head snapped around, but he kept his mouth shut, his lips pressing together into a thin line.

"It's not that much," she said hurriedly. "I'll pay it back and watch my back next time." She shrugged. "He wants someone to accompany me going forward. It'll be fine."

"Anything else?" Based on Josh's reaction, she was hiding something, but he didn't want to press her. Maybe Josh would enlighten him later.

"We told you because you need to watch your back." Kelsey rose. She squirmed and glanced at the door. "We gotta go."

Josh remained seated, but she put a hand on his shoulder. "Come on. Philip's busy. We'll see him at home."

Looking unhappy, the boy nodded and stood. "Yeah, sure. I got stuff to do anyway."

They walked to the door, and she opened it. She strode out without saying goodbye, but Josh hesitated, frustration evident on his face.

"Watch your back, Father. They might pay you a visit too." He frowned and fidgeted. After what was clearly an internal struggle, he added, "She didn't want to tell you until she realized they might target you next."

He left, closing the door behind him.

CHAPTER 23

Spying on Annabelle Lawson wasn't something Josh had planned to do. He'd simply gotten the urge to question Dakota's mother and headed to her property. Yet, instead of knocking on her door and confronting her directly, he found himself nestled in the bole of a tree outside her bedroom window. From that vantage point, he could sense everything in the house, though his vision was limited by what he could observe through the window. Currently, she wasn't in the bedroom, so he saw nothing of interest, but he certainly heard plenty. She'd just completed a fascinating call with Frank Evans.

Annabelle wants to get pregnant again. With Philip's baby. Not only that, but he'd refused her, and she'd called Evans to whine about it. The more Josh dwelled on what he'd overheard, the more the rage swelled in him until his fangs snicked out and he came near to smashing through the window and ripping out the stupid human's throat.

Pregnancy seemed to be a theme in his life at the

moment.

He was donating his sperm, and the less he thought about what happened with his little swimmers, the better. Dakota probably wanted to have a family with Culain. Even if she didn't want it, she was obligated to, and based on their previous discussion, she had no problem with that duty. Now he'd learned that her mother, too, wanted to get pregnant again. But Annabelle, like Josh, wasn't doing it to raise a child in a loving home. She did it for money.

Should he care? If he didn't care what happened with his donations, why should Annabelle's decision affect him? It shouldn't, except that he couldn't help thinking about how the woman's first foray into parenthood had affected his life and Dakota's life.

He dropped to the ground. Retracted the fangs. Strode around to the front and marched up to the door. Banged on it. Noticed the doorbell but didn't press it.

Footsteps approached the door. Stopped. The heartbeat on the other side was normal; then, the peephole darkened and the pulse quickened. She'd recognized him. The door opened anyway.

Annabelle looked young for her age. She was tall, slim, and her black hair cascaded in waves down her back. Her olive skin, deep-brown eyes, and ruby lips gave her an exotic look. Whatever she used on her skin, cosmetics, surgery, or magick, worked because her face and hands had no wrinkles. The dress she wore accentuated her breasts and showed off her flat stomach and shapely legs.

He wondered if she'd added the glamour for him or if she did it for anyone who appeared at her door. Since she wasn't a vampire, the glamour must've cost her a lot of money. She probably saw a local witch for all her beauty needs.

She gave him a beatific smile. "I remember you. You were a friend of Dakota's. James, right?"

"Josh." He noted her use of the past tense. "And Dakota's not dead."

Her eyebrows arched, and her mouth twitched into a smirk. "I never said she was."

"Then don't talk about her in the past tense."

Her expression sobered. "She moved out. That's all I meant. I'm afraid I can't tell you her new address. She ran away from home, and I haven't heard from her in ..." She gazed into the distance as though contemplating all the lost time.

He saved her the trouble of finishing her thought. "She's with the fae you sold her to. Don't pretend you don't know."

"That's nobody's business but mine."

When his fangs appeared, she gasped and took a step backward.

"You're a vampire?" Her gaze flicked to the lapel pin he wore. "Why are you here?"

"I want to know why you picked Philip to be her father. What's so special about his DNA?"

She blinked at him. "Why don't you ask him?"

"I did."

"If he didn't tell you, then I'm not going to. Did you try the Internet?"

Josh nodded. "I couldn't figure out when he turned. I couldn't find much about his family." They were wealthy and private. No social media accounts, no personal websites.

Her fear leached out and curiosity replaced it. "Philip turned you, didn't he?"

"So? I wanted him to. All the papers are in order." He pressed a hand to her chest and shoved her gently into the house. When he kicked the door shut, she squeaked out her fright.

"Don't touch me." She glanced around as if searching for someone.

"I know we're alone." He grinned. "I hear only your heartbeat." No boyfriend was in evidence—no sight nor sound nor scent of a man inside the home. She appeared to be completely on her own.

She backed against the wall, her eyes wide. "What do you want?"

"I told you."

"His family has prestige. Multiple communities value his heritage, fae included."

"Why?" He retracted his fangs and she visibly relaxed.

"Money. Land holdings. Business holdings."

"He has nothing to do with his family."

"Doesn't matter. His family has clout, especially in Kébec, and he passes on physical traits, bloodline."

"He's originally French Canadian."

She stared at him as if he were an idiot for stating the obvious.

"The accent's almost gone. Not everyone would notice it," he said a little too loudly.

She tilted her chin up. "Don't you live with him?"

"All right!" His fangs sprouted again.

"Sorry." She didn't sound as if she meant it, but he accepted it. "Are we done?"

"You want him to father another child."

She paled. "How did you know?"

"I just do. Why now? Why him again? Just for the DNA?"

"There's a demand. Why do you care?"

To show her he controlled the situation, he strode into the kitchen and opened her fridge. "I could use some blood."

"Help yourself." There was that squeak again.

He snickered, peered at her over his shoulder, and licked his lips. "You offering?"

"No. Left door for the donated storage."

He grabbed a bottle. Slammed the fridge door closed. "Nothing but the best for your guests, right, Annabelle?"

She shrugged. "I work hard for what I have. And I have important guests."

He opened the bottle and took a swig. A drop escaped, and he flicked his tongue out to catch it. "Perfect. Type O."

She blanched.

"So." He leaned against the fridge. When she made no comment, he carried the bottle to the kitchen table and sat. "Make yourself a cup of tea and sit with me," he invited.

She did as he bid and filled a kettle with water, probably to placate him. Her heart rate still registered fear. So did her shaking hands as she plugged the appliance in and turned it on.

"Large demand for dhampirs? Or babies of any species?" Ever since he'd received the order to donate sperm, a nagging feeling pursued Josh. It'd increased when he'd heard Annabelle asking for Philip to impregnate her again.

"How should I know?"

"Why do you want to get pregnant?" He glanced pointedly around the room, taking in the granite countertops, stainless steel appliances, and ceramic tile floor in one swoop. "You have everything you need. Surely you don't want to do that again."

"It pays too well, and my childbearing years are limited even with magick enhancements." She dropped a tea bag into a teapot.

Genuinely curious, he asked, "Don't you want to raise any of them yourself?"

She frowned. "You judging me? You?" She poured boiling water into a teapot.

That made him furrow his own forehead. "What do you know about me?"

"You became a vampire." Her eyes widened. "Not for Dakota, I hope. You changed, hoping that would make her love you?" She howled with laughter. "Surely, you didn't show up on her doorstep in fae country expecting to win her back?"

His face darkened, and he slammed the bottle down on the table.

At his snarl, she backed against the counter, her face turning vampire white. Her lips trembled, but she pressed them tight and stilled them.

"I'm sorry." This one sounded more sincere than the last apology, but he still didn't believe she meant it.

"Answer my question and I'll forgive you."

She cleared her throat. "What question?"

He asked the only one he wanted answered. "Why the sudden demand for babies to sell?"

She sighed. "I don't know. All I know is a request for baby mamas came through my channels. The pay went up, so I assume demand increased. That's all I can tell you."

He drained the remaining blood from the bottle, rose, and set the empty in the sink. "It's been lovely visiting with you." He drew close to her and let his fangs appear.

She swallowed but kept her composure. "Anytime." She smirked.

He leaned in and scraped a fang against her neck. She arched into it, and the urge to throw her to the floor and feast on her—in every way—became almost irresistible. He shoved her away, disgusted, and she grabbed the counter for support. This was Dakota's mother. The last thing he needed was to give the bitch her wish and knock her up.

Only one person could answer the question to Josh's satisfaction, but he didn't particularly want to confront Frank Evans again. He'd have to find another source of information.

He retracted his fangs and left Annabelle's house.

CHAPTER 24

Almost three weeks into the honeymoon tour, the royal caravan had covered over three-quarters of the towns on the circuit. They'd traveled through Eastern Realm, Southern Realm, Western Realm, and now cut through Northern Realm. Their current course would take them back to the road home to Central Realm. Culain's mood had improved after he'd revealed to Dakota what had distressed him, but that was only because she'd agreed to go along with his intention to pass a bill banning visits to the Earth plane. Once they were home, she planned to talk him out of it. In the meantime, things were more peaceful between them ever since he believed he'd won the argument.

While servants prepared for the evening feast on the chosen farmer's property, Dakota and Alina strolled arm in arm through the village market. Dakota rarely left the safety of the farmhouse at each stop, but she'd grown weary of watching others work. She'd talked Alina into taking her shopping. Naturally, two guards accompanied them, but Dakota had gotten so accustomed to her shadows she barely noticed.

"You planning to buy something?" she asked Alina, who held a multicolored silk scarf in her hand. They'd arrived recently and hadn't explored many stalls and shops yet.

"Maybe." Alina set the scarf down and selected another. "I promised my sister I'd bring her back a souvenir. She doesn't travel much." Meeting Dakota's gaze, she smiled. "She was jealous that I got to accompany you."

Dakota raised her brows. Alina sounded happy about her sister's envy. Did all siblings compete in every aspect of their lives, or was this unique to Alina's family? Her parents certainly prized success, which was why Alina and her sister insinuated themselves into courtly life with such gusto. From what Alina had said, their uncle—Alina's father's older brother—dictated to the family. He schemed and connived to get them status through arranged marriages for the girls. He determined what was suitable, and it wasn't love.

Alina grinned in return. "Yes, I find it invigorating. It's a competition I'm winning so far, and I'm happy about it."

"I can't relate. I have no siblings." That she knew of, anyway. It struck her that her mother might've done the pregnancy and baby sale before she'd had Dakota. Her intuition told her that wasn't so, but even if it was, it meant she grew up without siblings. Alina's family dynamic was foreign to the dhampir woman.

Alina set the scarf down, and the pair continued their stroll along the row of stalls.

Dakota paused to scan the area and take in the sights at once. The market's energy excited her. Rows of booths and tables, laden with the season's produce and other wares, surrounded them. Fae, dressed in colorful clothing and carrying bags containing their purchases, strolled along the lanes. At the center of the grounds, a faerie band played music, but not loudly enough to hinder conversation. Nearby, someone haggled loudly with a vendor about the price of a wooden cabinet.

The aroma of fresh herbs, baked goods, and spicy meats made her salivate. She pressed her lips closed, not wanting any of the blood-tinged saliva to leak out of her mouth. She wouldn't drool to vampire levels, but anyone seeing it might get frightened even if her fangs didn't show. With an effort of will, she kept the fangs inside her gums where they belonged.

She searched for a booth selling blood but didn't see one. Before this, she'd never worried about getting bottled blood. The royal caravan carried supplies, and when those depleted, a faerie in charge of purchasing goods did so at the towns they stopped in. Dakota never worried about running out of anything, including blood. Of course, Culain would let her feed from him whenever she wanted, but that wasn't always practical. Whenever she did that, it always led to sex. With vampires, feeding and sexual pleasure frequently intertwined. Dakota glanced at Alina. Dakota had never fed from her friend or anyone other than Culain. She didn't want to start now.

Most dhampirs in the modern age learned early that bottled blood sustained them and only those eighteen and older could, by mutual consent, feed directly on anything other than animals. The Earth plane had laws about it. She'd never verified fae laws regarding the issue but assumed they maintained a similar stance.

"What about this?" Alina brought Dakota out of her reveries, and the urge to feed passed. "I've always thought my sister could use a sword."

The weapon Alina held aloft had a curved blade and a jewel-encrusted handle.

Dakota grasped the hilt and examined it. "I know nothing of this type of weapon. It doesn't look very sharp." She almost tested the blade's edge with a stroke of her finger but thought better of it.

"Your Highness is correct," the fae woman behind the table said. "I'll include a sharpening with purchase. It's a great deal. My man is a talented smith. He's made weapons for countless battles, including the species wars."

"Why would your sister want a sword?" Dakota passed the item back to Alina.

"She wouldn't want it, but it's something she should have." The faerie woman turned the blade back and forth, lifted and lowered it. "It's got a good heft."

"You know how to use it?" The possibility stunned Dakota. "Are you trained in blade use?"

"Of course. Those of us who lived through the wars were all trained to fight—women and men. We had to protect ourselves. Humans are vicious. Sometimes I think they're worse than vampires." As soon as the words were out, Alina gasped. "I'm sorry, Your Highness. I meant no offense."

Dakota placed a hand on her friend's arm. "It's all right. I take no offense. I'm human and vampire, but I agree with you. Both cause enough harm to those around them, including their own kind, that you might consider them monsters." She dropped her hand. "But all species do. Humans and vampires just outnumber the others, so we notice it more."

"Yes, Your Highness. Thank you." Alina set the sword back on the table. "I'll think about it and come back," she told the vendor, who nodded politely and said, "Yes, ma'am." Her expression showed she doubted she'd see the women again.

As they turned away from the sword seller's booth, Alina said, "I'm truly sorry."

Dakota tucked her arm through her friend's. "I know." She stopped walking.

Around them, the current of people parted and flowed past. The guards stood patiently to the side and watched the exchange.

"I'm still getting accustomed this whole royalty thing," she said. "It's been months, and I'm used to the servants and the protocols. I can even handle people calling me Your Highness, though it sounds strange to my ears. But I don't want my friends to fear speaking their minds around me. What do you think I'll do if you anger me? Have you beheaded?" She chuckled, expecting Alina to join in the laughter. When her friend's expression remained sober, Dakota placed a hand on Alina's arm again. "Please tell me you don't believe I'd have you arrested."

Alina glanced around and then lowered her voice. "You wouldn't, my lady, but someone else within earshot might." She stared meaningfully at the two guards standing nearby.

Dakota didn't think they'd heard. "What do you mean? You're my friend. If I'm not bothered by something you said, it's not anyone's business to intervene."

"You don't understand. You're a princess. You're above everyone else except the prince and the king— and queen if we had one. An insult to you is an insult to the realm. Has no one explained to you that you are the realm?"

Self-conscious, Dakota studied the ground—grass trampled flat against rich black soil. "They've said it. Often. I didn't understand the implications." She released Alina's arm and met her gaze. "We'll keep certain discussions between us private, then. I'm your friend. I'll always be your friend. If you're in need, I'll help you. Believe that."

Alina gave her a weak smile. "I believe you, but be careful what you promise anyone, including me. A princess isn't a person, Your Highness. She's a figurehead. Never forget it."

"I won't," Dakota said but promised herself that she'd discuss this with Culain. Why should anyone suffer punishment for speaking their mind?

CHAPTER 25

They were in the journey's homestretch. They'd left the last town behind them, and before nightfall, Culain expected they'd arrive at the castle in Central Realm. The trip had gone as smoothly as such a big production could. Nothing plagued them except minor nuisances: a thrown axle on a carriage or shoe on a horse; running short of certain supplies that the purchaser assured him had been packed in plenty—the bottles of blood emptied far sooner than he'd expected, considering Dakota was the only one using them; a deep rut in the road exactly where culverts on either side prevented circumventing it. None of these significantly hindered their progress. A soldier accompanying them, competent with the carriage and horses, repaired both the axle and the shoe. They'd brought a servant responsible for making supply purchases on the journey when they needed more, so that wasn't a big issue. It did concern Culain that Dakota had consumed so many bottles so quickly—while also snacking on him at night. That recollection brought with it a craving to be with her, to have her feeding from him, making love to him. He hadn't known just how erotic letting a vampire feed from you could be.

He forced his thoughts back to the list of nuisances. No, even the rut hadn't slowed them down. A few men armed with shovels soon fixed that. But it didn't escape his notice that the axle and horseshoe had both been new, Dakota swore she hadn't drunk that much blood, and the rut looked freshly dug. He kept to himself the suspicion that someone was sabotaging their progress. Truly, none of it had slowed them down for long. None of it had forced them to change their route or cost so much extra that they had to tighten their belts for the remainder of the journey.

Just nuisances. Why would someone bother?

Even so, Culain ensured that the guards on horseback stayed close to the carriage in which he and Dakota rode, and he advised the pair riding inside the coach with them to stay vigilant. He'd had those conversations out of her earshot, of course—far enough out of her earshot that her dhampir hearing couldn't pick it up. No need to worry her over what probably was nothing.

They stopped for lunch at the side of the main road. On one side, a meadow, dotted with wildflowers, stretched far into the horizon. On the other side, a thick forest grew, full of evergreens, maples, elms, oaks, and birches. The servants dismounted to set up tents and blankets for a picnic. One chopped wood for a campfire and another visited a nearby stream for water.

Culain held out his hand, and Dakota took it with a smile. He helped her dismount from the carriage and led her away from the dusty road and over to the fire. The sun shone, and the air held no chill, but the fire provided a gathering place. The servants had set up logs around it where they could sit to eat. They didn't plan to stay long enough to set up camp tables or chairs.

"Looking forward to getting home?" he asked, simply to start a conversation.

She leaned into him and rubbed her cheek against his chest. "Oh, yes. I'm dying to get back to our own bed."

He whispered something suggestive and lewd in her ear, and she playfully smacked his hand. "My lord!"

Alina cut their jests short when she joined them, taking a seat on a neighboring log. "Such a lovely place." She inhaled deeply. This whole countryside is breathtaking."

"Yes, it is," Dakota answered. She tilted her chin up and stroked his thigh with her hand before sitting up with an expression of pure innocence on her face.

"You'll pay for that dearly," he muttered out of the side of his mouth.

She licked her lips in response, driving him mad with desire.

Alina laughed. "Should I leave? Return to the carriage and give you some ..." She looked around. "Perhaps it's you who should return to the carriages. No one's in them, and we're rather exposed here."

She'd meant that as a joke, but suddenly the hair on the back of Culain's neck prickled. He stood and walked around the fire's perimeter, staring into the trees, along the road, and into the meadow.

Dakota, too, rose. "What's wrong?"

Damn. She could always read him. That was usually

a good thing, but not this time. He wanted this trip to end on a positive, carefree note. Besides, it's not as if anything was wrong. Nothing had happened on the entire journey. Why should anyone bother them now?

He had a flash of his mother, pinned against a tree with a spear, blood streaming down her white gown.

Sometimes, he wanted to rip that tapestry down with his bare hands and tear it to shreds. His father insisted it remain displayed in the main banquet hall. *So we never forget*, his father had said.

How would I ever forget?

He realized Dakota had asked him a question he hadn't answered, and everyone, even nearby servants, was staring at him. He waved a hand in her direction. "Nothing to worry about. I'm on edge, that's all."

She sniffed the air like a hound on a hunt. He thought her eyes widened, but it happened so quickly he wasn't sure of what he'd seen.

"If you're sure, then it's probably nothing," she said.

He stared at her in silence for a moment, then nodded. In case his intuition hadn't failed him, though, he strolled over to the nearest guard and asked him to scout around.

CHAPTER 26

Josh was back in town. To be more accurate, in Central Realm, along the road back to the palace. Dakota had picked up the vampire's scent when she'd sniffed the air. She'd almost given him away by betraying her surprise and shock, but she'd cloaked it in time. Culain had asked no questions, but her sensitive hearing had picked up his instructions to the guard to patrol the area. Hopefully, Josh knew enough to stay out of sight.

Of all the stupid... She couldn't even finish the thought. Fury had her fists bunching and her foot tapping impatiently as she sat on the log and glanced furtively around the camp.

Idiot. She'd told him to never return. He'd promised her he'd never return. Why make such a promise just to break it? He'd been lucky so far to avoid capture. How long did he expect to get away with it? If they found him, they'd, at the very least, imprison him, and at the most, execute him. The fae had treated Josh and Philip leniently the first time they'd invaded

Autumnland, but they wouldn't receive such mercy for a second transgression.

A servant carrying a bowl of stew on a heat-proof plate interrupted her thoughts. She accepted the food with a smile and set the plate on her knees. The knowledge that her ex hovered somewhere nearby—near enough for her to have caught his scent—had caused her to lose her appetite. She dipped the spoon into the thick broth and took small bites so they wouldn't wonder why she wasn't eating. Surely, the fool wasn't planning to approach her while she traveled with the caravan. Whatever had brought him here, he'd better change his mind and leave. If he tried to talk to her again, she might pummel him.

She'd barely eaten anything when a frantic shout had her leaping to her feet, the bowl, spoon, and plate flipping onto the ground.

Guards rushed past her, one of them stopping long enough to order the princess and an equally shocked Alina and Lysandra to the safety of the carriage. Dakota's bodyguard grabbed her elbow, and with a brusque shout for the other two women to follow, he escorted the trio to the royal carriage.

"What's happening?" Dakota asked as he ushered her inside.

"I don't know, Your Highness. I'm only following orders. You three get down on the floor. I'll protect you." With pistols in hand, he and another guard shut the doors, leaving the women huddled on the floor.

Two other guards stood on alert outside the doors.

In the distance, Dakota heard shouts and thought she caught the word "kobold."

"Kobolds?" She placed a hand on the guard's arm. "Are we under attack?"

He cleared his throat. "Might be, Your Highness. This part of the country has them. We didn't expect trouble because we sent scouts ahead of the caravan and King Killian had these woods cleared out before we were due to arrive in the area. But we're always ready for any attack. You're quite safe in here."

She didn't bother to point out that she could kill a kobold in a fight though an armed band might cause her some problems. Dhampirs, like vampires, were difficult to kill, lethal in strength, and agile. She hadn't trained to fight, but she could wrestle down most faerie-realm inhabitants simply because of what she was.

This is the last time I cower behind a guard while my husband confronts danger.

Too bad Alina hadn't bought that sword after all. They could've used it, but a pistol would've been more practical.

Beside Dakota, Lysandra covered her face with her hands. Her shoulders shook, and a sob escaped her. Alina didn't cry or panic, but her hand trembled when she reached up to brush a strand of hair from her face.

Dakota draped an arm around each of them.

"Shh," she whispered in Lysandra's ear. "It'll be all right."

The young fae's sobs died, but she continued to quiver and kept her face buried in her hands.

"Look at me, both of you," Dakota said, her voice a command.

The women did as she bid.

"I won't let anything happen to you."

"Your Highness," Alina said. "It's our duty to die for you if we must."

Dakota shook her head. "Well, then, you mustn't."

When Alina protested, Dakota said, "Look at me. Look me in the eye." When they did, she let them melt into her gaze. Once they were well entranced, she bared her fangs. Neither woman flinched. "I'm a weapon when needs must. Do you understand?"

Alina responded first. "Yes, Highness."

"Yes, Your Highness." Lysandra's voice cracked, but her tears had dried, and she no longer panted with terror.

"Yes, Your Highness."

Dakota's gaze swept to the guard, who stared back at her, as mesmerized as the two women. She pulled in her fangs and snapped them all back into reality.

"We thank you for your protection," she said to the guard.

He nodded and said, "Yes, Your Highness," a look of astonishment on his face. She waved a hand at the window, and he resumed watching for any approach.

The sounds of whatever fighting she'd heard faded away. They could safely exit the carriage, but she waited for the guard to tell them it was all right.

They didn't have to wait long. A guard shouted the all clear; another opened the door and helped the women climb out. When they stood on the soft grass, the guards surrounding them, Dakota said, "Thank you, all of you, for keeping us safe."

The guards all bowed as one and, amid mutters of "You're welcome, Your Highness," she scanned the surrounding area for Culain. To her relief, she spotted him approaching but frowned when she scented fae blood. Quickly, she sniffed the air for any hint of a vampire's presence, and to her much greater relief, caught no trace.

When he reached them, she surreptitiously checked

him for wounds and found none. The fae blood spilled must belong to someone else.

"Are all members of our party present and accounted for, my lord?" she asked.

He met her gaze with his somber one, but said, "No fatalities on our side. One stab wound."

"Kobolds?"

"We slew one of a group of ten, but they attacked us, so it was self-defense."

"They're gone?" She asked as much for the two women listening with fear in their faces as she did for herself.

He patted her arm. "Yes, they won't bother us again."

He turned to the guards and the nearby servants. "Load up. Break camp. We'll move on." He lowered his voice and said, "I'll be happy to see the end of this journey. What a way to finish our honeymoon."

Now it was her turn to pat his arm reassuringly. "Worry not. We'll be safe in our bed soon enough."

With a grin, he pecked her cheek and whispered in her ear. "You always know how to get my blood pumping."

She gasped on a surge of lust. "So do you, husband," she whispered back. "So do you."

CHAPTER 27

Josh hadn't departed the faerie realm, but he'd left the vicinity of the royal caravan—after catching and feeding from a kobold or two. Or three. He didn't particularly love the taste of their blood, but it wasn't terrible. He'd waylaid the goblin-like creatures more to help protect Dakota than to have a meal. He'd also spotted something interesting, something she'd want to know as much as the news from home he bore on the wings of a broken promise. When she heard everything he had to say, she'd forgive him; he was sure of it.

He'd arrived in Autumnland that morning at nine—fae time. He wore his disguise, and so far, everyone he'd met seemed to believe his identity as half-fae, half-dhampir. After checking in at the palace, he learned the prince and princess were scheduled to return that evening from their three-week honeymoon.

How sweet. Josh scowled as he walked and kicked at a rock in his way. He probably shouldn't have tracked down the royal caravan and should've simply waited for Dakota to get home, but he feared if he did that, she'd go straight to the room she shared with Lover Boy. Josh wanted to talk to her and figured following them along the final leg of their journey would provide him an opportunity. No such luck, but fortunately for them, he'd been available to help dispatch the kobolds, even if no one in the royal party knew they'd had assistance.

After the tussle with the goblin wannabes, he dropped behind far enough that Dakota wouldn't pick up his scent. He waited for the caravan to start moving again, gave them a good head start, and then followed in their tracks.

They moved slowly, painfully slowly. Previously, he'd caught himself almost catching up to them— which was kinda how he'd spotted the kobolds tracking them and sounded the alarm. It had given the fae guards enough warning that no one in the royal party had been seriously hurt. A guard or two received minor flesh wounds, making Josh salivate and wish he could snack on some sweet faerie blood rather than the salty and slightly bitter kobold blood, but at least none had died. He hadn't worried about Dakota—she could take care of herself—but he'd helped anyway. What if the beady-eyed, green-faced little monsters got lucky?

Part of him had hoped they'd get lucky enough to kill Culain, but only a part. He wouldn't wish the loss of a husband on Dakota, and whether she was free or not, they were finished anyway. She was well and truly done with him. It made him sad, but it didn't make him change his mind about his mission here. He wasn't doing this as yet one more stunt to win her back. He simply believed she should know all the facts.

At least, that's what he told himself as he trudged

along. After what he'd seen before the kobolds attacked, he had to keep going. Even if he'd changed his mind about giving her the information he'd brought from the Earth plane, this fresh development affected not just Dakota but the entire royal family.

Satisfied he was doing the right thing, the ethical thing, he plodded on.

***

No sooner had the royal caravan arrived home—to great welcoming crowds and deafening cheers—than Edric Texeira, Culain's assistant, informed him that a welcome-home feast awaited them in the small banquet hall.

"Tonight? Now?" Culain sighed, stared wistfully at the sitting area in his bedroom, and then looked to Dakota.

She didn't seem as tired as he felt—probably her dhampir constitution—but her face fell, so he knew she was equally disappointed that they wouldn't get a night alone. Tomorrow their duties would begin in earnest. All Culain wanted that evening was a quiet meal in their room, a snifter of brandy, and his wife naked in his bed. At that thought, his wrist tingled and throbbed erotically in the spot where she usually fed from him. He grew hard thinking about her breaking his skin and latching on, and he almost moaned aloud, picturing what they'd do to each other.

"It's fine. We'll have our evening tomorrow." Her expression showed dismay and resignation all at once.

Culain nodded to Edric. "Very well. We need to rest, but we'll arrive at the hall before dinner is served. Have the servants bring tea."

Edric bowed. "Very good, Your Highness." He bowed to Dakota and left.

Now they were alone, the tension eased from Culain's shoulders. He sighed out the rest and met Dakota's gaze.

"I'm sorry you had to hide in the carriage while the kobolds attacked."

Her mouth dropped open. "How did you know?"

"I think I know you well enough to guess that you don't like to cower, and you're probably better in a fight than half my soldiers."

She laughed. "Does that mean next time I can join you?"

"No."

Her brows furrowed. "What?"

"I understand how you felt about it and recognize what you're capable of, but that doesn't mean you can fight alongside the men." He moved close to her and took both her hands in his.

She didn't recoil, which was a good sign.

"Before you get angry with me, hear me out," he said.

"Okay."

"Aside from the fact that you're a woman"—he held up his hand when she tried to speak—"we can't fight together. We can't risk both our lives at the same time. Ever. Unless circumstances dictate and we have no choice. If anything happens to me, you become queen—"

She sucked in a horrified breath, cutting him off. "Culain—"

"No, you agreed to listen. If something happens to me, you'll inherit the throne. If we have an heir, you'll be queen regent until our child becomes of age to ascend the throne. If we have no heir when that happens"—he swallowed and kept his eyes trained on hers—"you'll marry Colin."

Under normal circumstances, her skin was as pale as any he'd seen except her vampire father's. If possible, she went whiter still as soon as the words left his mouth.

Her hands slipped from his as she staggered backward. When she spoke, her voice cracked. "No. You can't expect that of me. Of your brother." She squinted. "Does he even know?"

"Of course he does. He's a member of the royal family. We learned the rules of inheritance as children."

"He knew when we married that if something happened to you he'd have to marry me?" Her voice had gone shrill.

"Yes. Everyone knows."

She staggered to the couch and dropped onto it, burying her head in her hands. Without looking up, she said, "Why didn't you tell me?"

"The possibility is remote. Not much will kill me, and we're both healthy. I'm sure you'll be with child soon."

She placed a hand on her belly. "I guess we have all the more reason to try harder."

"You wouldn't want to marry Colin?"

"I wouldn't want to marry anyone, my love. I wouldn't want to live without you." Her eyes dampened with tears, and she spun away from him, hiding her face. She jumped to her feet and ran into the en suite bathroom.

He followed her and found her dabbing at her eyes with a tissue stained red with her blood-tinged tears. "I'm sorry, bright one. I didn't intend to upset you or make you envision the worst." He drew her into his arms. "I merely wanted to tell you the truth."

She nodded, her face pressed against his shoulder. When she pulled away, a smear of red remained on his vest. She swiped fruitlessly at it with her tissue. "I'm sorry."

He grabbed her hand. "It's fine. The servants will clean it."

"My tears contain blood."

"I know," he whispered. "It's all right. Shh."

They remained standing in silence, holding each other. He took comfort from her body against his as she seemed to from his body against hers.

"Culain?" Her voice came to him small and timid.

"Yes, my love?"

"What happens if I die and we have no heir?"

He sighed. "I'll have to remarry, but we also have Colin as an heir."

"Why can't he become king if you die? And marry whomever he chooses?"

"Because the order of succession put you on the throne after me as soon as we married." He stepped backward and held her out at arm's length. "Dakota, my love, my life, we'll be fine. You'll see. This other will never come to pass." He hugged her again. "I have no intention of dying and leaving you to my brother."

Her voice, when she replied, was muffled against his chest, but he heard her loud and clear. "You damn well better not."

CHAPTER 28

The rectory's door opened to Kelsey's knock, and there stood Father Paul Bernside. When his gaze landed on her vampire pin, his eyes widened. She smelled his fear, but he stepped aside and politely invited her in.

"You're Kelsey Davis?" he asked.

"Yes, Father." *Letting me in would be a hell of a mistake otherwise.*

"I didn't expect a vampire."

"When I made the appointment with your assistant, I didn't tell her. I didn't think it should matter. No one stopped me from entering the church on Sunday."

No law made it illegal to turn a person away from a business or service based on their species, race, creed, or color, and some people put signs in their windows banning certain folk. Few revealed their racism that way, because business suffered, but some individuals hated anything or anyone different. It wasn't always humans who did it, either. Often, the worst offenders were the new members of society. Some hypernaturals believed themselves superior. Vampires had triggered the species wars because they'd viewed almost everyone else as their food supply.

"It makes no difference to me, which is why I invited you in. I enjoy the company of hypernaturals. Some of my close friends are not human."

Methinks thou doth protest too much, Father. Her only reply, though, was a smile.

She recognized Father Paul from the mass he'd led the Sunday before. Today, he wore his black priest suit—or whatever it was called—the black shirt with white collar and black dress pants. In church, robes covered it, but this man's line of work was unmistakable. She considered him almost too handsome for it: a full head of black hair, a square jaw, and bright blue eyes that sparkled even when he was afraid. She pegged him at around forty years. Younger than she'd been at forty-four when Josh turned her.

Kelsey held out her hand, and he clasped it firmly and without hesitation, but the stink of fear remained.

To seem as innocuous as possible, she'd worn a skirt and blouse to the meeting, perfectly embodying the good Catholic. She'd slicked her shiny blonde hair back into a bun, and her shoes were low heeled. The blouse she'd buttoned up to the neck. No cleavage showed at all. The sleeves were long, but that was more for sun protection than modesty. She wore a wide-brimmed hat and a kerchief tied around her neck that she pulled over her mouth and nose when out in daylight.

"Welcome, then." He released her hand. "Come. Sit. We'll have tea in the living room." He gave her a half smile. "You drink tea? Eat cookies?"

She chuckled. "Sometimes. That'll be fine. I

appreciate you meeting with me." She tried to sense another presence in the house and couldn't find one. One other priest, she knew from her research, shared the living quarters. Relatively small compared to Tkaronto's churches, St. George's nevertheless served a congregation large enough for two priests to share the duties.

"Where's Father Michael?" she asked.

"On an errand. He'll return shortly. Is that a problem?"

"No. The more, the merrier." She almost bared her fangs for effect but controlled the urge. She was here to ask for help, not frighten him.

The open-concept living room was sparsely but tastefully decorated. A navy three-seat sofa, matching loveseat, and two matching armchairs surrounded a square pine coffee table that held a tray with a teapot, milk and sugar, cups and saucers, and a plate of cookies. Beside the tray, a caddy held napkins.

The walls of the living area and the hall leading to the bedrooms were all a neutral beige while the kitchen was a lemon yellow. Everything was clean. Everything had a place and was in it. Behind the loveseat, a small office area had been set up. A desk butted up against a window, allowing whoever worked there to get a glimpse of the gardens beyond and perhaps feel closer to nature. At right angles to the desk stood a large, wide bookcase stuffed with books. Kelsey didn't recognize most of them, but she noted they were predominantly nonfiction and related to history, geography, theology, philosophy, and, to her surprise, the occult.

"You read books about magick and witchcraft?" She felt as surprised as he looked when she blurted out the question, but since she'd broached the subject, she sauntered over and pulled one off the shelf. She turned it over and opened it to read the inside cover.

"*The History of Witchcraft*." She stared pointedly at the father.

"You must know your enemy," he said.

She didn't reply to that. Didn't know how. It sounded like a quote, but she didn't recognize it as such.

Should've brought Philip with me. He had over a century of reading behind him. He could probably quote circles around this priest.

She stuck the book back on the shelf. When she glanced at Father Paul, she caught him watching her with an air of expectation.

She plucked another book from the shelf. "*Vampires: Separating Fact from Fiction.* Sounds interesting."

"Ah, yes, Vincent Muldoon. He presents an interesting discussion on vampires and how they evolved."

"Using Bram Stoker as his guide?" Stoker had gotten a lot wrong.

Father Paul smiled, which made him look younger and more handsome, and shook his head. "He references Stoker, of course, but as an illustration of how fiction influenced our beliefs about vampires."

"You've studied vampires?" Relief flooded through her. The hope that he could help her increased. "Do all priests study the occult and vampires?"

"My interest in the subject is personal, so yes, I've studied that subject, but not all priests do. Father Michael took the mandatory courses in seminary school on the subject, but he has no further interest in pursuing more knowledge on the subject. After the unmasquing, the Pope mandated that all seminary students study and learn about the creatures who revealed themselves."

"Your enemies?"

He held up a hand as if making a peace offering. "You're not familiar with Sun Tzu? *The Art of War*?"

She shook her head.

" 'Know your enemy and know yourself, and you'll never face defeat even in a hundred battles.' I'm paraphrasing, but that's the gist of it. I read it long ago, but it stuck with me."

She peeked at him from the side of her eye. "Am I your enemy?"

He stepped closer to her though his fear hadn't disappeared—it'd diminished but hadn't vanished. "Do you consider yourself an enemy to a man of the cloth?"

"No." She whispered it. "I've come for your help, Father."

"So you told my assistant," he replied. "Come and sit. I've prepared tea and cookies." He smiled again, charming her. "Rather, I made tea, and I opened a box of cookies. Baking's not my forte." He held his hand out, ushering her toward the living area.

She stared at the book she held, and his gaze followed hers.

"Would you like to borrow it?"

"You'd lend it to me?"

"I saw you in church on Sunday. You listened more attentively than half the congregation. You've come for what appears to be spiritual counseling. I trust when you've finished with the book, you'll return it to me and give me your review."

"Thank you. I will." She clutched the book to her

chest and preceded him to the living room. She took a seat in an armchair and set the book and her purse on the floor.

"If you're all right with it, I'll pour," he said.

She nodded, not knowing what else to do. She watched him fill each cup with the aromatic brown liquid.

"How do you take it?" he said, setting the teapot back on the tray. He betrayed surprise when she requested four cubes of sugar—in fact, his face puckered involuntarily—but he dropped them all in anyway.

"It takes a lot of sugar for me to get the taste," she explained. *I guess they didn't teach him everything at the seminary or in any of those fancy books.* She waved away the offer of milk. Her human self would've wanted the milk to cool the tea. Her vampire self didn't feel hot or cold, so she didn't need it. Even if it boiled, it wouldn't scald her flesh. Only direct sunlight could accomplish that—or gasoline and a lit match. She eyed the book, wondering what she'd learn about herself from it. Anxiety had her fangs protruding, but she focused and retracted them before they forced her mouth open.

Once they each held a cup and saucer, he relaxed on the loveseat across from her. He blew on his cup and took a sip of his tea. "Tell me, Ms. Davis, why you're here."

"Call me Kelsey." She didn't know why she wanted the familiarity, but she did.

"Very well. Kelsey." He leaned forward and set his cup and saucer on the table. "No more stalling, young lady."

That made her grin. She'd expected fire and brimstone. Castigation. Threats of hellfire and damnation. Instead, she'd received a warm welcome, tea and cookies, and a book to read. He'd already helped more than he could ever know.

"I want to become a member of your church. I want to attend mass and volunteer, and I want you to help me restore my soul so I can get into Heaven when I die."

***

No request for spiritual aid had surprised Father Paul more or sounded as sincere. Granted, in his ten years as a priest, he'd so far counseled only humans. He'd never expected the other species to have any interest in Catholicism. They had their own gods—or demons—to worship, and he preferred it that way. He had nothing against them—they were all God's creatures, whether they recognized the One or not; however, many of them not only made him nervous but also actually creeped him out. Not that he'd admit that out loud—he was a priest, after all. A good Christian who preached and practiced tolerance and prided himself on walking his talk.

When this vampiress had appeared on his doorstep, though, terror had come close to overwhelming him, but he refused to turn away anyone asking for help. This one had come to him asking for salvation. Wasn't that his job? Counseling those with souls—believers who committed no mortal sins—that was easy. The job became much harder when the damned came to him for help. If Jesus forgave his killers, then wouldn't He also forgive a vampire?

Yes, but would He allow her into Heaven? How did one save the soul of someone who had no soul? Would she even exist in the afterlife? He was sure he'd never encountered the answer in one of the dozens of books on his bookshelf.

He'd start with the basics. "Tell me about yourself."

"Perhaps you already know some of it. Do you recognize me at all from news reports? My son and I were missing for a while."

He studied her face. Now that she mentioned it, she did look familiar. He couldn't pinpoint why, though, so he shook his head.

"My son got into some trouble, and when I tried to help him, we wound up involved with some dangerous people." She stopped talking and sipped from her tea. She chose her words carefully, thought everything through before speaking. He could tell she kept much to herself, revealing only what necessity decreed.

An excellent lesson for us all, but it shows she doesn't completely trust me. He could understand that. He had no legal or spiritual obligation to keep her secrets at the moment.

As if she'd read his mind, she said, "Whatever I tell you is confidential, yes?"

"Unless you admit to anything illegal. This isn't the confessional."

Immediately, she said, "Forgive me, Father, for I have sinned. It's been two years since my last confession."

He nodded. "Very well, but if you reveal something criminal, I'll encourage you to turn yourself in."

"I don't think you'll need to do that, but I want the guarantee that whatever I tell you stays between us."

"If you haven't broken man's law, I have nothing to say to anyone. Your secrets are safe with me."

"Thank you." She set her empty cup and saucer on

the coffee table. She settled back in her chair and folded her hands in her lap.

"Tell me what happened." Part of him didn't want to hear it. Part of him wished she'd booked this appointment with Father Michael instead. *Lord, I know it's your will, and I prayed for more spiritual work, but did you have to send me a vampire?*

The story she relayed chilled him.

She told of a dhampir girl sold into marriage to the fae. Of her son turned into a vampire on Kelsey's insistence when a sadistic killer shot him. That same son had turned his own mother into the vampire sitting here.

She left out many details, leaving questions he refused to ask. She never told him who the vampire was who'd saved her son's life. That was irrelevant. Father Paul already planned to get on the Internet when she left and verify her story.

He identified inconsistencies in the narrative she spun, but he didn't pry. For now, the highlights would suffice.

"I'm sorry for all your pain and suffering," he said when the story wound down.

"Will you help me? I'm a vampire, but I want *me* back. I was mad at God." She hung her head. "After I became a vampire, I hated God. I wanted to doubt His existence. I was happy to not care what He thought about how I behaved."

She looked up again and met his gaze. "I'm here because it's His will. Isn't that what the Church teaches?"

For a moment, he was speechless. He'd thought it himself that her presence here was God's will. He couldn't argue that point with her.

He tried to picture her at the church socials. *Maybe she'll join the Catholic Women's League.* His heart rate sped up, and he had to swallow his panic.

"I'll do everything in my power to save your soul." He'd have to research how he might achieve that, but he didn't know if the information existed. To his knowledge, vampires had no souls. Death wouldn't be the salvation for her that it was for living creatures. She'd have to survive until they found a way to retrieve her soul.

But where had it gone?

CHAPTER 29

The day after their return home from their honeymoon, Dakota felt the stirrings in her belly as she sat in her old room reading a book and sipping a bottle of A-negative. Little butterfly kicks tickled her insides, making her sit up and place a hand on her tummy.

Was she pregnant? It'd been over three weeks since their wedding night, and dhampirs went through a shorter pregnancy than humans. This could very well signal a life growing within her.

Or it's indigestion. She tittered at that. Dhampirs didn't suffer from that—they didn't even fart. Their vampire half ensured it. Their feces didn't stink. Most people never wondered how a cross between a vampire and a human worked. In general, dhampirs received what one might consider the best of both worlds.

Except periods, but without those, I'd never carry a child to term.

So how did female vamps conceive and carry a child when they bred with humans? Two vampires couldn't reproduce, but a vampire and a human could—hence dhampirs. Hypernatural physiology baffled her. No wonder interspecies doctors—and mages and hedge witches—made big bucks.

Excitement and an urge to tell Culain immediately made her set the bottle on the coffee table and drop the book on the couch. Once she was on her feet, though, she remained frozen in place.

Should I tell him now?

What if she was wrong and raised his hopes for no reason? She strode to the bedroom door and opened it.

The two guards outside snapped to attention.

"My lady," the taller one said and bowed. The other man followed suit.

Unable to say what she needed, she shook her head and shut the door.

Alina. She'll help me get a pregnancy test without alerting the entire palace. Once more, Dakota opened the door, but this time, she stepped into the hallway. With the guards trailing behind her, she walked to the nearby women's apartments where Alina lived.

Before she knocked, she listened for her friend's heartbeat. As soon as she detected it, she rapped soundly on the door.

Alina opened it, wearing a casual dress that indicated she had no plans to go out—at least, not soon.

Dakota slipped inside so quickly that Alina let out a startled gasp.

"Shut the door." Dakota scampered into the sitting area. Behind her, the door thumped closed, and the lock clicked into place.

"What's wrong?" Alina hurried to the princess's

side.

"Nothing." Dakota placed a hand on her faerie friend's arm. "But I need your help." At Alina's look of alarm, Dakota said, "No, it's nothing bad. I need you to keep what I'm about to tell you confidential."

"Doesn't sound like nothing, then."

"Will you keep this to yourself?"

Alina's lips curled into a pout. "Of course. You know you can trust me. You don't even have to ask."

"Yes, I do. It's important no one learns of this."

"Okay. Tell me."

"I think I'm pregnant."

Alina's face beamed. "Why, that's wonderful." She stared more closely at the princess. "Isn't it?"

"Yes, but I don't know if it's true. I don't want to get excited about it or tell anyone, especially Culain, if I'm wrong."

"Ah, I see. You need a pregnancy test." Alina crooked a finger. "Come with me."

The fae woman led the princess into the en suite bathroom. She opened a drawer in the large vanity and removed a package. "I got this from a medicine woman. We mix the herbs and steep them in water. You'll pee into the mixture, and if it turns red, you're pregnant." She handed the package to Dakota.

"Isn't that for fae?"

"It'll work for dhampirs, too. Once the fae started breeding with your kind, we needed something effective for all of us, not just faeries and humans."

Dakota frowned. How could it work for all three species? Once again, the physical workings between the species had her stumped.

Alina chuckled. "Don't worry. It'll work." She plucked the package from Dakota's hand. "Come on," she said, excitement in her voice. "Let's get this done."

When Dakota's expression turned to worry, Alina put a hand on her friend's arm. "Really. Relax. In twenty minutes, we'll have an answer. The royal physician needs to verify, but at least you can share the good news with Culain."

"All right. You mix it together. You know how to do it, right?"

"Absolutely." Alina led her into the kitchen and put on the kettle. "Grab me the teapot. I'll put the herbs into a tea strainer." She gave Dakota a sidelong stare. "Relax. I've never seen you so worked up."

"Part of me believed I wouldn't get pregnant." She dragged the teapot from its corner next to the fridge and set it on the counter beside the kettle.

Alina quickly filled a mesh strainer on a long chain with herbs from the package. She set it inside the teapot, letting the chain dangle out from under the lid. Both women watched the kettle anxiously.

"A watched pot never boils," Alina commented.

"That can't be true."

Alina laughed. "It's a saying. Have you never heard it before?"

Dakota shook her head but said, "Feels like it might be true enough. How long have we been staring at it?"

"Not long enough, obviously."

Dakota closed her eyes and tried to settle her nerves.

Did Annabelle feel like this when she thought she was pregnant with me? Probably not. Annabelle hadn't planned to keep her child. *No, wait, she probably did feel this way—over the money she'd earn from it.* Once again, thoughts of her mother instantly spoiled what should've been an exciting and happy moment.

***

Josh stared at the half-finished bottle of blood and the book lying haphazardly on the couch. *As if she had to drop everything and leave.* The thought that something distressed her enough to bolt from her sanctuary worried him. What could've happened? He knew she came to these chambers to relax and take time for herself, mostly when her husband—he refused to name the faerie prince who'd stolen her away—was busy with realm business.

Maybe something had happened to the prince. The thought didn't particularly cheer him up. Even if the prince died, Dakota would remain here. She'd married the muttonhead. She'd be a Shiels forever. Divorce wasn't possible, and death would not do them part— not from the Shiels family, anyway.

Josh sniffed the air, as if trying to pick up the incident's spoor. He caught a hint of Dakota's citrusy perfume but nothing else. If she'd left the room upset or frightened, he couldn't detect it. *So probably not either of those, then.* That relieved him, even if it meant Prince Douchebag was fine.

Tempted to finish the bottle of blood, he picked it up and sniffed it. And instantly set it down again. It'd sat out for too long.

The door opening caught his attention, and he moved vampire quick into the walk-in closet. He kept the door open a crack to see who'd arrived. It was only Dakota, so he stepped out and, clearing his throat to grab her attention, revealed himself.

Her reaction was less than he desired: she stalked up to him and slapped his face.

"Ow, hey. What the hell was that for?" He rubbed his cheek. She hadn't actually hurt him, but it smarted that she'd attack him like that. He'd come here to help her. Tempted to walk out and leave her ignorant of his news, he glared at her as he waited for her to respond.

"You promised you'd never return."

"To be fair, I never actually said the words."

"Don't be daft. You shouldn't have come back. If they catch you, they'll kill you. They might kill me, and I ..." She averted her gaze, her hand traveling to her solar plexus.

It hit him like a battering ram to the gut.

"You're pregnant." He tried to listen for the second heartbeat, tried to sense the other life within her, but failed. It didn't matter. She'd have Culain's baby. Josh let out a low growl, and his fangs appeared.

"Stop it." She stepped backward but not in fear. "Get out."

Fury made him walk toward the window, which he'd left wide-open for a quick exit. The sheers billowed ghostlike in the breeze. Before he reached them, he retracted his fangs and turned around to face her again.

"I can't. Not without telling you what I came to say."

She gritted her teeth. Finally, she said, "Spit it out and go."

"You're not the only one who wants to have a baby."

Her already pale face went white as marble. "Who?"

So she at least suspected but needed to hear him say it anyway before she could believe it. At first, he couldn't vocalize the name. He held off telling her because he knew it would hurt, but she deserved to know. Wasn't that why he'd risked his life to visit her one more time?

"Annabelle." He refused to say your mother. That woman was no true mother to Dakota.

Dakota shrugged. "Why should I care?"

"She wants your father to get her pregnant again."

Dakota dropped to the floor where she stood, and he raced to her side. He kneeled beside her and put an arm around her shoulders. When she shrugged him off, it wounded him, but he understood. He stood and stepped away.

"One more thing." He backed toward the windows.

She looked up, and his heart ached to see the blood-tinged tears leaving tracks down her cheeks. "What?"

"You have a traitor among your guards."

"How do you know?" Her expression told him she knew the answer to that, too.

"Must you force me to say everything out loud?"

"Isn't that why you're here?"

"I was there when the kobolds attacked your caravan."

"Kobolds live out in the wilds. In the caves. They waylay travelers. It's not unexpected to run into them on the road. What makes you suspect a guard was involved?"

"I saw it, Dakota. I tracked you down hoping to— I don't know—see you. Make sure you're okay. I ... couldn't wait to see you, so I followed you instead of waiting for you here." He shook his head. "Not important. What's important is that one of your guards slipped out of camp when you stopped, and he met with a kobold. He led the band right to your party. I alerted the guards on sentry with some noise, giving away the kobold band's location. Without my intervention, the fae would've had much less time to react."

"Thank you. I don't suppose you can identify the traitorous guard?"

"They all look the same to me in those uniforms. He looked like a faerie." He thought for a moment. "White skinned. I'd say he's from either Central Realm or Northern Realm. Slight chance he's from Eastern or Western. Unlikely to be from Southern, because they have dark skin." Like the skin tone he'd chosen for his disguise whenever he entered the faerie world.

He spun around and strode toward the window— not at vampire speed; he had a reluctance to leave her because this time it would be forever. He intended to go without another word.

"Josh?"

The plea in her voice halted him, but he kept his back to her.

"Thank you. And I'm sorry. Sorry for what we lost and sorry because we can't see each other again," she said. Her gown rustled as she rose to standing. "Stay safe."

He left without a backward glance and without promising to never return.

CHAPTER 30

Silence blanketed the apartment Philip shared with Kelsey and Josh. Philip paced around the living room. *Of course it's quiet as a tomb in here. No one else is home.*

Josh's absence didn't bother him as much as Kelsey's did. The boy was out either walking the lake or working for Evans. Philip disliked the idea of his son donating sperm, but he couldn't forbid it, so he put it out of his mind. It didn't seem to bother the kid, so why stress about it? Philip had enough problems without taking on extra worry on behalf of others.

No, what irritated him was Kelsey's comings and goings. She'd slipped out without a word.

Not even a goodbye. As if they weren't a couple. *We're not—not as far as she's concerned.* Isn't that what really irritated him?

They not only shared a bed to sleep, but they also had sex together daily, sometimes multiple times per day. While it'd started out as helping Kelsey release tension and deal with controlling her urges, Philip hoped it meant more to her than simple satiation. Ever since he'd helped her get to where she could go out unsupervised in public, he'd seen a change in her. He'd fantasized that attitude shift included developing feelings for him.

I love her, damn it. It hurt that she didn't reciprocate, especially since, before Josh had turned her, she'd admitted to Philip that she loved him.

His cell phone's ring tone for Frank Evans halted Philip's steps. He snatched it from the coffee table and answered the call.

"Yeah?" He was in no mood for a conversation with the crime boss, let alone receive an assignment from him.

"I hear you're reluctant to renew your association with Annabelle Lawson."

Philip froze. "You heard right." No conversation that involved Annabelle would turn out well for him. That Evans wanted to discuss Philip's relationship with her shook the vampire. Surely Evans wouldn't order him to ... Philip couldn't finish the thought.

"I have your next assignment."

"Don't push it, Frank."

"Now, now, you haven't even heard what it is." The crime boss sounded more amused than angry.

Philip's fangs flicked out, and he hissed into the phone. "Then tell me so I can say no."

"You don't have the luxury. Donate your sperm. There's a huge demand for dhampir children, and we all know how popular the fruit of your loins is."

"Fuck you. No one else gets any fruit from my loins." He retracted his fangs before he chewed through his own lips or cheeks.

"What do you care? You won't have to raise the kid

or worry about it."

He couldn't help asking the obvious question that arose from that instruction. "Why wouldn't I care about my own child?"

"You're much too sentimental for a vampire, you know that?"

"I'm not doing this. Ask anything else but not that. I won't put another child through that. If I'd known what Annabelle's scheme was back then, Dakota wouldn't exist." He strode to the fridge and retrieved a bottle of blood to distract himself. If he didn't, he'd crush his phone, race over to Evans's house, and slaughter him and possibly his family. "You're stepping over the line."

"I don't think I am. You owe me. All of you."

Rage overcoming him at the thought Evans implied he'd demand this of Kelsey, too, Philip hurled the bottle against the wall, spraying glass and synthetic blood on the wall, floor, ceiling, and kitchen table.

"Stay the fuck away from Kelsey. She's not your private breeder."

Silence except for the human's slow, steady breaths.

"With all due respect," Evans said at last, "she most assuredly is. I can order her to do anything I want, and if I want her to bear a child for the business, that's what she'll do. Besides, it's not your call."

"I'm warning you. I'm setting a boundary, and you'd better respect it."

"I'll make you a deal."

Philip allowed the silence to hang while he frantically tried to think of something, anything, to wake himself from this nightmare. Unable to, he said, "I'm listening."

"Do this one thing for me, and I won't order Kelsey

Davis to have a child."

Philip closed his eyes. If he agreed, it would at least buy them some time. "Deal, but only if none of it goes to Annabelle Lawson."

"Fine. I'll text you the details."

"Sure." Evans had capitulated suspiciously quickly. "Frank?"

"Yes?"

"I want it in writing."

Evans chuckled. "You got it, sport." After a moment's pause, he said, "One more thing."

"What?"

"Find out why Kelsey is hanging out with priests. I find this development … interesting."

The line went dead as an icy dread spread through Philip. He stared at the bloody mess he'd made. *Guess I'd better clean that up before Kelsey sees it.* He planned to take the knowledge of this deal to the grave—figuratively speaking.

***

Instead of heading home after her visit with Father Paul, Kelsey went to Crossroads, the book he'd loaned her tucked safely in her bag. Some time spent working on her business would distract her overloaded brain. Her spiritual burden felt lighter after her chat with the priest but only because he'd agreed to help her. Neither of them had any idea what that help would look like.

But he's a man of the cloth. He works for God. If anyone can help me, he can.

At least someone out there believed she wasn't necessarily damned. What did other Catholic vampires do? More of her kind must exist. *Maybe I'll start a support group*. She laughed aloud at that.

Bells jingled as she pushed open the door and entered the store.

Chase stood behind the counter, serving a customer.

Kelsey waved a greeting, and after he acknowledged it with a nod, she strode through the maze of tables, past the shelves full of books, and into the staff room. She tucked her purse away and took a moment to slip into her office and verify the next day's deliveries. Satisfied everything looked in order, she returned to the front of the store and joined Chase behind the counter.

"Enjoy your day," he said to a customer as he handed her a latte.

After thanking him, the woman strolled to a table, where she sat down and pulled out a novel.

"How are you doing?" Kelsey asked. "Everything all right with Jaycie and the baby?" Chase's girlfriend was pregnant—about six months along. Past the morning sickness stage and well into the more enjoyable middle months.

"Everyone's fine." He poured himself a coffee and sipped without adding anything. Kelsey permitted her staff to help themselves to coffee and food while they worked. "Can I get you something, boss?"

She shook her head. "Thanks, but no. I came in to get away."

"Most people want to escape from work."

She shrugged. "Mind if I ask you about your religion?"

His mouth popped open, but he recovered himself and smiled. "Sure."

She scanned the store. No one was within

earshot—not unless a vampire or lycan hid behind a bookshelf—but she didn't sense anyone other than the handful of humans at the tables or browsing the books.

"You believe in many gods," she said. It wasn't a question because she knew the answer already. As a mage, Chase worshipped the old gods.

He, too, glanced around the room before speaking. "I'm acquainted with a few of them." He looked as if he wanted to add something to that but changed his mind.

"What does that mean?"

"Some of them visit the Earth plane. Not only that, but it's possible for a mage to travel between this world and the next. We're not supposed to, but it happens."

She gasped. "When Jaycie was missing, she went ... where?" If she'd had a beating heart, it would've been pounding.

"Don't let her know I told you. I trust you, boss. You've always looked out for me. This has to stay between us."

"Of course."

He hesitated still. "Even vampire you?"

She gave the question serious consideration. "Vampire me is actually more trustworthy. I don't care about gossip—less so now than as a human—and if you break moral, ethical, or legal laws, I don't care. I'm not your conscience or a cop." *Or a priest.* She recalled Father Paul's words about his obligations in the confessional and figured it was good enough for her, too. "If you've committed a crime, I might encourage you to turn yourself in, but you never know. I might not care enough."

He chuckled. "That's not what the old Kelsey would've said."

"That woman is long gone." The truth of that statement didn't make her sad. She enjoyed living without the anxiety that had ruled her former self. "Vampires are pretty Zen, I find. Unless you cross them."

"All right. Jaycie and I went to Hades."

A chair scraped against the floor as one of two men at a nearby table rose and approached the counter. Chase's distraction with the customer gave Kelsey time to consider what he'd just revealed.

Chase and Jaycie went to Hades. It exists. That meant the old gods existed. Could she conclude from this that her God didn't exist? No one went to Heaven and returned with reports of it. *Yes, they do. Near-death experiences.* She waited impatiently for the customer to get his order and return to his seat. When he was finally gone, she waited, foot tapping, for Chase's attention to return to her.

"Hades?" she whispered as soon as he settled beside her again. "How?"

"You're aware I had some trouble this past winter? The dean expelled me when he thought I'd summoned a demon during a final exam. Another spell I did later went just as badly."

She nodded, remembering the news reports of his expulsion but also of the reports of Jaycie's disappearance and the slamming shut of the doorways between the worlds. A faint image of floating above a lake and watching Josh pull her body out onto the ice snapped into sharp focus. The shock of recovering that memory almost buckled her knees. When it'd happened, she'd wondered what would become of her spirit since it couldn't cross to the other side with the doorways shut.

"I had a near-death experience."

Chase stared at her, puzzled. "When you became a vampire?"

"Yes. No. Before that. I died." To occupy herself, she strolled to the small fridge where they kept bottles of donated blood. Synthetic blood they stored in the main fridge, but plasma needed special storage. She removed a bottle and popped the cap. She returned to Chase's side so she could keep her voice low.

"I fell through the ice and drowned." He needn't know that a vampire chasing them shot Philip, who was carrying her, which landed her on the frozen lake. The vampire had then tossed a boulder after her, breaking the ice so she'd fall through. *The son of a bitch killed me. He intended to kill me.* She tucked that away for future reference. Evans was lucky she hadn't remembered that tidbit when she'd confronted him in his home after or he might not have survived that night.

"Josh rescued you and turned you?"

"Something like that." The memories returned, fast and vivid.

Philip had tried to stop the boy, but he'd been too late. The change had already started. The memory of the overwhelming hunger from that moment had her chugging the entire bottle.

Chase's eyes bugged out when some of the blood dribbled from her mouth and trailed down her chin. She swiped at it but only smeared it with her hands. He handed her a napkin, and she wiped herself clean.

"I'm sorry. I'd forgotten everything that happened from the moment I hit the ice to the moment I woke up as a vampire. It all came rushing back."

"Are you okay?" He placed a hand on her arm, and

she appreciated he wasn't afraid to touch her.

She tossed the bloodstained napkin into the garbage. Another chair scraped along the floor, and a woman approached the counter.

From the side of her mouth, Kelsey said, "Is the blood gone? Do I look okay?" *Wouldn't want to scare the customers.*

Chase gave her a quick glance. "You're fine."

"Then if you've got this, I'm going home." The urge to find Philip almost had her reaching for her purse at vampire speed, but she controlled it.

"Go," he said. "I'm here until close." As she turned to leave, he grabbed her arm. "Anything I can do?"

To her surprise, his concern touched her. She shook her head. "I'm fine. I need to get home after all."

"If you need anything, you know where to find me."

On a day full of surprises, she astonished herself one last time and hugged him. She left him staring after her with his mouth hanging open and the customer calling him out of his daze.

CHAPTER 31

Morning dawned on Dakota, who greeted it with mixed feelings. Living with the fae had transformed her from a night owl to a morning person. *It's not natural.* At least she didn't have to avoid the sun to the extent her father and Josh did.

She slipped out from under the covers, glancing at Culain's side of the bed, and discovered she didn't need to move cautiously. He wasn't there for her to jiggle awake.

Dakota scanned the room and found him at the desk, his head buried in his arms, tiny snores wafting out. She smiled affectionately and tiptoed to his side. She placed a hand on his shoulder and shook him gently.

"Culain?" She almost whispered the name, reluctant to wake him but hating to see him sleeping in such an uncomfortable position. What was so damn important that he hadn't come to bed?

He still didn't know he was going to be a father. She'd wanted to surprise him with the news when he came to bed, but she'd fallen asleep waiting for him.

That wouldn't have happened if I kept vampire hours.

She shook him again, this time not as gently, and he stirred and grunted.

"Culain? Wake up." She no longer whispered.

He raised his head and smacked his lips. "Stay back. Morning breath." He stretched, his bleary gaze meeting her alert one.

She chuckled. "I can smell ya from here, dear. I mean, my lord."

He pressed a hand to his mouth and blushed. "I'll go brush." He stood and turned toward the en suite bathroom, but she restrained him with a hand on his arm.

"You slept at the desk. It's not healthy to bring work into the bedroom."

"I didn't intend to. It just happened."

"You should've come to bed."

He raised his brows. "Yes."

She released him. "We need to talk. When you're dressed." Realizing she too still had her nightclothes on, she added, "When we're dressed."

He threw her a startled look. "Something wrong?"

"Not at all. I'd like a word before we start the day." She glanced at the window. Sun seeped in around the blinds. She'd tell him about the baby, but the other news would take finesse. How would she tell him about her mother or about the traitor amid their guards without revealing her source? She'd have to lie about how she learned the information, but what she'd say remained a mystery. She recalled the various nuisances they'd encountered on the final leg of the journey home. They didn't seem so coincidental now.

She followed Culain into the bathroom to brush her

teeth and wash her face while he showered. The child within her stirred, and she pressed her hand to her tummy. It hadn't rounded out yet, but in a few short weeks, she'd show. The entire realm would buzz with the news as soon as it got out. How long could they keep it to themselves? King Killian would probably want to make the announcement immediately.

Minutes later, the water in the tub stopped, and Culain's hand emerged from behind the shower curtain. He felt around, and, to save him the trouble, Dakota pressed the towel into his fist.

"Thanks," he said.

"I should've joined you in there to save time."

"My dear, if you'd joined me, it wouldn't have saved us any time."

She laughed. She loved how he joked with her. How he talked to her. He respected her, which, if Alina was to be believed, was rare among faerie men and their wives.

Easy enough when I'm not responsible for all the chores.

He stepped from the shower, naked as a Greek statue but much better hung.

She smiled lasciviously. "Suddenly I'm hungry for blood, Your Highness."

His reaction was instant, and when she saw his hardness, she forgot everything but biting into his thigh. She dropped to her knees.

As it turned out, her shower was delayed, but when she finally stepped into the stall, he joined her after all.

***

Culain returned to awareness in the shower after what had felt like an out-of-body experience. Dakota, once again, had driven him to heights he'd never experienced before. Her lips, her tongue, her teeth— the way they all worked together to bring him pleasure no woman had ever provided. He'd almost swooned when she'd broken the skin on his thigh with her fangs. He hadn't cared how close she'd gotten to his testicles. In fact, he'd wanted her to ... Culain swallowed, his manhood growing hard again. They lacked time for another round, and she'd said she wanted to talk. Whatever was on her mind couldn't be too bad if she'd given him such body-shaking pleasure.

After getting dressed with the help of his valet, whom he immediately sent from the room as soon as they were done, Culain met up with Dakota in the sitting area of their bedroom.

She sat on the edge of the sofa, her hands pressed to her knees. Her palms rubbed back and forth on the gown she wore. It was one of her more casual outfits. Lysandra was nowhere in sight, which meant his wife had dressed herself. He knew she preferred to, but most days, she bowed to convention.

Not today.

He sat down beside her and smiled encouragingly. "What's going on?"

She cleared her throat. "I have news."

"Clearly." He frowned, growing worried again. "What's on your mind?"

She scrunched up her face at that but quickly smoothed it out again. When she spoke, excitement flooded her words. "I'm pregnant."

Joy filled him and he gasped. "Are you sure?"

She nodded. "I did a test yesterday afternoon." She averted her eyes, shooting her gaze down at her hands. "Alina helped me. I'm sorry you weren't the first one to find out besides me, but she promised to keep it a secret until I told you." She raised her head. "I didn't know who else to ask for help. I trust her."

"That's fine, my darling. I'm so happy. How far along?"

She grinned at that. "That we don't know. I suppose I could guess. I'd like to believe it happened on our wedding night."

Unable to restrain himself, Culain pulled her into a tight embrace and covered her hair and face with kisses.

She laughed, breathlessly, and returned the hugs. "I guess I'll have to see a doctor, who'll tell us everything we need to know."

"Of course. We'll get one in right away. He'll visit you here." He frowned. "Unless you have a midwife or hedge witch you'd prefer? They're rare in our world, but they do exist."

"Whoever you trust is fine with me." She tilted her head to the side and wrinkled her brow. "I suppose we'll have to wait, then, to make the announcement?"

"Yes, which is why we'll summon that doctor here immediately. I need to verify this and then announce it to my family. King Killian will make the formal announcement at the next banquet."

"Okay."

He stood. "I'll send a guard to get the doctor for you." He hurried to the door and made the request. After the man scurried away, Culain returned to Dakota, who'd remained seated where he'd left her.

"Is everything all right? Do you feel okay?" What if she had morning sickness? He didn't think dhampirs experienced that, but he knew little about their physiology. She was still half human, and humans certainly suffered from that.

"I feel fine. I overheard something concerning that I think you should know."

"All right." He waited, giving her all the time she needed.

"I don't know who said what. I was too far away, but ... you understand I have exceptional hearing."

He strode over to stand before her and dropped to one knee. Taking her hands in his, he said, "Just tell me. Whatever it is, I'll take care of it."

"I could be mistaken. You need to verify whatever I tell you. If it's not true, I don't want to have anyone unjustly accused."

"My goodness. What has you so worried?"

"Don't patronize me. I won't tolerate it." She pulled her hands from his.

"I didn't intend to. Stop dancing around it, then, and tell me."

She cleared her throat again, a sure sign she was nervous. "You might have a traitor in the guard unit. One who journeyed with us on our honeymoon."

He instantly sobered. This was indeed serious. If she was right, they'd need to ferret out the guilty person quickly before damage was done. He quelled the urge to storm out. What if she'd overheard a baseless rumor? As far as he knew, all his guards were loyal to him and to everyone in his family, including Dakota.

"Tell me what you heard and how you heard it."

Her pupils shifted from side to side as her gaze darted everywhere but at him.

Interesting. What wasn't she telling him? He sensed she was hiding something, but he loved and trusted her. She'd shown herself as loyal and trustworthy as any fae. *Except maybe one of the guards.* He shoved that aside. She was part of his family, and he trusted family implicitly. He waited her out.

When she spoke, her eyes had ceased their darting, and she folded her hands calmly in her lap. "I've heard rumors that after the kobolds attacked and we were verifying that everyone was present and accounted for, a guard was spotted returning from the forest. They deem the behavior suspicious and question if the problems we had before the attack were sabotage."

Rumors weren't proof, and staff gossiped more than was good for anyone, but his mind connected various pieces and drew a conclusion. "To slow us down? Ah, yes, and allow the kobolds to attack us at that location and time." It'd seemed too perfect an ambush. He'd assumed they'd had a scout or had followed the caravan's progress through messages from villagers. He'd refused to accept one of their own party could've set them up.

She stood and approached him. "Why would someone do this?" Her tone held not just puzzlement but also sorrow. "To what end? To kill you? Me? Or to hurt us even if they don't kill us?" She folded her arms across her chest. "If the alarm hadn't sounded when it did, if they'd caught us unawares, they could've killed someone."

"That didn't happen. Those protecting us did their jobs and got us all home safely. The only casualties were among the kobolds, and they brought that on themselves. I feel no guilt for it."

"Nor I," she said.

He put a reassuring hand on her arm. "Leave this to me, my love. You have enough to concern you, and I won't have you stressing yourself and our baby needlessly." *Our baby.* He rejoiced at the notion. It went beyond relief at producing an heir so quickly though that certainly was a factor. He loved Dakota so much he wanted to start a family with her immediately. He promised himself he'd give any children they had the fatherly attention he'd missed from King Killian. Even if Killian passed the crown along to Culain tomorrow, the faerie prince vowed his children would love him rather than fear him. Respect was important, but one didn't earn it through sternness and punishment.

An image of the king standing nearby as a servant put the strap to Culain's bare bottom flashed into Culain's head. *Never. This child will never feel the lash's sting.* His father would disagree—vehemently—and accuse him of spoiling his children and making them weak, but Culain didn't think he'd learned strength from beatings his father meted out. And for what? Sneaking a sweet from the dessert table before eating dinner? Part of him wondered if his father had enjoyed lording his power over his two sons.

"Culain." Dakota leaned in close and brought him out of his reveries. "Are you okay? I'm sorry if I've upset you."

He kissed her lips, but distractedly.

"I need to go." He spotted a trace of worry in her expression. "Tell me what the doctor says. I'll see you here before dinner." He left the room to find out what the hell was going on.

CHAPTER 32

Kelsey slipped into their penthouse unit at nightfall. The days were getting longer, and by this time of year, the sun set around 8:30 p.m. She relished the night. Tonight, she planned to start a new program: fight training. Evans had hired a personal martial arts instructor who lived in the building to meet with her four nights a week in the gym downstairs. This was one more thing she'd keep from Philip—not that he'd object, but she feared he'd want to interfere. She'd never noticed his control issues before she became a vampire because she'd had too many of her own, but the red flags had existed. Or perhaps they'd only started when she was no longer human. She supposed that had to be it. He certainly hadn't interfered in her downward spiral back in the cabin. He'd let her slide until it was almost too late. She wondered what he'd have done if she'd actually taken her life. Would he have turned her if he'd been the one to hold her dying body in his arms?

She closed and locked the door. Philip was home—

she sensed his presence in the living room—but darkness and silence blanketed the entire apartment.

His voice shattered the quiet, and he appeared before her as a silhouette her vampire vision detected, standing in front of the couch. "Where were you?"

She snarled in response. What right did he have to question her comings and goings?

In a flash, he pressed up against her. "Where were you?"

"Out." She bared her fangs. That brought with it a surge of lust in her loins. Her body trembled with the desire to bite into the neck so near her mouth. A low growl rumbled out of her.

He grabbed her around the throat and pushed her against the door. "You want me? Tell me where you were."

Her mouth opened; her lips drew back over her gums. Saliva oozed from the corners of her mouth. She pressed a hand to his crotch and cupped his testicles through his pants. *Thank God, he's not wearing jeans.* She stroked his hard cock. "Meeting with another man."

His rage was as immediate as his lust.

He snarled and his fangs sprang out. Releasing her throat, he pressed his nose to her neck and sniffed a line down her body. He stopped when his face reached her crotch. "I smell no other man on you."

"I said I met with another man. I didn't say I fucked him. Or fed from him." She moaned when he rubbed his nose against her thigh.

"Take off that prissy skirt before I chew through it, darling." He pulled away, giving her space.

His physical absence made her feel empty and achy, so she obliged, unzipping it and letting it drop to the floor. She stood before him in only her blouse, stockings, and shoes. Those she kicked off so only the blouse and stockings remained. And the bra. Frantic to get it all off, she tore off the material and flung it aside.

Using her vampire speed, she vanished from his sight into the bedroom and reclined on the bed. He followed an instant later, naked as a newborn.

Everything became a haze of wild lust after that. They bit, they sucked, and they made love until they wore each other out.

Kelsey spared a moment to wonder if this would damn her further in the sight of God, but the thought didn't slow her down. Perhaps she'd confess it the next time she met with Father Paul. She didn't dwell more than a second on thoughts of the priest, though. Philip saw to that. He ravaged her, but when she tried to wrest control from him, he fought her for the first time since they started having sex.

"Not today," he said with a growl. "Today you do it my way. You do what I tell you."

His words alone almost had her climaxing. She ended her struggles and went boneless under him.

In an agony of ecstasy, she said, "Tell me what you want."

For the next half hour, he did just that.

***

"I need to go." Kelsey rolled out of bed, no trace of weariness or lust in her voice.

Philip pricked up his ears and sat up, the sheet pooling in his lap. Just as well it hid his groin. He was as flaccid as a wet noodle. While that didn't make him self-conscious, he didn't need her gaze landing on it. That would activate it again, and he was sure she didn't want that. Resenting how much her opinions affected him, he followed her movements with his gaze. With effort, he kept his fangs in.

"Where you off to?" He thought he'd kept his tone neutral, but he must've failed because her fangs slid out and she snarled. He held up a hand.

"Peace. I'm just making conversation." He wasn't—he wanted desperately to know where she was going and what she'd be doing.

"Gym." She strode to her dresser, clearly unselfconscious of her nakedness.

His libido stirred.

God, her breasts are perky, and her ass is tight. And those legs. She's a fucking goddess. Of course she was. She had the perfect body of a vampire. She looked twenty-five though she'd turned at forty-four.

He raised his brows. "You know we can't build muscle. What you were reborn with is what you get for eternity—but you're hella strong, anyway." He flexed his arm. He at least had some definition, but his build as a human had been the skinny rock-star type. Not quite heroin chic but nowhere near bodybuilder. "Vampire strong."

She laughed, and it relieved him to hear it. While not carefree, it wasn't forced or constrained, something he was used to hearing in her human laugh. Her vampire laugh mostly sounded sinister. The genuine glee in it figuratively warmed him.

"I know. I'm ..." She frowned. "Damn it, why must you know everything I do? What's with you lately?"

He sneered. "Nothing. Why can't you—?" Why couldn't she—what? Be more of a girlfriend? He almost laughed.

Christ, if Dwayne could see me now. Philip wondered

vaguely where his former business partner and onetime best friend might be hiding. Sometimes he actually missed the scum-sucking traitor.

She pulled a sports bra, panties, a tank top, and a pair of leggings from her dresser. "I have to jump in the shower before I get dressed. I don't want to go down to the gym smelling like sex."

"How practical and considerate of you."

"Every vamp in there will smell you on me if I don't."

"Is that so bad if they know you're mine?" He tossed the sheets aside and rose from the bed. "Why don't I join you?"

Before he could even blink, she tossed her clothes onto the bed and pinned him against the wall. She scraped her front teeth down this throat. "You think you can handle more?" she teased.

His fangs broke free in response. He tore his wrists from her grasp and picked her up by the waist. Carrying her wriggling body into the bathroom, he showed her exactly how much more he could handle.

CHAPTER 33

"How now, brother?" Colin waved, drawing his sibling's attention from the report he was reading at the desk in his office.

Culain finished writing a note in the margin and set down his pen. He leaned back in his chair, stretched his legs out, crossing them at the ankles, and laced his fingers behind his head.

"I need a break from this mind-numbing reading." At times, he hated that the fae refused the most modern technology. Dakota had complained about a lack of Internet connectivity and a dependence on physical books rather than digital. He agreed with her, but they couldn't connect to the Internet without exposing their world to the outside one. None of the fae wanted that.

Colin dropped into the chair in front of the desk. "I have news."

Culain had confided in his brother about the traitor among the guards—not about where he'd heard the information, just that he'd received it that day. His brother had promised to discreetly investigate. From the look on his face, he must've learned something important.

"Well?" Culain asked. He held his breath.

"Your information was wrong."

That didn't sound right. "Are you sure? My source was a good one. I doubt the person got it wrong." *I'll have to investigate it myself.* He frowned. One more thing to add to his packed to-do list.

"Positive." Colin stood and paced the room. He'd always been a restless boy, and he'd become a restless man.

"How exactly did you investigate this?"

"I nosed around the guards' quarters. Asked the servants working there." He stopped pacing and stood, hands clasped behind his back, facing the window. Silence reigned for a moment before he added, "Your Highness."

"Knock it off." He'd heard the mockery in Colin's voice and had no time for petty jealousies.

Colin dropped his hands to his sides. "I investigated everyone's finances. No one has money or possessions he shouldn't have. No one's comings and goings arouse suspicion. I checked the logs. Everything's in order where the guards are concerned." He tilted his head to the side and studied Culain. "Perhaps your source is the traitor's attempt to throw off suspicion or frame an innocent. Or maybe it's revenge for an imagined slight. You know, accuse your enemy of treason—that kind of thing."

"Impossible."

"Why?"

Culain rose. "It just is."

"Who told you this? Perhaps if you shared the name of your informant with me, I could evaluate and give you a more objective opinion on his loyalties."

"I'm sure the person was simply mistaken. They told me they weren't certain."

"You're going to an awful lot of trouble to avoid using the word *he*. Perhaps your source is a woman? Dakota, maybe?"

His brother's accurate guess had Culain frantically trying to come up with a reasonable response. "Of course not."

"You can tell me. She's my sister-in-law. If you don't deliver an heir, she could one day be my wife."

Had Colin's eyes brightened a bit too much at that prospect? Culain was tempted to tell his brother his chances of that had dimmed significantly since this morning, but he kept the news of the pregnancy to himself. It would've offered him satisfaction to wipe the glee from his brother's face, but he had to follow protocols. Once the doctor verified the news, King Killian would hear it immediately. Despite a desire to punch his brother over the remark, Culain simply said, "I don't plan on dying without an heir."

"No one plans on dying," Colin promptly replied. "Happens, though. All the time."

"Few things can kill a fae. My odds are good. Unless you plan on giving destiny a hand?" He tried to make it sound like a joke, but it came out somberly.

Colin shook his head. "Even after all this time, you suspect me of wanting to usurp your position."

Yes. Because your every act and utterance reveals it. "Wouldn't you?"

"Tsk. You think I'd want to be king? My time is better spent elsewhere." He wrinkled his nose. "And I don't want a secondhand wife, either."

Culain decided the conversation needed to end before it devolved into fisticuffs—something that had happened regularly when they were boys but that they needed to avoid as grown princes. "Is that everything you had for me?"

"Aye. If I were you, I wouldn't worry about your men. They're loyal to you. If the threat exists, it's from elsewhere." Colin bowed—facetiously, it seemed to Culain, who ignored the gesture.

"What's your agenda for the rest of the day?" he asked.

"Not that it's any of your business, but I'm seeing Alina. I'm taking her on a picnic in the garden."

"Colin ..." He didn't finish the thought. He didn't need to.

"I don't care. You married the woman you love."

"If you court Alina, she'll expect you to marry her. Her family will as well. Father, however, expects you to marry a dhampir or a fae of higher status."

Colin growled in response and slammed a fist onto the desk. "Damnation, if you beget an heir, I don't see why I shouldn't be with the woman I love."

"Father would suggest you can marry appropriately and keep the woman you love on the side."

"Father," Colin scoffed. "Why do you think he never remarried? Not even to a dhampir? Mother was the love of his life. He married the woman he loved, yet he denies me the same courtesy."

Culain sighed. "You know how it goes. We marry the family, not the woman. Mother's family was well connected. They owned half of Eastern Realm. The wealth and connections our family received from the marriage filled more than our coffers. It gave us and our children wealth, power, and security."

"I don't need all that."

"Don't you?" Culain recalled all the times they'd played pretend together as children. Colin always wanted to be the dashing highwayman who kidnapped Alina while Culain played the knight who rescued her. Over half the time, she'd wanted to stay with the highwayman. "No, I suppose you don't." He grinned. "Don't despair. When I have an heir and I'm king, perhaps I'll change the rules for you."

Colin's expression turned quizzical. "I hope you're not teasing me."

"I wouldn't. Alina is Dakota's closest friend. She's a friend to me as well. If it weren't for her family's lack of wealth and status, the two of you would already be engaged." That was a lie. If her family had the wealth and status, his father would've married her to Culain, and they'd never have purchased Dakota. Where would the dhampir girl be then? The thought sent chills up his spine. Her mother would still have sold her; Culain was certain of it.

"I'll hold you to that, brother." Colin headed for the door but turned back when he reached it. "I'll do some more digging, but so far, your guards are above reproach."

Since Colin sounded as if he genuinely meant it, Culain removed investigating the guards back off his mental to-do list. He trusted his brother. Why not? They had their differences, but they loved each other. And if you couldn't trust your own family, then who could you trust?

CHAPTER 34

Glamour didn't work as effectively for dhampirs as it did for vampires. Dakota could enhance her appearance, but she couldn't veil herself in another identity the way Josh could. She shouldn't even be considering it, but she was anyway. Ever since she'd learned Annabelle wanted to get pregnant again, thoughts of confronting her mother had plagued Dakota. She became so distracted that Culain started asking questions. While she insisted nothing was bothering her, she could only blame her desire to have a child for so long. Consequently, she made plans to indulge her obsession and venture into the world.

A disguise was her only means out of the faerie realm. Getting permission from the king wasn't a consideration. He'd never allow her to leave Autumnland. Married to the prince or not, she remained a virtual captive to the fae. No Running Loose for her. As far as Culain and his family were concerned, her whole life before the fae bought her was one giant Running Loose, and she should've had her fill.

As if. Her mother had kept a tight rein on Dakota right up to the moment the fae claimed her.

She waited on the sofa in the sitting area of the bedroom she and Culain shared. Any moment now, he'd appear and she'd confirm the pregnancy for him. The doctor had verified it, to her great relief. She hadn't doubted she was pregnant, but it helped to have the doctor's tests verify it.

The bedroom door swung open, and Culain stood in the entrance, staring hopefully at her.

She laughed. "Close the door. This news is for your ears, not the guards'."

He did as she bid and then hurried to her side. "The tests were positive."

She jumped to her feet and threw herself into his arms. "Yes. We're going to have a baby. You're going to have an heir." Thank the gods for that. While she enjoyed trying to get pregnant, she hated the pressure-filled wait for the child to be conceived.

He whisked her into his arms in a bear hug and swung her around, rounding it off with an impassioned kiss.

Breathless—or as breathless as a dhampir who drew in little air could be—she laughed. All her tension and thoughts of her mother vanished with his infectious joy.

He set her down again and had to grab her when she staggered at the sudden halt of their motion. She laughed again, thrilled at how it felt. So free and easy. What she loved most about him was his freedom of emotional expression despite the fae tendency to squelch it. In private, Culain was a delight.

"We must find Father immediately and tell him."

Her stomach fluttered nervously at the thought of facing King Killian, but at least the news was what he wanted to hear. Her father-in-law wasn't a cruel man, but he was somber, and that made him brusque and, at times, harsh. More than once he'd made her feel unworthy of her husband-to-be despite the Shiels family having paid so much to get her. She believed that was exactly why he expected much and demanded everything from her.

Dakota had lost her temper over it once when the king had ordered her servants to burn the embroidery the dhampir girl had worked on for three weeks. Granted, it did look as if a three-year-old child had sewn it, but she'd worked hard on it. In her mind, she'd done it well enough that she'd felt a touch of pride when he'd asked to see it.

He stared at the uneven stitches, the slightly dirt-smudged white of the cloth, and the frayed lace for a moment. Then his face turned red.

"You call this sewing? My sons could've done better when they were three." Then he told Lysandra to feed it to the fire and ordered Dakota to redo it.

Okay, so it looks like a two-year-old child sewed it. That thought started a whole tsunami of sentiments that everyone present was probably lucky she didn't voice. But she couldn't hold it all in.

"How dare you?" Her bellow startled them both, but the old man hid it much better than she did. "That stupid scrap of fabric took me forever to do. It's not good enough for you? Oh, so sorry that I'm not cut out for embroidery." She was on her feet by this point, her fists thrust firmly against her hips.

"A woman must excel at such things," he replied.

"It's not that I care what the damn thing looks like; it's that you're failing at women's work."

She sputtered as she tried to collect her thoughts to focus on the most important one. What came out was "Women's work? Teach me how to wield a sword, then that'll be women's work too!"

He'd clutched at his chest then, and for a moment she feared she'd given him a coronary. With her dhampir senses, she listened to his heart. It beat a little rapidly, but fae didn't succumb to such things as myocardial infarctions. He wasn't in any danger. She'd shocked him, but that was all. She expected him to rage at her, to put her in her place, and she braced herself to respond in kind. What she didn't expect was what he did: he roared with laughter. Tears trickled from the corners of his eyes.

"Gods love you, girl. You take after my Alessia. She hated this fussy stuff too." He dabbed at his eyes. "Well. Swords, you say? My wife never requested that of me, but we'll see. I suppose a dhampir isn't a fae and never will be, but that's not a bad thing, is it?"

She didn't know how to respond, but he waited until she filled the silence. Things usually went badly for her when she spoke impulsively, but she did all right this time.

"I never liked to sew, Your Majesty, but I enjoy sports, and I've always wanted to learn swordplay." If she'd known how to fight, she wouldn't be here. Maybe. It hadn't occurred to her until they'd kidnapped her that self-defense was a necessary skill to have. If they wouldn't teach her martial arts, perhaps she could convince them to teach her how to use a sword.

King Killian had indulged her, but only to a point.

He'd let her take fencing lessons if she agreed to continue with her sewing, and only until she married. "A princess has protection around her. She has no need to fight."

She agreed to his terms but vowed to change his mind later. She also didn't point out to him that had his wife known how to protect herself, she might not have lost her life. Dakota hadn't picked up a saber since her marriage. Now that she was pregnant, King Killian likely wouldn't allow her to resume those lessons. She intended to confront him on the subject but decided to wait until after she had the baby.

With all those thoughts racing through her head, she linked her arm through Culain's and said, "Shall we go tell the king, then, husband? I'm sure he'll be thrilled."

CHAPTER 35

Against his better judgment, Philip followed Kelsey on a bright July Sunday. He disguised himself and kept a fair distance behind her as she made her way to wherever she disappeared to on Sunday mornings. That it turned out to be church shocked him as much as if she'd been having an affair despite his conversations about it with Josh and Evans.

While he watched from behind a tree, she waited for all the humans to enter before she strolled in herself. No one stared at her or treated her as if she intruded. A greeter at the door handed her a schedule and, smiling, let her pass.

Philip hadn't set foot in a church since well before he'd turned. A lapsed Catholic from the time he left for Montreal's McGill University in what was then Quebec, he'd tossed religion aside along with his bedroom at his parents' house. His parents had been disappointed—vocally so—but what did he care? He no longer lived under their roof.

He'd gotten his degree in dentistry and had actually

run his own practice for ten years before the pandemic hit and the hypernaturals came out of the closet. The vampire who'd turned him had appeared in his life during the species wars and had almost ended it. Not all vampires turned their victims, and when they first swarmed among the human population, they killed many. It'd been a dark time with casualties on both sides since humans already knew from folklore and legend how to kill the undead.

Decades later, Philip met Frank Evans, and they saved each other's lives even though one was a vampire and the other was a human. Some might consider what they'd done a betrayal to their species, but at the time, it'd made sense. They'd survived; though it often felt to Philip as if he'd made a deal with the Lord of the Flies himself. No doubt Evans felt similarly about his own situation.

Which of us is Satan in this scenario? After all, Evans was considered to possess a soul while Philip was viewed as a monster.

Considering his current situation, he felt as though he'd come full circle. It chafed, and he resented getting mixed up with the mob boss again just as he'd wanted to end the relationship.

Whenever his memories dragged him back to those times, Philip shook off the recollections that followed his turning and the obligation and friendship that had developed as a result. His life took a leap forward then as Evans helped the vampire adjust to a society in flux. Philip preferred to forget the years between his rebirth as a vampire and the present day, but his accursed brain refused to cooperate.

Kelsey had long since vanished into the church. He hung around a while longer and almost crossed the street to follow her in but changed his mind.

The entrance was shut and the congregation would already have taken their seats. His appearance at the doors he'd have to thrust open, no matter how stealthy he tried to be, would attract attention.

At least she hadn't spotted him. He could only imagine her fury at catching him following her to church.

Why the hell come to church? Is she really visiting the priests?

Without a decent answer to that, Philip turned on his heel and walked away.

***

Father Michael led the mass that Sunday morning at Father Paul's request. The older priest—a decade separated Michael from Paul—had agreed to the schedule change without complaint, but questions were inevitable. Paul didn't want to lie to his friend and mentor, but how could he tell the man the truth? Father Michael was an exceptional priest, generous, and kind, but he viewed hypernaturals as soulless devil spawn rather than God's children. While the pair's discussions on the issue until now had been theoretical, Father Paul dreaded dragging them into reality. Kelsey Davis would test the priests' friendship and their work relationship—which was why Father Paul watched the sermon from inside the confessional at the rear of the church.

He felt foolish huddling in the booth where he sat when he heard confessions. He'd felt even more ludicrous when he first crept into the church and hid— a full thirty minutes before the start of mass.

As on previous Sundays, Kelsey entered last. She

strode to the pew nearest the exit as she always did. This provided Father Paul with a decent angle for viewing her profile if she faced right or left, her back when she faced the front, and her expression if she faced the back. He hoped she never turned toward him, but if she did, she shouldn't be able to see him.

She genuflected and took her seat, keeping at least three feet of distance between herself and her neighbor. The woman, who sat with her husband and four-year-old son, barely glanced at the vampire.

The pew in front of Kelsey had no one near her either, and since she'd seated herself in the last pew, no one sat behind her. She'd deliberately chosen a spot that allowed her to avoid interacting with other members of the congregation. Even so, during the salutation, the family sharing her pew would likely offer their hands to her. Father Paul had never observed any problems when he'd led the mass in the past. On reflection, she always secured a seat far from others.

After Kelsey's visit to the rectory, he'd wondered how the rest of the congregation tolerated the member of the undead in their midst. Hence the cloak-and-dagger escapade. He could see she'd managed the situation herself. He needn't have worried she'd disrupt the mass. She'd caused no trouble so far.

The feeling of foolishness amped up. What was he doing here? What did he hope to accomplish? Spying on a member of the church? What did God think of that?

God wouldn't want the vampire in his house. Father Paul doubted the words even as he thought them and why he needed to observe for himself how she behaved in God's house and how others treated her.

Father Michael and his attendants entered the

church then. The procession moved up the center aisle, and the priest bowed at the altar. He moved behind it, the altar servers standing at attention in front of their seats.

A peek in Kelsey's direction showed her frowning at Father Michael's presence, but she settled into her seat as the priest finished greeting the congregation. As mass proceeded, she appeared to hang on every word said, the way she did when Father Paul led the mass.

I guess I'm not as riveting as I thought.

He'd been flattered to think she'd believed him wise or intelligent. Now he realized she was obsessed with whatever anyone leading the mass said about God and the scriptures.

No one around her paid her any mind. She obviously knew the routines and responses, so she hadn't lied to him when she'd told him during their meeting that she'd attended mass since childhood.

Father Michael began the Penitential Act.

"Brothers and sisters, let us acknowledge our sins and prepare to celebrate the sacred mysteries."

He fell silent then, leaving only the sounds of shuffling, clearing throats, and a child saying "Mommy?" followed by a soft shush.

All spoke the response, the vampire included. "I confess to almighty God and to you, my brothers and sisters ..."

As Father Paul listened to her say the words and watched her fervent expression, he took a moment to reflect on how unfair it was that such a good person, someone so dedicated to her spirituality, had become one of the undead. She'd told him she hadn't broken any laws, and when he'd investigated her story after she'd left, that appeared to be the case.

She and her son had become legal vampire citizens after a hearing presenting their extenuating circumstances allowed it, but something about that bothered him. Others had tried after-the-fact defenses and ended up in jail. Why had Kelsey and her son escaped such penalties?

The mass passed smoothly. The offering of peace passed without incident.

Kelsey moved even farther away from the family— practically standing in the aisle to avoid interacting with them. The woman closest to the vampire glanced once in her direction, noted the distance between them and Kelsey's obvious reluctance to touch anyone, and offered her hand to someone else nearby.

The time for Holy Communion arrived.

Everyone kneeled.

Each row stood up in turn and moved down the center aisle to where Father Michael waited. Kelsey kept her head bowed as though in prayer. She'd removed the sunhat she'd worn into the church. Father Paul couldn't see where she'd placed it, so he assumed it sat beside her on the bench.

The family sharing Kelsey's bench moved out, the father carrying the child, who asked in loud whispers if he could have one of the crackers to eat today.

Father Paul smiled. He'd heard the boy ask the same question, and the parents always patiently explained that he'd have to wait until he was six.

Kelsey kept her head bowed through the exchange, stirring only to stand to prevent tripping people as they passed her by. With the pew emptied, she stood alone. She returned to her position on the kneeler. Hands clasped in prayer, she tilted her head forward.

Father Paul almost took that opportunity to sneak

away but feared Father Michael might spot him even if Kelsey didn't. He shifted in the cramped quarters, searching for a more comfortable position, but froze when Kelsey's head snapped up and turned toward him.

She heard me. The thought discomfited him. To his horror and fascination, she then sniffed the air.

Her gaze landed directly on the confessional.

He swallowed past the lump in his throat and held his breath.

After a moment of staring, during which he almost believed she glimpsed him through the screen-covered section of door, she moved from the kneeler back to her seat on the pew. She faced front again as if dismissing the presence lurking in the confessional.

She knows I'm here. He grasped the handle on the door, ready to open it the moment Father Michael spoke again and distracted the congregation. Distracted Kelsey.

At last, communion ended, and the remaining stragglers returned to their seats.

No one disturbed the vampire on the return trip. When they returned, her seatmates entered on the opposite side of the pew.

The boy slipped onto the bench first, and as he drew close to Kelsey, she faced left and stared down at him.

He stopped. Smiled.

Father Paul sucked in a breath. Held it. And released it when she returned the smile—close-mouthed. If her fangs were out, no one saw them.

Father Michael started the concluding rites, and everyone once again faced the front. When his fellow priest reached the announcements and fixed his gaze on the paper before him, Father Paul quietly slipped from his hiding place and hurried to the exit. He opened the door only enough to allow egress and stepped outside. As he pulled the door closed, he glimpsed Kelsey's ice-blue eyes watching him leave.

CHAPTER 36

I have no shortage of stupid ideas. Josh clambered through the windows in Dakota's private rooms. He closed and locked the pane and raced with vampire speed into her closet when he heard the rattle of the bedroom door's lock. He cracked the closet door open and peered out in time to see a guard stride to the window. The lad, who looked young and green and probably had never confronted anyone, let alone a prowler, touched the lock. Turned it to the open position. Shoved the window up. Leaned his head through it.

"Well?" Another guard entered the room, this one older and likely thinking himself wiser. "Nothing, right?"

"Not nothing. I swear I heard a noise in here." He pulled his head back into the room and secured the window.

"Probably a rat."

Green Boy shook his head. "She's dhampir. No rat would dare intrude in her rooms." Josh heard the whisper with his vampire hearing as if it were a shout.

Wise Man laughed. "A myth, that. You think she eats them for dinner when no one's looking?" He smirked.

"I think she's a lady and wouldn't do anything of the sort."

"A soft spot for Her Royal Highness?"

"She'll be our queen one day."

Wise Man shrugged. "Don't I know it. Crazy bunch, them royals."

Green Boy raised his chin in defiance. "You'd do the same if you could afford the bride price."

When only silence met the statement, Green Boy gave a slight, smug smile as he scanned the room.

Josh quickly used his vampire powers of illusion to make the closet door appear shut tight. *Don't need to give that nosy bugger any reason to investigate the closet.* He could incapacitate them or entrance them and erase their memories, but it was simpler just to avoid a confrontation.

He tensed as Green Boy took a step in the closet's direction, but he only paced the perimeter of the room. When he landed back at the window, he peered out of it again.

"For the love of Puck, lad," Wise Man shouted, "the damn room's empty. You heard rats. Or the wind blowing through your ears. Are you done yet? What if the lady returns? How'll we explain our presence in here?"

The boy strolled silently past his partner to the door. Opening it, he gave the room a final scan and stepped outside. The other guard followed him. The door banged closed, and the lock snicked into place.

Josh waited a moment, and when he deemed it safe,

he stepped from the closet. That was close. He didn't need to worry about camera surveillance in the fae realms, but clearly the guards checked on these rooms as part of their rounds. They might not enter every time, but they obviously stopped outside and listened.

He dropped onto the couch—silent as a mouse, not noisy as that imaginary rat—and waited for Dakota's return.

***

Ever since King Killian had announced to the entire realm that Prince Culain and Princess Dakota were expecting, Dakota's days had become hectic even while her friends, Culain's family, and the servants all pampered and doted on her. She found peace and privacy only in her quarters. She headed there now, hoping to spend an hour or so reading. Culain knew where he could find her if he needed her, but he wouldn't disturb her. This day, duties had kept her especially busy, and to her surprise, she felt tired and irritated. All she wanted was to hole up in her room and decompress. Two guards accompanied her and unlocked the bedroom door for her. One of the pair stepped inside and wandered through it, poking his head into the bathroom and the closet to make sure no one hid inside. When he gave her the all clear, she entered the room, and he left.

"We'll be outside if you need us, Your Highness," he said, as he always did.

"Thank you," she replied—as she always did.

She closed the door and locked it even though they had the key. Locking it gave her a sense of privacy and control. She made her way to the bookcase to retrieve the novel she was currently reading but froze halfway there. *Josh*. She'd caught his scent in the air. He'd been here—recently. In fact ... She closed her eyes and reached out with her dhampir senses.

He's still here.

How could the guard have missed it? Of course, the fae didn't have her sense of smell or her acute hearing, but he'd looked in the closet. Could he have missed a person hiding in there?

Dakota rushed to the closet, but before she reached the door, it swung open and Josh emerged.

He stood before her, a guilty smile on his face.

"This is getting old," she snapped. "I told you never to come back. You promised."

"Actually, I didn't."

She frowned, trying to recollect their last conversation. He was correct. She never should've let him get away with that. "Promise me now and leave."

"How's the child?" He stared pointedly at her belly.

Instinctively, she laced her hands over it. "Fine, though it's none of your concern."

"It's my concern how you are though." He peered at her through squinted eyes. "Are you healthy? Are they treating you well?"

"You didn't come here out of concern for my well-being. If you were worried about that, you'd have stayed away. What do you want?" It came out gruffer than she'd intended, but she was tired of having him pop up unexpectedly in her private rooms.

"You're right. I do have news."

After a moment of silence, she prompted him. "Well?"

He whirled away and strode to the couch. "Come." He patted the seat next to him. "You might want to sit for this."

Her belly flip-flopped. "What is it?" *Mother. It has to be about her.*

For a moment, she hoped he'd tell her that her mother was dead. It would make her life so much simpler. "Just say it. I don't have time for this." She glanced at the door.

All was silent in the corridor, but if she listened hard, she heard the shifting of the guards in their places as they stood sentry.

He looked fixedly at her. "She did it. She's pregnant."

Dakota kept her gaze on his face.

He bore a neutral expression, his eyes showing no compassion. That didn't mean he didn't care. He wouldn't have come to her if he didn't care. What she couldn't understand was why he felt so obligated.

"Why tell me?" She walked to the sofa and sat down, leaving a cushion-width of space between them.

"I thought you'd want to know."

"Why?"

"Because she's your mother. This baby will be your brother or sister."

"No." She shook her head for emphasis. "Why did you risk our lives to come tell me this? What's in it for you?"

He froze, his eyes widening. His mouth popped open and his brows rose. "Come again?"

"What could you gain from bringing me that information?"

He glared at her, his lips twisting into a sneer. "I get nothing, Dakota. Just like I've always gotten from you."

"What do you expect? We ended things. More than

once. Why can't you give up?"

"Well, don't we think highly of ourselves?"

She stood, waving her hand dismissively. "Don't turn this on me. This is your issue." Mocking him, she said, "We need to break up, Josh. It's not me; it's you." As soon as the cruel words escaped her, she regretted them. "I'm sorry."

She rushed back to the sofa. Sat next to him. When she tried to take his hands in hers, he yanked them away from her.

"Don't touch me. I know I'm the problem. I'm not trying to get you back. I'm trying to tell you what your mother's done."

"Why? What can I possibly do about her?" But she knew. Hadn't she considered sneaking out of the fae kingdom and facing the woman who'd given her life and then sold her? In all the time since she'd left her home—was forced from her home—she'd wondered what her mother felt. Had craved confronting Annabelle to learn what made her capable of doing this to her only child.

Not the only child for much longer. Her mother intended to do this again.

Dakota had no illusions that Annabelle was creating a child out of love and intended to raise it.

"That bitch wants to sell another kid into slavery." It wasn't a question.

"Yes. If you want to stop her, I'll help you."

Dakota dropped her head. Josh was skilled at sneaking in and out of the faerie realm undetected. He could teach her. She lifted her face and met his gaze.

"I want to stop her," she said. "I want to rescue my brother or sister."

CHAPTER 37

Three weeks after the king announced Dakota's pregnancy, dawn found Culain, in his pajamas and robe, pacing in his office. The realm's subjects had rejoiced at the marriage and took joy in the impending royal birth. Culain himself thrilled at the thought of having a son or daughter to love and nurture. With a healthy child, his duties in that area would be half complete. One additional child and he'd have a spare, too, negating the risk Dakota would have to wed Colin should the worst happen. But that wasn't what caused Culain's mind to race and compelled him to rise so early. Worry over Dakota and secrets he suspected she was keeping from him had.

For about a week, she spent more time in her private rooms. He'd promised her that her old bedchamber could remain a haven for her when she needed it, and he'd vowed to himself that he'd adhere to that promise. In truth, he hadn't expected her to draw away from him to such an extent. She swore she simply needed the quiet, peace, and solitude she found there, and that she wasn't escaping him but taking space to recharge.

It all sounded legitimate and logical, but he didn't believe a word of it.

Tempted to have the guards spy on her for him, he dismissed that shameful course of action immediately—no matter how often the urge flooded him. She loved him. She was loyal to him. He owed her faith and trust in return. Hadn't she given herself to him in every way? Didn't she still give herself to him in every way?

Yet even when she'd lived in those damnable rooms, she'd never spent so much time in them.

She's pregnant. Fatigued. He froze in his pacing. Did dhampirs get fatigued? Only when pregnant? *Probably. She's half human.* Vampires didn't get exhausted. Dhampirs might. Perhaps this worry was for nothing.

He wanted to ask her but didn't want her to think he distrusted her or didn't believe her explanation. He could ask her physician, who would explain what she experienced now and what to expect during the rest of the pregnancy. Culain didn't know how long she'd carry the child before giving birth. Vampires only conceived with a partner outside their species, so he had no idea how long a typical vampire pregnancy lasted. Humans carried for nine months. Faerie pregnancies also lasted nine months.

Happy that he at least had a course of action, he headed for the door to return to their bedroom when someone knocked on it. He yanked it open, and Colin entered without waiting for an invitation.

"Morning." He scanned Culain from head to toe. "Casual day at the office?"

"Funny." He eyed his brother in turn.

Colin wore a white shirt with ruffles at the throat and wrists. His black cotton pants bloused loose down the thighs and fit tight along the calves. Fancy buttons traced a decorative path up the outer side of the calves.

"Thinking about becoming a pirate?" Culain said.

Colin huffed out a laugh. "Now who's funny?"

"What are you doing here so early?" Come to think of it, how'd his brother know to search for him here?

"I have news you need to hear."

"How'd you know where to find me?"

Colin's eyes narrowed. "I went to your bedroom. Your wife answered my knock. She's perturbed that you left without alerting her."

Culain stared at the floor. "I didn't want to disturb her rest."

"Why don't I believe you?"

"Why wouldn't you? I left our bed before dawn. She slept. Why disturb her simply because I can't sleep?"

"No, you're right. But when we're done, you might want to go to her. She seems distraught."

Culain sighed. "Very well." He stroked a hand through hair that hadn't yet seen a comb. He hadn't even brushed his teeth or showered. "What's your news? I need to get dressed. I'll get no more sleep today, that's certain."

"We've had a security breach."

"Where?"

"Someone from outside has entered our realm."

"How do you know?"

"Ever since Dakota's father and her so-called former boyfriend invaded, I've had our security team working on a more advanced surveillance system. We've always avoided the electronics on the other side since tapping into their networks would lower the vibration of our world and shift us closer to their world. Before long, we'd become part of that plane. No one wants that. The unmasquing was bad enough."

"Okay. So what did you do?"

"We recreated the system they have but use magick to run it and keep it contained within our own world."

"And it works?" Culain was impressed. He tried to imagine a fae World Wide Web and failed, but the prospect of having modern technology as a tool buoyed his spirits.

"Well enough to mount surveillance cameras at every portal."

Culain realized where the conversation headed. "You caught someone."

"Yes."

"Who?" Culain held his breath.

"Someone dressed as a faerie lord but who is most likely a vampire." Colin put a hand on Culain's shoulder. "I'm sorry, brother, but I believe Dakota's had visitors."

Culain puffed out the breath he held, feeling as if his heart would stop beating. Dakota's insistence on hiding out in her private quarters suddenly made horrifying sense. If this were true ... he didn't want to contemplate the ramifications.

"I guess we'd better verify that your information is correct," he said. He refused to believe it until he caught her in the act. She loved him. She wouldn't allow vampires into their realm. Her contract forbade it. Outsiders weren't welcome anywhere in Faerie. She knew that. She'd accepted it when she agreed to marry him.

"If you need my help or learn anything of relevance to security, you'll let me know?" Colin's tone was neutral, his expression revealing nothing of his thoughts.

The brothers locked eyes.

At last, Culain nodded. "Of course. But I trust my wife. She isn't a part of this."

"I never said she was. I'm simply reporting the information to you. Would you rather I approached the king with it?"

Culain's face clouded and he scowled. "Naturally not." He softened his expression, reminding himself of that old adage about shooting the messenger. "You did the right thing, and I'm grateful."

He stared vacantly as he considered. When he spoke again, his voice was firm, and he met Colin's gaze steadily. "If she's a party to this, I promise you she'll be punished to the full extent of the law. I don't shirk my duties, and my wife wouldn't get a pass just because she's my wife. But fear not; she's loyal. She'd never sneak around behind my back, and if her father or that Josh character returned, she'd tell me."

Colin's expression remained neutral. "Very well. I'll report to you again in the morning. Perhaps a little later, this time."

Culain grinned. "Yes, this time tomorrow I hope to still be abed. But if you have urgent news, wake me."

The pair said their goodbyes, and Colin left the office.

Guess I'd better speak with Dakota, Culain thought. The prospect of that conversation unsettled his stomach.

CHAPTER 38

The rectory's door opened. Father Paul and Father Michael entered, the latter pausing his speech to allow the former to close and lock the door.

Kelsey smiled smugly at the wasted move. They'd locked themselves inside with a vampire, which put them both in danger and yet safer than ever. She could kill them if she wanted to, so quickly they wouldn't realize they were dead until they met the God they worshipped, the God she wanted to believe in. But she wouldn't, and were anything to attack them in her presence, she'd protect them with her life.

Still, she had a point to make. When they turned toward the kitchen, Father Paul suggesting he put on the kettle, she stepped from the shadows and blocked their path.

"Good evening, Father Paul." She nodded politely at the man she addressed and then to his partner. "Father Michael. Lovely to finally meet you."

Both men gaped at her, wide-eyed. While Father Paul's expression reflected surprise more than anything else, Father Michael bristled with terror. She could smell the fear so strongly she could taste it.

She licked her lips. Let her fangs flick out. She opened her mouth to show them off. "Worry not, Fathers. I haven't come here to snack on servants of the Lord."

While Father Michael spluttered, his fear turning to fury, Father Paul spoke. "What are you doing here? Why would you break into our home?"

She waved a hand toward the living room. "Please, come in. Sit down. I've already made tea and set out cookies. They're from your pantry, but I'm sure you understand."

Neither priest made a move.

"I'll explain myself when you've made yourselves comfortable."

"In our home," Father Paul said. "I want answers, Kelsey. Vampire or not, you had no right to break in here."

She bared her fangs again, and then to show them what a good sport she was, she visibly retracted them.

Father Michael flinched, but to Father Paul's credit, he remained impassive, and his heart rate stayed normal.

"Did you have a right to spy on me in church on Sunday? Does Father Michael know you hid in the confessional during his mass?" she said, keeping her tone conversational. She once again waved her hand toward the living area and the thoughtfully set up service for tea and cookies.

Father Michael finally found his voice. Rounding on Father Paul, he said, "You know this demon? How did she get in? Did you give her an invitation to enter?"

Before Father Paul could respond, Kelsey said,

"Demon. Is that nice for a priest to say about another being?" She batted her eyelashes at Father Michael. "I've attended mass at your lovely church for over two months. No one told me I couldn't. Don't you want to save my soul?"

His face flushing crimson, Father Michael said, his voice low and contemptuous, "Save your soul? You have no soul to save. Get out, demon. You're not welcome here."

"Michael, wait." Father Paul placed a hand on his mentor's arm. "She came to me—to us—for help. Would you turn away someone who seeks salvation?"

Father Michael shook his head. "She's tricking you. Seducing you. It's what they do."

"If I wanted to trick you, I'd mesmerize you. It'd be simple." She stared into his eyes. He struggled to avert his gaze, but she held him. When his shoulders relaxed and his jaw slackened, she broke the connection.

He backed away from her. "Get away from me." He rounded on Father Paul again. "Did you see what she did? She overpowered my mind."

"She released you. I believe she proved her point."

"What point?"

Kelsey broke into the discussion. "Don't be dense, Michael. I could've had you clucking like a chicken. Instead, I released you. I'm not here to harm you. I'm here for answers. And for help."

He glowered, his disgust for her evident in his expression. "Breaking into our home isn't the way to get it."

"Would you prefer I hung out on the front stoop until your return?"

"I'd prefer you made an appointment," Father Paul said. "You're here to speak with me, I assume?"

"I wanted to speak to you both." She took the seat she'd occupied the last time she'd visited and stared pointedly at the two men.

Slowly, Father Paul sat down on the couch. Father Michael continued to stand, his hands fisted on his hips.

"I don't drink tea with devil's spawn." He continued to mutter under his breath, and she realized when she caught the words with her vampire hearing that he was praying.

She laughed. "Didn't you rescind my invitation, Father Michael?" She stood and stalked to stand before him. "Yet here I still am. I enter the church every Sunday." She strode to the front door, above which hung Jesus on the cross. "Your redeemer allowed me to pass." She plucked the cross from the wall and held it to her face. "I can touch it." She gave him an evil grin, her eyes sparking fire. "I can fondle it. He doesn't care."

Father Paul left his place on the sofa and approached Kelsey. "He doesn't mean to hurt your feelings. He doesn't understand." Gently, he pried the cross from her hands and replaced it above the doorway. Linking her arm with his, he guided her back to the armchair.

"Please," he invited, "sit. We'll talk. Shall I pour the tea?"

When she nodded, he filled three cups. "Just sugar, if I recall." He added plenty to her taste. "Sit, Michael. At least hear her out. She hasn't broken any laws—not those of God or man."

That you know of, good Father. The errands she ran for Frank Evans and his crew she'd keep to herself. Since she had no option at the moment, she didn't want to sully her relationship with Father Paul, but it would eventually come out.

"What have you learned?" Her eyes met his though she refrained from mesmerizing him.

He averted his gaze anyway. "Nothing helpful yet. I wanted to ask Father Michael's advice." He turned to the other priest. "I'm sorry. I didn't know how to broach the subject with you. Kelsey came to me for help. As she said, she's attending mass and wants to be an active member. She wants to recover her soul."

Father Michael's gaze locked on hers, all fear gone. "Impossible."

"What is?" She gritted her teeth and swallowed the urge to release her fangs.

"You lost your soul when you died. It's impossible to recover it once it's gone. You're not human. You're undead. Who knows what entered your corpse when you resurrected from death or what animates it now."

At his words, memories came crashing back: the fall through the ice; her struggle to get to the surface; losing the battle and floating above the scene; Josh jumping in and pulling her out; and when he bit into her, sucked out her blood, and then fed her his, she was yanked into her body.

"It was me. I came back into my body."

Both men stared at her, incredulous.

"Impossible," Father Michael said. He rose from his seat. "God wouldn't allow it."

"I assure you, He did," she retorted. "He allowed Jesus back into his body. Or did a demon enter his corpse, too?" Both men gaped at her, Father Michael sputtering with fury. She ignored them and carried on. "The door between the worlds was shut. I had nowhere to go. My spirit was still there. I watched what happened from above, and when my vampire father gave me life, I returned to my body and accepted it."

Father Michael strode across the room until he stood before her. "Get out. I never want to see you in my church again."

She stood. He towered over her, but his fear diminished him. "You don't own the church."

"I'll have you formally excommunicated. The Church doesn't recognize vampires."

"Do you think I need your permission to follow God? To follow Jesus's teachings? You think no other vampires attend church? I'd bet a priest or two has been turned over the years."

"You need my permission to enter my church, and if I have you excommunicated, you'll never step foot in another Catholic church." He thrust his hand out, pointing at the door. "Get out, demon. I don't care if you don't need an invitation to enter. If you don't leave immediately, I'll call the police, and they'll arrest you for trespassing."

She smiled, baring her teeth and releasing her fangs.

His terror rose, and he took a step back.

"Michael. Kelsey. Wait. Don't."

She moved around Father Michael, whose gaze followed her every step, and she strolled to stand next to Father Paul, who stood in front of the couch. For his sake, she sheathed her fangs and closed her mouth.

"Will you keep digging? Find out what the church knows?"

"He won't. Not without repercussions," Father Michael said.

Father Paul didn't hesitate. "I won't stop." He looked at his fellow priest then. "If we help her, we can help others of her kind. Imagine vampires turning to

God. Think of how much good that would bring to the world."

"Paul"—Michael's voice cracked—"they drink human blood. They'll never get into God's kingdom. They're children of Satan. Don't let her bring division into our church. You don't know what you'll unleash."

Kelsey smirked. *Doesn't he see the irony?* She recalled Jesus's words to his apostles: *This is my blood. Drink this in memory of me.*

Before anyone could say another word, the door blew open, and Philip stepped inside.

CHAPTER 39

Kelsey stood next to one priest while another glared at them from the opposite side of a coffee table. At the sight, Philip's rage escalated even as it perplexed him. He didn't know what she was doing in a Catholic church's rectory, and he had no idea why her presence in one should upset him so much.

Without stopping to evaluate it, he snarled at the trio, flashed across the room to Kelsey's side, and grabbed her arm. "Let's go."

She hissed at him and yanked free of his grip. "What are you doing here?"

"I'd ask you the same."

"Saving my soul. Saving our souls."

He laughed then. Couldn't help himself. The idea was preposterous. "With the Catholic Church's help?"

"It's my church."

"Not anymore," Father Michael said.

Philip turned his attention to the priest. "I agree, good Father." He turned back to Kelsey. "We'll discuss this at home."

Her expression grew thoughtful. "Home."

Unease crept into his belly. "Yes, home."

"And then what?"

"We figure this out." Whatever this was. What was wrong with her? Why would a vampire care about religion?

"How did you find me?" She took one step toward him, brushing past the priest next to her.

When her arm jostled him, the priest grasped her arm and held her back. "I'll help you. I promise."

She met the man's gaze. "Thank you, Father Paul. I'd better leave now." She sounded distracted, but Philip was relieved she at least agreed to leave.

He put an arm around her, gratified when she didn't shrug him off, and led her out the door. As he closed it behind them, he heard the priests begin their argument.

The moment they reached the walkway leading away from the house, Kelsey threw his arm from her shoulders and whirled around to confront him.

"What are you doing here? How'd you find me?" She thrust her fists onto her waist and snarled at him, her fangs sliding out.

"You'll never guess."

The sarcasm in his tone had her mouth opening and her hands rising, her fingers clawing the air. "Probably not."

"Frank Evans."

That made her pause. Fear skimmed across her face, but it vanished instantly. Her brows furrowed and the scowl returned. "What does he care if I visit a priest?"

"It interests him highly, and when Frank Evans gets interested in something, I take notice—especially when it concerns you."

"He's having me followed?"

"No, he told me to find out why you're hanging out with priests."

"And you followed me?"

"I had to. I didn't want Evans to send someone else."

She gave what amounted to a sigh without breath. Her fangs retracted. She hung her head, but he didn't think it was in shame.

He waited her out.

Finally, she said, "I want to know God doesn't hate me. That I can go to Heaven when I die."

"Darling, we don't die."

Unwilling to continue the conversation on church grounds, he hooked his arm through hers and led her toward the large wrought-iron gates. They always stood open, welcoming all God's children—children the Catholic Church didn't consider hypernaturals a part of.

The issue had arisen before. Even priests and nuns could become vampires, but he doubted that had happened since the laws regarding turning humans were set in place—at least, not that he'd heard. Holy rollers who'd turned before the unmasquing hadn't volunteered for it, so wouldn't at least one of them have reacted as Kelsey had? What about other former-Catholic vampires? Did they care as much as she did that, according to the church they'd devoted their lives to, their God now rejected them? Hadn't he heard of an all-vampire church? He'd never cared about religious vamps and so had never paid attention. He decided he'd better start.

"We can be killed," she said, jarring him from his

musings.

Startled, he said, "Do you fear that?"

They reached the sidewalk, and he turned her in the direction they needed to go. The walk would take hours without vampire speed, but for the moment, he wanted to keep the dialogue open.

"Fear?" She shook her head. "No. I'm not afraid of dying. I'm afraid of dying and not going to Heaven."

"You believe there's a heaven? One that allows only Catholics to enter?"

She paused her steps. "I ... not only Catholics. That can't be right."

"Then Christians. Is that it? A holy club only Christians can enter?"

"I don't know." It came out as a cry of despair. "All my life, it's what I was taught. Grown men and women believe it; some dedicate their lives to it. How can they take it so seriously if it's nonsense? Nothing more than a fairy tale like Santa Claus and the Easter Bunny. How can it be absurd even if it sounds so?" She stopped and faced him. "Father Paul and Father Michael believe it."

"Ah, the good priests you turned to for help. Why go to the priests when they believe you damned?"

"Father Paul doesn't. Not damned for eternity. He promised to help me."

They reached the downtown core. Bloor and Yonge. Neither suggested taking the subway. Philip quickened his pace, and Kelsey automatically matched it.

"How will he help you?"

"He's researching. He has access to church documents and books—old books from before the unmasquing. Surely, they contain something about vampires and how to save them."

"Believe me when I tell you he won't find it, and then he'll turn on you. I've seen it before."

She stopped walking and grabbed his arm, halting him. "What do you mean? Other vampires have tried this? Why doesn't Father Paul know? What did they do?"

"They failed. Or they kept quiet about it." He took her hands in his. "Stay away from this. I'd advise that anyway, but considering Frank Evans has taken an interest, I hope it's not too late."

"Why should he care?" she whispered, so low he only heard the question because of his vampire hearing.

"Think about it. We work for him. We're dangerous. He's always going to search for new and inventive ways to exploit us." What if Evans had set a tail on them and already knew they'd met with the priests tonight?

Philip scanned their surroundings: the bright lights, the traffic jamming the street, the buildings so tall you had to crane your neck to see the tops. Most had shops at their base. Some were office buildings; others were condos.

Kelsey wrinkled her nose.

The breeze wafting past their location on the sidewalk brought with it every disgusting street stench but mixed with food and perfume aromas—a stomach-turning combination had they functioning stomachs to turn. The racket around them threatened to drown out his thoughts. None of his senses picked up a tail, but that didn't mean they weren't being watched. He searched the tops of the buildings. Nothing hinted at an observer.

"Let's go." He waved for Kelsey to follow, and to

his relief, she did so without protest. Perhaps she was mulling over the implications of Evans interfering in her quest.

"Now that I know, I'll take more care to hide my visits to Father Paul."

He halted again. "Stay away from him. I thought I'd made it clear to you that this path is too risky to pursue."

"I need to know."

"Then I'll help you."

Her expression turned dubious. "How?"

"You think vampires don't have resources? I've lived almost 150 years. I can get into archives these priests don't even know exist. Church archives."

"Why didn't you—"

"Tell you? You think I'm crazy?" He folded his arms across his chest. "Why didn't you tell me what you were doing? Don't you trust me?" That hurt. He didn't want to admit to her how much, and he'd thought he'd kept it out of his voice, but she flinched. He hoped it was from guilt.

She averted her gaze, but he remained silent, pressuring her into a response. Finally, she said, "I trust you. I thought the church was my best path to salvation."

He almost laughed, but he didn't want to insult her. What he said, though, turned out to be not much of an improvement. "The church isn't anyone's best path to salvation."

"That's not what I believed."

He noted the use of the past tense. "What do you believe now?"

She gave her head a violent shake. Paced the sidewalk, her hands waving. "I don't know. I need help.

The priests were supposed to help me." Her voice had risen and dripped with desperation. "He loaned me a book. It's supposed to be full of facts, but I don't know how accurate it is. It maintains vampires can't eat garlic, for one."

"Well, when was it written?"

"Before they learned about the enzymes we can take to digest it, I guess, but that means it's probably full of other fallacies."

He stopped her with an arm across her chest, and when she whirled around, he grasped her shoulders. Staring into her eyes, he said, "Darling, I'll help you. Whatever it takes. Just lose the holy rollers. Yeah?"

Her shoulders dropped. "Yes. Okay. I won't go back as long as you help me."

Thank God. But he didn't say it out loud. Philip didn't think God cared enough to have played any part in her acquiescence, and he didn't want her to think he'd ask God for anything. Linking his arm through hers again, he continued their stroll home, his steps lighter than they had been for weeks.

CHAPTER 40

The house Dakota stared at from behind a tree sat on a sizable property.

Annabelle has come up in the world. At my expense. Was that really true, though? Annabelle had sold her daughter to the faeries, but it'd turned out better than Dakota could've hoped for or expected. Did she need to exact revenge if she wasn't, in fact, a victim?

No, it's the principle of it. She hadn't had any control over what'd happened to her, and though she'd lucked out, her sibling might not. Someone had to stop the woman, and the only one who cared enough to do it was Dakota. She glanced at her partner. At Josh. He'd insisted on helping her even if he had no real stake in the outcome. For him, it was truly vengeance, and if a true victim existed and had suffered from Annabelle's actions, it was Josh.

As much as her dhampir physiology allowed, she breathed deeply and felt the baby stir inside her. It'd become active in the past week—just little flutters, but they grew more frequent as time passed. She loved to feel it brushing against her tummy. Just knowing she and Culain had created a new being, part fae, part dhampir, excited her. Her husband, too, was thrilled. Every morning, he asked her how she felt. Asked her if she needed anything or if he could do anything for her. His concern touched her, but it also firmed her resolve to rescue the child her mother had created and planned to sell.

"She sure as hell doesn't need the money," Dakota muttered, uncomfortable and irritated in the jeans and T-shirt she wore. She missed the reassuring layers of her fae clothing.

"Annabelle?" Josh asked.

"Who else?" Dakota glared at the sprawling ranch house set back fifty feet from their hiding place across the street and bordered by a white picket fence and a landscaped garden. "She even has a fucking cherry tree."

"Language, Your Highness," he said. "This rage doesn't become one of such status."

"Fuck off, Josh." She couldn't help herself. He'd pinched the right nerve with that comment. *I shouldn't be here. What would Culain say?* She couldn't think about him now, though he was never out of her head. He was so present she might as well have brought him along.

"My God, did you get that mouth from living with the fae? I thought they were a right holy bunch."

"Their beliefs are pantheistic, so you can leave God out of the discussion."

He gave her a sidelong glance. "You're stalling. Are we going in or not? You've risked everything to get here. Do what you came to do."

Yes, she'd already waited too long. A human-vampire pregnancy lasted mere weeks, the fetus growing at a phenomenal rate. It meant Annabelle could pump out a dozen kids before retiring her uterus.

Dakota nodded. He was right, after all. She hadn't risked everything just to wimp out. Her fangs threatened to pop out as she considered confronting her mother. She wouldn't allow them to yet. Her mother would receive the full effect of Dakota's wrath, but the dhampir girl didn't know what she'd do when they finally came face-to-face. They hadn't seen each other since before the mob kidnapped Dakota and sold her to the Shiels family.

Taking a moment to sense the lives on the property, she confirmed two heartbeats on the main floor and one in the backyard. The human in the backyard was a groundskeeper. He wouldn't bother them. He was far enough from the house he'd hear nothing. All the windows were closed against the summer heat.

"Come." She moved as soon as the word was out without verifying Josh followed. In a flash, she reached the front door. She tried the doorknob, but the door was locked with a deadbolt.

"Cameras," Josh said, indicating the one above the door. "She's likely getting an alert about us."

"Then let's not waste time talking." She kicked in the door and, with dhampir speed, reached the spot where she'd sensed Annabelle.

A second pregnancy and childbirth hadn't affected Annabelle Lawson's slim build, and it certainly hadn't taken away her innate beauty. Tall, slim, with cascades of black hair and deep olive skin, she had a face that, while it wouldn't launch a thousand ships, could probably break a thousand hearts. Unfortunately, her personality, once you got to know her, spoiled the effect. Most who knew her well didn't consider her beautiful, and at least a few of them, Dakota included, thought her downright ugly.

When the dhampir girl burst into the bedroom where her mother hovered over the crib of a baby boy, Annabelle shrieked. The child stirred at the sound, and his eyes popped open.

The size of a normal six-month-old, he'd grow ever more quickly as the weeks passed. Soon he'd look and think like a toddler, then a five-year-old. At five, he'd be a teenager. He was a cute boy with his mother's dark hair and the pale skin of a dhampir despite the touch of olive in his complexion. His eyes were large and dark brown and somehow familiar as was the shape of his mouth.

Dakota rounded on the vampire standing next to her.

"You fathered this baby?" She couldn't accept that, but what else could she conclude? The kid resembled Josh too much for it to be a coincidence.

"Not deliberately," he said, his brow furrowed.

"Did you know before we got here?"

He opened his mouth to reply, but Annabelle interrupted. "What are you doing here? Get out of my house. Do you want to get us killed?" Her mother's voice held no fear, something Dakota wanted to rectify immediately.

"No one knows we're here, *Annabelle*." She refused to use Mom or even Mother. She wondered where Philip was and if she should visit him during this unsanctioned furlough. Him, she was willing to call Father though not Dad. Funny how the labels revealed so much about a relationship.

But back to what mattered.

"When did you know this child was yours?" she

said, keeping her tone mild and conversational. After all, why should anything Josh did bother her? Except that it did. If he'd known the child was his, he should've told her.

"Not until I verified it just now. I still don't know for sure except that he resembles me, and odds are good he's mine. I put the pieces together after I learned Annabelle was pregnant. Without looking at the DNA record, we can't verify it."

Dakota addressed her mother. "Did you know?"

Annabelle grinned. "I requested it."

Dakota let her fangs slide out then, and she opened her mouth, stretching her lips away from her teeth for full effect. With a snarl, she flashed to stand behind Annabelle and grab her by the hair with one hand while the other wrapped around her waist. Dakota pressed her mother against her chest, exposing her neck at the same time. When her daughter's fangs pressed to her carotid artery, Annabelle shuddered, and finally, Dakota sensed the woman's growing terror.

But you wouldn't know it from her voice. When Annabelle spoke, no tremble betrayed the terror she successfully controlled.

"Let me go. Why come here? We're done, you and I."

"You might be done with me, but I say when I'm done with you." Dakota scraped a fang along Annebelle's skin, scratching it to form a thin track of blood an inch long. It was just a trace, but the scent of it filled Dakota's senses. She pulled her mouth away before she plunged and plundered and tasted. The thought of feeding from her mother revolted her, but the visceral pull of the fresh blood was almost irresistible.

Her gaze met Josh's over her mother's shoulder. He shook his head.

"I'll let you go if you promise to answer my questions."

"Make it quick. I have a business meeting this afternoon, and I can't be late."

How tempting to rip into her mother's throat—and not just for the sweet blood. Tearing open this sad excuse for a mother's flesh and destroying her would be gratifying.

"Making a deal to sell your second child?" Dakota added a hiss to the snarled words.

"What's it to you?"

"That's my brother you're planning to sell to the highest bidder."

"So? I have to make a living. It's my right to do what I want with my property."

Dakota fought the urge to tear Annabelle apart with her bare hands. "He's not your property. I wasn't your property."

"You did fine. You're a princess. Instead of threatening me, you should thank me."

Dakota flung her mother to the floor, but she managed to keep from sending her through it, and Annabelle wasn't hurt. Much. She did cry out in shock and pain, but Dakota didn't regret the move.

For as long as she'd lived with the fae, Dakota had wondered what she'd do if given the opportunity to confront her mother. Now she knew, and she was just getting started.

CHAPTER 41

It was true. The kid in the crib was his son. It'd seemed awfully suspicious that Frank Evans had ordered Josh to donate sperm exactly when Annabelle wanted another child. The strategy had provided a back door to Philip Belanger's DNA through his vampire son. When one vampire created another, the parent contributed DNA to the child, much as human parents did to their offspring. Josh had verified Annabelle's application to the lab. They'd paired her up with a vampire who sounded remarkably like himself. The forms simply identified him as a number—all donors were kept anonymous. Except if Frank Evans wanted a specific father for a specific woman, he could arrange it, and Josh was certain he had. The proof of it lay in the crib he stood beside.

The room itself was sparsely furnished. It held the bare necessities for caring for an infant: the simple crib, a small dresser, a changing table. No baby monitor. Did she let the child scream? Did she neglect it? The possibility bothered him, and he didn't know if he was finally growing a conscience, developing empathy, or if he had an issue with someone mistreating the fruit of his loins.

Suddenly, he understood his own mother's devotion to him. What became of this child mattered to him, and it puzzled him that the woman who'd given birth to it obviously didn't feel the same.

"You're a shallow bitch. Did you think I wouldn't find out you had my child?"

The woman on the floor shrugged. "You weren't supposed to. I can only surmise you compromised the private files. If you leave immediately, I won't mention it to your boss."

"Your boss?" Dakota stared at him, her brows raised, her tone suspicious.

Shit. He'd never told her he worked for Frank Evans. She'd hate knowing her first love worked for the man who headed the organization that facilitated her sale to the fae. He remained silent, but Annabelle didn't.

"You don't know? He's worked for Frank Evans ever since they returned from wherever they'd disappeared to." She smirked. "As does your father, my dear, and Josh's mother."

Dakota shook her head. "No, Father wouldn't. He tried to rescue me."

"He's not the saint you like to think he is. He's worked with or for Frank Evans for decades." Annabelle stumbled as she rose, as if afraid Dakota would interfere with the attempt. "Go ask him." She steadied herself with a hand on the crib.

The child stirred, yawned. Opened his eyes.

"What's his name?" Dakota asked in a whisper. When no one replied, her voice rose, and she whisked to Annabelle's side, gripping her mother's arm so tight she cried out. "Answer me."

"Haydon. His name's Haydon."

"I'm surprised you took the time to give either of us a name. I hear you shouldn't name your livestock. It might make you care about them." She flung her mother's arm away and stepped to the crib. She smiled at the baby and gently stroked a wisp of hair from his forehead. "Hi, Haydon. I'm your sister." She glanced at Annabelle, then bent into the crib so her lips brushed the baby's ear and whispered, "I'll protect you. I promise."

Josh caught the words, but he doubted Annabelle had—not that it would matter to the human if she'd heard it. She probably figured Evans would keep them all in line. She was mistaken. Dakota had thought Josh didn't have a stake in what happened to Haydon. Now she knew better. Together they could rescue the child. Take off with him. Josh stopped short of picturing domestic bliss with a pregnant Dakota. She loved the fae prince—she'd made that perfectly clear. But he'd have his child even if it meant going into hiding from Frank Evans, the mob, his mother, and his vampire father. Hell, if he had to hide from the entire world, he'd do it.

Dakota interrupted his musings.

"You don't deserve to raise this child. I'm not leaving him here so you can sell him."

"You're not taking him." Annabelle thrust her chin up. "If you do, I'll have the mob down on you. You think the cameras didn't upload your images to the cloud? I have proof you were here. Does your husband know where you are?"

Dakota went still and silent, but Josh stepped into

the breach. "You don't want to do that."

Annabelle gave him a smug smile. "Why not?"

"Because I'll kill you." He picked up the child and hugged him close.

The boy struggled, but Josh stared into his eyes and quieted him.

"Put him back." She raced over and grabbed for her son. "You think the mob won't notice a missing dhampir child? They'll hold me accountable."

"You think we care what happens to you?"

"You'd better because if I don't make this deal today, Evans will hear about it. He'll hunt you down, and if you think he and his men can't make a vampire disappear, you're more naïve than I thought." She placed her hands on the baby's waist. "Come to Mama."

"Mama," Dakota scoffed. "Is that what you expect him to call you?"

"You did."

Dakota stepped back as if she'd taken a hit and sucked in a breath. Her eyes grew wide and round, and her jaw gaped open as if she struggled for air.

Josh opened his mouth and reached his hand out to offer comfort, but she whirled away from him and zipped to Annabelle's side. She grabbed her mother by the throat with one hand and lifted the human off her feet. "You made me love you. You were a shit mother, but I loved you anyway. Then you betrayed me. Treated me as if I were nothing to you."

Annabelle sputtered, unable to respond. The wheezing sounds coming from her nose and mouth indicated she took in enough air to breathe but with difficulty.

"You're not doing this to any more children."

Dakota's eyes flashed, and she raised her other hand, the fingers bent into claws, the nails extending long and razor-sharp.

The odor of urine filled the room as Annabelle saw death in her daughter's eyes.

"Dakota, release her. Don't do it." Josh was tempted to physically stop her, but refused to interfere. He'd leave the decision up to her. If she killed her mother despite his pleas, he'd help her cover up the crime. Working for a mob boss might finally work to his benefit.

He didn't care if Annabelle died, but he didn't want Dakota arrested for the crime. The laws on this side of the veil were one thing; but if the humans turned her over to the fae, she'd be executed. Simply leaving the faerie realm doomed her if she was caught, but he didn't believe for a moment that the fae would catch them, and if they did, they could fight them off together. Josh had no concerns about bringing Dakota here. He was a vampire. She was dhampir. They could handle anything thrown at them. Hadn't he spent months in hiding with Philip and Kelsey?

Once again, he pictured himself with Dakota and Haydon, but this time, her baby joined them in his fantasy. So what if the child belonged to another? Josh could grow to love it if he raised it as his own.

The hand holding Dakota's mother aloft trembled. The nails remained lengthened and menacing.

"Let her go." He spoke casually, as though he simply offered a suggestion.

Dakota kept her gaze focused on Annabelle but spoke to Josh. "What about Haydon? He can't stay here. If I let her live, she'll send Evans after us."

"I don't think so." He stepped close to the pair and

gazed into Annabelle's eyes. They stared at one another until her eyes glazed over and her jaw slackened.

Dakota slowly lowered her mother so she could stand on her own, and then Josh spoke quietly into the human's ear.

CHAPTER 42

Her opponent's fist hurtled at Kelsey's face. She dodged it, but she wasn't swift enough to avoid the follow-up blow. It landed squarely in her solar plexus. Since she was a vampire, it didn't wind her, but she doubled over from the force. That gave her trainer the opportunity to use his foot to send her flying into the gym's wall. Her head smashed against the brick. Again, her vampire strength and physiology kept her from serious pain or injury. This time, though, it rattled her brain, and she sank to the floor.

"Get up! I didn't say you could take a break," Bryer McGraw, the vampire training her to fight, said. "Move it. No one'll give you a hand up in a real fight."

She groaned and staggered to her feet. Deciding to brute it out, she launched herself at him with no idea of what she'd do when she reached him.

It didn't go well.

Bryer slapped her aside with ease, and she plowed into the wall again. "That was stupid. I never taught you recklessness. What're you gonna do if we introduce knives or swords? You'll need a medic standing by and vampire blood." He scowled in obvious frustration.

"For what? We heal spontaneously?" she snapped back though she knew he'd exaggerated to make a point.

He snarled and, in a blink, had her in the air over his head. Whirling her around while she screamed and struggled, he tossed her onto the floor, which thankfully had a mat over it. Something snapped in her arm anyway as she landed with it twisted underneath her.

She howled, more from rage than pain.

"I think that's enough for today," Bryer said as though they'd just finished waltzing and he hadn't possibly fractured her arm. "We'll pick it up again in three days. You need a couple of nights to heal that injury."

Had to be the right arm, too.

"Swell." That put them into the weekend. "So, Friday?"

She tried to think if she had any plans with Philip, who, to her utter amazement, hadn't complained when she told him she'd booked training sessions with the building's resident fight expert. She hadn't told him Evans had referred the trainer and ordered them to work together.

When she questioned Philip's lack of surprise, he explained most vampires eventually trained in martial arts or developed some sort of fighting skills.

"We're a violent bunch. Laws hold us in check when it comes to humans and the other species, but we attack each other surprisingly often."

"Aren't there laws against attacking anyone, including other vampires?"

He laughed. "Of course, but we live by our own code. Have you ever heard of vampires going to court?"

She blinked at him as she considered it. "No."

"Because it doesn't go that far. We have secret tribunals. We mete out punishment accordingly. It flies under the mainstream radar and is harsher than anything humans can throw at us."

"They kill us for illegally turning a human into a vampire. They'd have killed you for turning Josh if Evans hadn't intervened," she pointed out.

"Believe me," he said, "there are worse things than a stake through the heart during a public execution."

She'd had no reply to that. When she recalled the fight between Evans's vampire and his two thugs against Josh and Philip that had resulted in her death and turning, she agreed he had a point. The mob also had its own code, and every day brought new opportunities to break it. They needed to prepare for the moment everything turned to shit—and she was positive it eventually would. Evans wasn't easy to work for. He and his goons pissed her off daily. Only concern for what might happen to her son and Philip if she betrayed the mob boss kept her in check. Josh had resumed boxing as soon as they revealed their return to society, but she'd initially thought that was out of nostalgia more than anything else.

As if vampires get nostalgic. Her eyes widened. Then why seek salvation if not from nostalgia for her old life? Could it be that simple? That trite? Ever since she'd promised to stop seeing the priest and going to church, she'd questioned her decision to go in the first place.

The trainer snapped her out of her reverie.

"Aye, Friday. Ten o'clock. Sharp, eh?" He meant ten o'clock at night. Bryer kept strict vampire hours. He slept from dawn to dusk.

"I'll be here."

"Sharp."

"I get it. I've only been late once, and that wasn't my fault."

He frowned but let the comment slide. "We'll have to practice rolls again."

She grimaced.

He revealed he'd read her expression correctly when he said, "I don't want to hear it out of you. You snapped your arm when you landed. That's your fault, not mine. If you don't know how to land after all the practicing we've done, it's on you."

"I know. I didn't argue it."

He chuckled. "You wanted to. Go have it set when you leave here so it heals correctly. The resident doc should have you fixed up in a minute." He strode to the edge of the mat, where he kept a mini fridge for synthetic blood. He tossed her a bottle before he snagged one for himself.

She snatched it out of the air with her left hand, all the exertion from their session suddenly making her gut gnaw with hunger. She ripped off the cap and chugged.

"Slow down or I'll take it back. Do you want to puke?"

Kelsey, unable to reply because feeding preoccupied her, forced herself to ease up and took sips instead of the gulps her ravenous hunger compelled. When at last the emptiness in her gut eased somewhat, she paused and removed her mouth from the bottle.

"I'd rather hunt and drink real blood." She sipped from the bottle again and then tipped what was left into her mouth. Not enough remained to affect her digestion.

"It's all I can store here." He put an arm around her shoulders, and she stopped short of hissing at him and wrenching away. He didn't seem to notice her reaction and walked her to the door.

Taking the empty bottle from her hand, Bryer released her from his too friendly hug. "Go see the doc. It'll heal if you don't, but you need a splint so you don't accidentally jar it out of alignment."

"Yes, boss," she said. The trainer wasn't such a bad guy. Had she not owed her life and loyalty to Philip, and had they not shared so much history, she might've considered taking Bryer to bed. Before her body reacted to that thought, she waved farewell at him with her good arm and scurried away.

CHAPTER 43

Night deepened, shadows darkening in the dead-end alley in downtown Tkaronto where Philip waited behind a dumpster for his quarry. He hated thug work, especially when it felt as if he bathed in the stench of rotted garbage to carry it out, but it was all Evans threw his way. For now. Eventually, the situation would change, and Philip would hate that even more. The longer his tenure with the crime organization lasted, the more the indentured vampire detested his life.

Life. Could anyone really call this living?

He glanced again at the photo he held to fix the target's face firmly in his mind. Wouldn't do to threaten the wrong person.

He sensed a disturbance in the airflow. Someone stood at the mouth of the alley.

The alley divided two stores, one a hockshop and the other an abandoned unit, in a shabby section of the downtown core. They were off the main Yonge Street drag where the more successful businesses got most of the foot traffic. The only customers entering the hockshop would be the desperate trying to sell personal possessions, thieves trying to sell their stolen goods, and the poor trying to find a deal.

Two people stepped into the alleyway. He'd expected only one. He tensed but remained hidden, assuming the pair had entered the alleyway by chance, perhaps to make a drug or sex transaction. Hopefully, they'd get it over with quickly before his target showed up.

"Philip Belanger?" The feminine voice was cold and hard. "We know you're here. You might as well show yourself."

He stepped from behind the bin.

"You have me at a disadvantage. You know my name, but I don't know yours." In the dim light, his vampire sight showed him a male accompanied the woman. Neither matched the person whose photo he held.

Philip sensed immediately the man was human.

He wore a gray suit and red tie, and his shaggy hair was a yellow that could've only come from a bottle. Red flecks adorned his chin stubble, and freckles dotted his face. His eyes flashed green. No gun bulge, but that didn't mean the man wasn't armed. The jacket fit loosely, likely to help conceal a weapon.

The woman had dark-brown skin, and her waist-length hair was styled into dreadlocks. She had an ethereal quality. *Not human.* She wore head-to-toe black leathers, her boots thick-soled and tough. Under her tight-fitting jacket, he noted the shape of a holstered weapon. Using all his senses, Philip drew in her essence.

"What's a daemon doing here and dropping my

name from its lips?"

The lips in question, crimson and glistening, peeled back in a snarl to show bright white teeth and a pair of fangs. "Careful how you speak to your betters, vampire. You're almost a daemon yourself."

Ignoring the comment but filing it away for future consideration, he repeated his question. "How is it you know my name, and what do you want?"

"Other than to teach you some manners? We're the target you came to rough up."

Philip frowned, annoyed at the daemon's arrogance and the man's fearless stare.

He held up the photo. "Which one of you is Juan Sanchez?" He couldn't keep the sneer out of his voice and off his face.

"Both of us." She smiled, but it was mocking rather than friendly.

"I'm tired of your riddles. Get to the point."

As she reached into her jacket, his fangs slid out and he crouched, ready to spring.

"Relax." She pulled out an envelope. "Here's the money you were expected to beat out of Sanchez."

Suspicious, he didn't reach out to accept it, but he did draw in his fangs. "I don't understand. Did he send you?" How could a lowlife gambling addict afford to hire a daemon to run his errands?

She laughed, and the throaty chuckle reverberated through the alley.

Philip looked around uneasily. Little chance they'd be overheard in this deserted, shitty location, but it wasn't the police or law-abiding citizens that concerned him. She held ten grand in that envelope—if it was indeed all there. Daemon or not, he didn't need her to attract attention from whatever species of creature inhabited the streets here. Daemons were formidable, but they could be overwhelmed if their attackers appeared in numbers, especially if they were powerful hypernaturals. At the very least, she'd escape while he and the man fell under the assault.

"There is no Sanchez, my little vamp. He was simply a means to draw you out from under the watchful eye of Frank Evans and his people."

He resented the implication in her statement.

"No one watches me," he said through gritted teeth. His fangs remained in check but only with effort.

"Easy there." She arched her perfectly sculpted brows and winked at him. "Don't get testy." She waved the envelope at him. "Take it. Evans is expecting it. I consider it money well spent as long as you agree to play ball."

"And if I don't?" What could they possibly want from him? Whatever it was, it couldn't be anything good, especially if it involved doing something behind his boss's back.

"You won't be happy with the results." Her face never lost its smile as she said the words, but her tone chilled him.

"Get to the point, darling. I haven't got all night." Now it was his turn to smile, and he gave her one that would've frozen flames.

"We want you to work for us."

He snatched the envelope from her hand and peeked inside, did a quick count. It was all there. He slipped it into the inside pocket of the leather jacket he wore. "As you can see, I'm already gainfully employed."

"That's what makes us want you working for us," she replied. "I know your history."

"Do you now?"

"Born in old Quebec to a Métis family, you became a dentist and opened a practice for a decade. Pressure from your family had you start and sell various ventures before the pandemic hit. Your family benefited from the unmasquing and the species wars. One of the few human families to profit from the disaster, they accumulated money and property. You met your maker during the wars, and she turned you into the dashing undead creature I see before me." She put her arm around him, and when he recoiled, she hugged him tighter.

Unused to dealing with someone stronger than himself, he growled low in his throat, and his fangs snicked out.

"Easy, dumpling. I won't hurt you. We need to talk, but I've had enough of this alley's sewage stench." She draped her other arm around the human's shoulders.

Before Philip could respond, a surge of energy zapped through him—not uncomfortable but definitely disorienting—and he found himself standing in a spacious living room.

Everything in it was white except any furniture that was made of wood or contained metal. Even the marble fireplace mantle was white. It crossed his mind to wonder how the owner managed to keep the plush carpeting clean.

He wrenched free of the daemon's embrace, his fangs flicking out and a growl escaping him. "Where are we? Who are you? What do you want?"

"Relax," she said. "I'll explain."

CHAPTER 44

Sneaking back into faerie country wasn't as easy as slipping out. Dakota huddled in moonlight among the trees near the faerie ring and waited. She kept still and out of view of the cameras Josh had warned her watched from every angle. From the outside, she appeared calm and steady. Inside, her mind raced, and for the first time in her life, she felt genuine fear—not worry, not unease, but outright terror.

What had they done? What had she agreed to?

If Culain learns I left Autumnland and confronted my mother, he'll have me arrested. If they found out she'd continued to meet with Josh, they'd put her to death, perhaps without a fair trial first. She might even agree with the verdict.

Taking care to remain still and silent, Dakota reached out with her vampire-like senses.

Nothing stirred in the surrounding forest. She heard only birdsong and the breeze wafting through the trees, making them whisper and rustle. In the distance, a brook bubbled. Wispy clouds obscured some of the stars but not the full moon. A sound from the bushes nearby didn't startle her. She immediately recognized the fat waddling shape emerging into the clearing as a raccoon.

She extended her sensory reach through the faerie ring into the kingdom beyond. Sentries guarded the land there, making her crossing tricky. On the way out, she and Josh had mesmerized the guards without actually confronting them. They'd shielded themselves with illusion projected into their minds and then entranced them one at a time before slipping past them. She needed to reverse the process on the return trip, but this time, she didn't have Josh to help her, and projecting the illusion from outside the circle challenged her dhampir skills. Being only a half-vampire had its advantages when it suited her to play up her human side, but at the moment, she'd have preferred the skill boost full vampirehood afforded. She couldn't resent Josh for leaving her to return alone. She'd refused his help, insisting he take the child into hiding immediately.

Daylight dominated on the other side, so she draped her cape's hood over her head and slipped on a pair of gloves. She'd changed back into clothing she wore in the faerie realm and had tossed the clothes she'd worn to Annabelle's in a trash bin on the way home.

Her jaw clenched, and she projected the illusion of the empty surroundings into the minds of the two guards standing at attention. Another pair slept in the nearby guardhouse at the portal into the faerie realm. Instantly, she passed through the ring, focusing all her power on upholding the illusion.

She stepped in front of first one sentry and

mesmerized him and then the second.

So far, so good. She paused. Did she really need to mesmerize the sleeping pair? Josh had insisted on it before, but she didn't understand the point. What harm would it do to let them lie in peace? The longer she lingered here, the greater the risk of exposure. As it was, her control of the illusion slipped for a second.

Easier to leave than keep this up. Decision made, she vanished from the site, heading for the castle in the distance.

She reached her private room without anyone stopping to ask questions, and she glamoured the two guards standing outside her door. She closed and locked the door behind her. After she waited a respectable twenty minutes perched on the edge of her sofa, she opened the door once more.

"Your Highness," the guard on the left said. Both men bowed.

"I'm ready to go to the dining room. I'm sure Prince Culain will already be wondering where I am." He'd definitely be wondering where she was, but she couldn't help it. She'd needed to wait long enough to ensure the spell had worn off the guards and they'd returned to full awareness. Interacting with them too soon after glamouring them might make them realize they'd lost time.

She strode purposefully to the dining room where she found Colin sitting next to Alina, King Killian at his position at the head of the table, Alina's parents on either side of him, a few other couples who were related to the Shiels family or were close friends, but no sign of Culain.

Hurriedly, she took her accustomed seat, and with a sideways glance at Colin, said, "Sorry I'm late. I'm afraid I had an overlong nap. My alarm didn't sound." She stared pointedly at Culain's empty chair.

"Not to worry," the king said. "We haven't started yet, and your husband seems to be as tardy today as you are. Will he join us soon?" He smiled reassuringly at her, giving the impression she hadn't arrived annoyingly late.

"I'm sorry, but I don't know where he is. I was ... alone in my room, napping." She didn't want to reveal she'd been in her private chambers but didn't want to lie and say she'd napped in their shared rooms in case Culain was there. To demonstrate an unspoken excuse for her fatigue, she placed her hands protectively over her belly in a gesture she hoped they'd assume was instinctive.

I should've checked our bedroom before coming here. It'd been careless of her to assume Culain had beaten her to the dining room. They could've arrived together.

"He's at the portal," Colin said, causing a sinking sensation in her stomach.

Servants appeared then with serving carts but hesitated upon seeing the empty chair.

Colin waved them forward. "Might as well serve it up. No telling how long he'll be." He met Dakota's gaze. "Seems someone breached the portal and slipped past the guards."

Alina gasped. "How is that possible?"

"We're not sure. That's what Culain's investigating."

The king's voice was gruff as he said, "Why wasn't I told?"

"We didn't want to worry you, Father. Culain wanted to verify what happened. Could've been a false alarm. He took guards with him and an expert in vampire lore."

"Vampire lore?" Dakota repeated as a serving girl placed a salad before her. Her human half had her stomach growling with hunger despite the fears that threatened to overwhelm her. "Why?"

She felt as though she'd just emerged from a trance herself. What if they learned she was the one who'd slipped past the guards? Could they prove it? She mentally retraced her steps. Josh had met her at the portal and guided her out. She was certain they'd given nothing away. He was a master at coming and going from Autumnland. If a mistake had been made, she was the one who'd made it.

I should've taken the time to glamour the sleeping guards. That had to be it. *But they were asleep! Why would that make any difference?* Yet, if it wasn't important, why had Josh done it? She should've asked him, but at the time, she'd cared only about reaching her mother.

Colin studied her. He rubbed his chin and squinted. "Obviously because a vampire once got past our security. We need to ensure it hasn't happened again."

She brazened it out, playing the innocent. "Didn't you plug the holes? Surely the portal is secure."

He tilted his head, still staring at her as if he suspected she toyed with him but wasn't quite sure why. "You'd think so." He leaned forward, resting his elbows on the table. "We can't take any risks, though, can we?"

She shook her head. Under the table, her fingers twisted together until she realized she fidgeted. She folded her hands firmly in her lap and forced calm into her demeanor. "Of course. You can't be too careful."

The door swung open, and Culain strolled in. His gaze remained focused on Dakota as he strode to his seat next to her. He leaned in and kissed her on the cheek before he sat down. When he'd taken his seat, he gazed around the room.

"Sorry I'm late," he said.

Colin met his brother's gaze but remained silent. When Culain said nothing more, Colin shook his head. In a tone dripping with exasperation, he said, "Well? What news from the portal?"

Culain waved his hand. "Later, brother. We'll have our meal first."

King Killian turned his gaze from one son to the other, settling on Culain. "What have you, laddie?" He scanned the table. "We're all friends here. If there's news, share it."

"I'd rather speak privately, Father—with you and Colin and any of his security team as would need to know."

A lump formed in Dakota's throat. She swallowed painfully.

The serving girl placed a salad before Culain. Instantly, everyone at the table clasped hands and bowed their heads. King Killian started the blessing to the goddess.

As he droned on, Dakota tuned out, listening instead to Culain's breaths. They were normal, as was his heartbeat. His hand in hers exhibited no sign of stress. His grip was strong, yet comfortable, and remained moisture free. A sidelong glance at his face showed he'd closed his eyes, as had everyone else sitting around the table. Reassured, she shut her eyes and returned her attention to the blessing just as it wrapped up.

King Killian waved his hand. "Please," he said, "enjoy your dinner."

But as everyone dug in, his expression turned grim, and he rose. "Boys, let's talk in my office. I'll have them send our meal there."

Relief flickered across Culain's face. "A wonderful idea, my lord." He rose quickly and gave Dakota another peck on the cheek. "Later, my darling," he whispered. "I'll join you in our room as soon as possible. Please await me there."

She nodded. That sounded like an order. Her gaze followed the departing men from the room.

CHAPTER 45

P hilip stared at the daemon, who met his gaze without flinching or turning away.

"I don't believe you." He could think of nothing else to say. How was it possible that a daemon had attached to him? She'd referred to herself as a familiar, a spirit animal. She looked nothing like an animal.

She shrugged, her shoulders looking surprisingly delicate for one so powerful. "I can't help that. You'll have to adjust your beliefs as we go along."

He shook his head. "We're not going along."

"I can't have you continuing to waste your life." She sank to the sofa and put her feet up on the coffee table. The way she reclined made her look almost human.

"Aren't you worried those boot heels will scratch your table?" Not an important question, considering, but he had to fill the silence as he processed everything she'd said. He tried to recall his daemon lore. Did they lie? Were they evil? Demons certainly were, but they tended to go after Christians who believed in them.

Daemons, however, fell more in the middle, neutral rather than evil or benevolent.

She chuckled. "Not my table."

"Where are we, if not in your home?"

"A safe house, I suppose you'd call it." She smiled, making his blood pulse as if he had a beating heart.

"Safe from what?"

"What've you got?"

He dropped into the armchair across from her and stroked the smooth armrests with nervous hands. It felt solid, but that didn't make him trust they'd remained on the Earth plane.

"Quando, dear," she said, turning to the man who'd appeared in the alley with her, "please get us some refreshments."

He bowed and left the room.

She smiled at Philip. "Quando is such a loyal servant. I don't know what I'd do without him."

"Don't you mean slave? How can he be your servant? He's human."

She stiffened. "He's a slave to no being. He knows his place and appreciates the life I've provided. Yet humans were born to serve us, were they not?"

"Us?"

She waved a hand, encompassing herself and Philip in the gesture. "Us. Those of us at the top of the food chain."

"I don't even know your name or why you're interested in me."

"You may call me Dianeme."

"Is that your name?"

"It's what you may call me."

Forgetting he couldn't sigh, he tried to push one out. Annoyed he'd slipped back into baby vampire ways, he rose, towering over her and baring his fangs.

"You know what? I don't care anymore who you are or what you want. Return me to the alley. I have work to do."

The door opened, and instinctively, he turned to see who'd entered. He expected Quando with a tray of food.

The servant had indeed returned, but he wasn't carrying a tray or pushing a tea cart. He escorted two young women, one on each arm.

"Your refreshments, Mistress," he said.

Philip took a step backward, his eyes flashing rage. He snarled. "What the hell is this?"

"Hell? No, not that." Dianeme rose to meet his gaze, and in those high-heeled boots, she stood almost as tall as Philip. "For us, there is no hell. Come. Don't act as if you've never supped from humans. They're quite willing." She approached one of the two women, who stepped away from Quando and eased her body into the daemon's embrace. "It's what we do. It's our nature to eat this way."

He shook his head, unable to speak. He'd spent years weaning himself off of feeding directly from humans. Too much paperwork and too arousing, though that wouldn't matter here since they weren't on the Earth plane. But if he took one taste from a pulsing human vein or artery, he risked falling back into his old ways. He desired to direct-feed only from Kelsey.

He found his voice. "No. We don't have to do that. They're not cattle. Do you want to return to the days of the species wars?" It was why humans had fought so viciously when the hypernaturals appeared in their world, and who could blame them?

Another thought occurred to him then. His brows

furrowed. "You're a daemon."

"Daemons feed from humans but not on blood." She tilted the head of her chosen victim up, but instead of biting into her neck, Dianeme placed her mouth over the young woman's, covering it completely.

The girl moaned, and her eyes rolled back, much as he'd seen his own past victims do.

Dianeme remained still, her eyes closed, the only sound the girl's lust-filled groans and sighs.

Philip stood poised, ready to act, but he didn't know what to do. Should he interrupt a feeding daemon? What would happen to the victim if he did? His hands practically itched to tear the pair apart, but without knowing the consequences, he didn't dare.

"Your dinner, sir."

Philip turned to face Quando. "Thank you, no. I'm not hungry."

Dianeme interrupted her feasting and lifted her head. "Don't be daft. She's prime, ripe. Perfect for you."

"If we're done here, I'd appreciate a lift back to the alley, darling."

The daemon eased the young woman to the sofa and gestured to Quando. "When she recovers, return her to her quarters. Take the other to the dining hall. No doubt someone there is hungry or could use some company."

As Quando guided Philip's would-be meal from the room, Dianeme stroked the unconscious woman's face with delicate fingers.

"Thank you, my dear. Delightful, as always."

"What did you do to her?" Philip stepped closer to the pair but didn't move within arm's reach. Not that he expected an attack, but his fight training had taught him to keep his distance.

"You take their blood; I take their essence. It's temporary and causes her no harm. I've fed from this one often." Dianeme licked her lips. "She's quite delectable. If you want to sample her, you're welcome to. Just wait until she gets her strength back."

"What the hell is wrong with you?" His voice was devoid of anger and held mostly curiosity. He genuinely wanted to know.

"Tsk." She stood. "There's that word again. Don't talk to me of hell." For the first time, her face clouded in anger. "You know nothing about it. I know you're not a Catholic—not even a Christian." She tilted her head and studied him. "What are your beliefs? You gave up your native roots before you turned. What gods do you worship?"

He laughed. "None. What have they ever done for me?"

"You neglect your spirituality to your detriment."

He couldn't believe she was actually lecturing him about religion. "You're a daemon, darling. Don't tell me you worship the gods."

She smiled indulgently. "The old gods. Before the Christ came along and took over." Then it was her turn to laugh. "They thought he was the son of God."

"Isn't he?"

She nodded. "Yes, as much as any of us. Some believe he was also dhampir."

"What?" He blinked, uncomprehending.

"They accuse Lilith of being the first vampire, and so she was. How do you think Jesus gained the ability to resurrect after three days? How do you think he healed others? Raised the dead?" She sauntered to his side and put an arm around him. "This is my blood," she whispered into his ear. "Drink this in memory of me."

He wrenched from her grasp, rage beyond anything he'd experienced surging through him. His fangs sprang free, and his hands curled into clawed fists. "Blasphemy. His mother was human."

"Yes, *she* was. You deny the evidence?

"What evidence? He was human."

"Oh, Philip, it looks as if I got to you just in time. Your little vampire girl—what's her name? Kelsey?— is on the right path. She'll find out."

He backed toward the door, but Quando had returned and blocked the exit. Unless Philip wanted to climb out the window, he'd have to go around the servant. *Or through him.* He shook off the thought. He certainly had the strength and ability to mow down the man, but he lacked the desire. Besides, he didn't need the daemon chasing after him.

"How the he—how do you know about Kelsey?" The desire to escape and track down Kelsey to make sure she was okay became an obsessive itch.

"I know all about you, love. You're mine, after all."

"Knock it off. I'm not yours."

"I'm your spirit animal." She grinned. "As I've said."

"About that. How does that work? You don't look like an animal."

In a flash, her clothes flew off and a grizzly bear stood in the daemon's place. Before Philip could react, it lunged at him.

CHAPTER 46

Culain stalked back and forth in front of King Killian's massive oak desk.

"Stop your pacing, boy. It's distracting me."

Culain did as his father ordered but couldn't help fidgeting in place. When he realized he'd replaced one display of nerves with another, he repositioned his body so it faced his father, who sat behind the desk, and Colin, who stood behind their father. Culain clasped his hands behind his back and inhaled deeply, forcing stress and frustration out on the exhale.

His father acknowledged him with a nod. "Thank you. Much better."

Two members of the security team stood inside the door, and the vampire expert, Edwy Cardinal, stood a few steps in front of them. They'd helped inspect the portal and its surrounding areas with Culain when he'd received the notice that the guards suspected a breach, so he felt he could speak freely in front of them.

"Well? What evidence have you that our security was compromised?" the king asked.

"The guards off-shift noticed strange behavior in the on-shift guards at shift change."

The room fell silent. King Killian waved a hand, indicating Culain should continue.

"They suspected someone had mesmerized the guards. That shows vampire activity, which gave us cause to inspect the surveillance video from the cameras outside the portal." He started pacing again. "Enough anomalies showed up that we called in the vampire expert." He nodded to Edwy, who stepped forward and loudly cleared his throat.

"Your Majesty." He bowed to King Killian.

The king gave the man a nod of acknowledgment. "What did you find?"

"Evidence of two vampires near the portal. Someone entered, and when they left, another accompanied them. Only one returned."

Colin, his expression neutral, met his brother's gaze. "How does Dakota spend her days, Culain?"

The fae prince gave a snarl that would've made any vampire proud. "What are you implying?"

"The obvious. You eased up the surveillance on her, and she's taken advantage of it."

Despite already having drawn the same conclusion, Culain resented hearing it from his brother. He instantly protested, defending his wife not only to everyone else in the room but also to himself. "Dakota loves me. She'd never betray me."

Colin's expression morphed into one of pity and understanding. "I don't doubt she loves you, brother, but we all know women can be swayed to evil, and that vampire ex-boyfriend already trespassed once. He's likely done it again and either coerced or convinced her to help him."

"Help him with what?" Culain snapped. "She's pregnant with my child."

"Is she?" As soon as the words were out, Colin's expression turned to shock. He staggered backward as Culain rushed him and grabbed him by the lapels.

"Never say that again. Not in my presence. Not to anyone else. Got it? I'm the father of that child. No one can question that."

"My apologies. I mean not to imply she'd betray you in that way."

Culain released Colin, but as he did, he gave his brother a disgusted shove. "She wouldn't." He gave another snarl for emphasis.

"Enough." King Killian rose from his seat and glared at his sons. After a moment, he turned to Colin. "Princess Dakota's DNA tests revealed her as the best mate for Culain. I doubt not the child in her belly is Culain's." Then he turned to Culain. "What we didn't learn was the existence of that boyfriend, and we couldn't foresee his turning. Now he's a vampire—one who's already trespassed on our land—we can't assume he hasn't influenced her into some sort of betrayal." He shook his head. "I'm sorry, son. We'll have to investigate, and if we discover she's continued to see that boy or, worse, stepped through the portal into the Earth plane, she'll be punished to the full extent of the law."

Culain felt as if his heart had stopped. Softly, he said, "What of the child if the mother is executed?"

King Killian's expression softened with compassion. "The child is yours, my son, and your heir. She'll give birth before we mete out her punishment."

"She hasn't betrayed us, Father." Culain averted his gaze to the floor to hide the doubt in his eyes.

***

Dakota wasn't used to trembling with nerves or fear. She'd felt both before but never to this degree. After a tense meal, during which she ate little and spoke even less, she returned to her private quarters to worry and pace. Culain had disappeared into King Killian's office with Colin and three of the security people, convincing her the jig was up.

They know. They know and they'll execute me. Why the hell had she ventured out of Autumnland? But she knew the answer: to confront her bitch of a mother and let her know her baby-selling days were over. She hadn't expected to steal the child—*my brother*—but she also couldn't leave an infant to Annabelle's mercies.

Should she run away? Escape to the Earth plane? If she did that, she'd abandon not only Culain, the love of her life, but also her obligations to Autumnland. She strode to the window and gazed over the land she'd grown to love almost as much as her husband.

But they bought that love with money, and I traded my freedom for it.

Yet if she fled, where would she go? Josh had vanished with the child without telling her where he was going.

"The less you know, the better," he'd said.

She'd agreed at the time, but now she wished he'd told her because then she could follow him into exile. Perhaps she still could. Without thinking, she already had a purse out and was stuffing whatever gold coins she had in her possession into it. When she realized what she was doing, she flung the bag against the wall.

"I won't leave him," she whispered. "Even if they

kill me, I won't leave him." She was no coward. Whatever she'd done, she'd done for the sake of that baby and all others that might come after. Her mother had to be stopped. She experienced no shame over what she'd done, and the only regret came from the possibility that she'd be caught. Given the opportunity to do it over, she'd make the same choice.

Come what may, she wouldn't let them break her for doing what was right.

She scurried to the purse lying on the floor and bent to pick it up. She froze at the tap on the door.

It opened and Culain strode in. Worry creased his face, but his overall expression was that of concern.

"We need to talk," he said.

She stood straight, the purse in her hand. Strolling to her closet, she opened it and tossed the bag inside. She turned to face him, meeting his gaze steadily, confidently.

"Of course." Her heart rate increased from the slow, intermittent thump that was normal for dhampirs. She tossed a prayer of thanks to the goddess who ruled over the fae lands that Culain wouldn't be able to sense her fear or nervousness. Dakota swallowed and stopped short of licking her lips.

Get a grip. Stop acting so guilty. He might not know you were involved. She strolled to the couch and sat, turning an expectant face to him. She tried to show puzzlement, curiosity. *I wish I were a better actress.*

He took a seat next to her, something she hoped was a good sign.

"You're aware we've had a security breach." A statement, but she'd been sitting right there when he'd announced it in the dining room, so why wouldn't he state it rather than phrase it as a question?

Catching herself overanalyzing his every utterance and every move, she vowed to let him speak without trying to read subtext into it. "Yes. Have you resolved it?"

"To a degree."

The silence lingered. Was she supposed to fill the void with a confession? She controlled the urge to do so. This was probably a test to gauge her reaction. She tilted her head forward and tried to appear expectant.

"A vampire—or dhampir—passed through the portal. In, then out, but when he left, another went with him. Unfortunately, we determined his partner returned, and we see no sign that this person went out again."

She pressed a hand to her mouth, suddenly nauseated. Since she hadn't had morning sickness, she knew it was terror and not pregnancy. She swallowed the rising bile, refusing to leap to her feet and rush for the bathroom. He'd definitely assign guilt to such behavior.

He placed a hand on her knee. "My love, do you know anything about this? Has anyone from the Earth plane visited you here?"

She wrenched her knee away, indignant that he'd accuse her yet overcome with shame and guilt because his suspicions were justified.

Before she could respond, he said, "I'm not accusing you, Dakota. I simply want to learn if you've seen anything strange or had any dealings that, in light of these developments, you might view differently. The possibility exists that someone came to spy on you— or us."

He was giving her an out. She could throw him a few "suspicious" incidents, and he'd believe she had nothing to do with it. Would believe her an innocent victim to a stalker. She thought of Josh and how he'd fought to save her and protect her when she first went missing and refused to betray him. Yet that meant betraying Culain and his family. She tilted her head to the side as though contemplating, but she'd already decided against revealing anything.

Finally, she said, "I'm sorry. If anything out of the ordinary happened around me, I was oblivious. I have so many people entering my space that I wouldn't recognize anything abnormal."

He drew closer to her and pulled her into a tight embrace. "All right, my sweet. It's fine. I'll let security know you've noticed nothing strange but that they should watch you more closely."

She took that as a warning. She returned the hug, pressing him to her as though she never wanted to release him. She didn't.

"Yes, thank you." She tilted her face up and kissed him. When she released his lips, she said, "I'll try to be more aware of what's happening around me. If I see anything I can't explain, I'll tell you right away."

Relief flooded his expression. "Thank you."

He released her and stood. "I'd better get back. Security's in an uproar over this. They'll add one more guard to the duo who accompany you, and they'll check any room before you enter it."

"They already do." Not thoroughly, but they always preceded her into every room to verify it was empty before allowing her to enter. If Josh wasn't a vampire with the ability to vanish from mortal sight, they'd have likely caught him.

"Ah, but this third guard is different. He's a dhampir. If a vampire or another dhampir is in the vicinity, he'll know it." He held his hand out, and she took it, letting him pull her to her feet even as her mind raced.

After hugging Culain once more, she followed him with her gaze as he left the room.

Goddess, please keep Josh from returning. One slight consolation was that Haydon occupied his attention. Perhaps that would be sufficient to keep him away. She dropped back into her seat and, in despair, buried her face in her hands.

CHAPTER 47

Josh didn't know what mess Philip had gotten himself into, but whatever it was, it froze the young vampire in his tracks. The bond, both psychic and physical, between maker and child was strong. Josh felt it in his own body when terror surged through his sire. He instantly tried to home in on the elder vampire's location, but no matter how hard Josh tried, he couldn't get a lock on it.

Probably sensing Josh's distress, the infant in his arms struggled and squalled.

Oh, great. That's all I need. Josh cuddled Haydon more tightly to his chest. Whatever was happening with Philip, Josh needed to find out immediately, but he couldn't take a baby with him. How could he do that without revealing the child's presence? It would not only raise unwanted questions but give away his position before he'd even begun to hide.

"Fuck!"

The shouted curse only made Haydon squeal louder.

Josh scanned their surroundings.

He stood amid a grove of trees in the Algonquin woods, the cabin he'd rented visible through the foliage. He'd contacted a real estate agent Philip had dealt with over a year before. The agent helped Josh secure the small home in Algonquin Forest with all transactions done remotely. Holing up in a remote cabin was the best plan he had. They'd hide there until the kid was old enough to communicate verbally. With a dhampir child, it wouldn't take long—the kid would be a young adult by age five. A few days would seem like months. Staying isolated with only an infant to keep him company would have his nerves frayed. To top it off, he'd still have to do work for Frank Evans without letting the mob boss know Josh had stolen Evans's property.

"What the hell was I thinking?" The moan that accompanied the words cut through the forest, silencing the birds and sending a small animal rustling for cover through the underbrush. But he knew what he'd been thinking: help Dakota. Everything he did was always for her despite his understandnig on an intellectual level they'd never be together. It was his heart that refused to give up.

Terrific. The world needs a lovestruck vampire. Josh grinned darkly.

Haydon had stopped squealing and struggling and now slept with a cheek pressed against Josh's chest.

Cute kid. Even if he's a product of that bitch Annabelle. Josh grimaced. *He's my son. Mine. I should have a say in how he's raised and who raises him.* He should, but he didn't. He'd lost that right when he donated his sperm. The law wouldn't recognize his claim, Annabelle wouldn't recognize his claim, and, most especially,

Frank Evans would probably kill him for stealing the child and the money he'd generate.

Pain flared through Josh's body as though he were being torn apart. *Philip.* He had to find Philip.

Someone else flashed through Josh's mind then—someone he didn't want to turn to for help but someone he'd have to approach.

He cursed again, under his breath so he wouldn't wake the baby, and veered away from the cottage that would've offered him immediate safety.

***

The lycan found Josh before Josh found the lycan. He burst from the trees in his wolf form, his mouth slavering, his eyes flashing death. Vampire and wolf collided, Josh twisting his body so that when he landed on the hard ground, his body cushioned the blow for the baby. Haydon woke up, naturally, but Josh had no time for a squalling infant. He lay pinned under the wolf. If he hadn't been holding the boy, Josh would've flung the beast off and leaped on him. As it was, he could only grip the struggling babe tight to his chest and splutter at Patrick, whom Josh recognized from his smell.

"Get off me, you jerk," he spat out.

In response, the wolf bared his teeth but retreated nevertheless. In a flash, the animal vanished, and in its place stood a tall, muscular, naked man.

Josh struggled to his feet, Haydon's cries turning to gulps. Streaks of blood-tinged tears stained his cheeks and Josh's T-shirt.

"Why are you darkening my doorstep, vampire? The agreement was you'd all disappear." Patrick sniffed the air and scanned the surrounding area. His features relaxed as he detected no other presence.

"I had nowhere else to go," Josh said. He didn't want to launch into a request for babysitting, but circumstances forced it on him. Philip's pain had become a dull ache, but it hadn't disappeared. Somewhere, he was suffering. Josh tried to send reassuring feelings telepathically, but since he received no response and Philip's fear level remained steady, he suspected the messages hadn't reached their target.

The wolf-man glared at the vampire, then shifted his gaze to stare at the baby. "You've stolen a child." He growled and bared his fangs.

"Quit jumping to conclusions." Josh didn't deny the allegation, so technically, he didn't think he lied. He was just warning Patrick against making assumptions. That the wolf had assumed correctly was beside the point.

"This is my son." Again, not a lie but not the truth. "Please. I need your help."

"Find someone else. I don't want to get entangled in your mess."

"Just let me explain." He took a step toward Patrick, but the low, menacing growl from the man stopped him.

"I don't want to hear an explanation. I want you gone as you promised."

Josh scowled. "Philip promised. I made you no such deal. I'm taking shelter here, as are you. No one will bother you." He barreled ahead with the request. "I need you to watch my baby."

Patrick jumped as if he'd been goosed, and shock flooded his face. "You want me to what?" The menacing tone had vanished, replaced by utter surprise.

"Babysit." There, he couldn't make it any clearer.

"Are you insane? You want to leave a dhampir child with a lycan?"

"You going to eat him?"

Patrick huffed out a breath, his nose rising with an offended air. "We aren't baby eaters."

"Then why is leaving him with you a problem?"

"I'm not a nanny. I want nothing to do with ..." He ended with a sputter. "Watch your ... are you ...?"

"Cut it out. I don't have time for this. Philip's in danger. I have to track him down. You took in that dog, damn it. I know you have it in you to help a creature in trouble."

Patrick scowled. "A dog. Not a human, not a vampire. A *dog*. And he was injured."

"Yet you kept him. My mother told me you rescued him, dressed his wounds, and gave him a home."

"She shouldn't have told you anything."

"Relax. She didn't betray your trust. She told me nothing about you other than you didn't harm her and you saved the dog."

Patrick shrugged.

When the lycan said nothing further, Josh angled his head toward the once more sleeping infant. "Please. I need to keep him safe while I find Philip. If you don't help me, I have nowhere else to turn."

"What about your mother?" Patrick's tone had softened.

Josh was certain he was close to wearing down the wolf-man.

"I can't let her know I have a son."

Patrick's brows rose, and his mouth opened and closed as if he wanted to comment. After a moment, he said, "Far be it for me to judge or pry, but you're asking too much."

"I'm desperate," Josh cried out. "Do you think I'd be asking a naked lycan to watch a dhampir baby if I wasn't?" He swiped a strand of hair from his eyes. "They grow quickly. The kid'll be ready to walk within days. Talk, too. You'll have him toilet trained by the end of the day if you push him."

Patrick's face darkened. "How long do you expect me to care for him?"

"Not long. I need to track Philip and make sure he's okay. I'll return immediately." Josh held the baby out toward Patrick and met the lycan's gaze. "Please."

With a growl, Patrick accepted the precious package. Startled at the new development, the baby opened his mouth and howled in rage.

"His name's Haydon," Josh said and vanished before Patrick could change his mind.

CHAPTER 48

Last stop for the day. Kelsey entered the variety store on Yonge Street near Dundas. She barely acknowledged the store's owner as he handed over the sealed envelope. She shoved it into the inner pocket of her leather jacket and left without having said a word.

Outside, the night air was cool—or so she assumed based on the light jackets the humans around her sported.

Her arm had healed nicely, so she'd returned to training with Bryer. She strode along the main drag, taking in the sights and smells, some pleasant, some quite disgusting, when a surge of fear made her freeze. Josh. He was anxious. Afraid. Not for himself, she could tell that much. The intuition she'd acquired since becoming a vampire gave her the answer: Philip. Something had happened to Josh's sire to make the boy frantic with worry.

Since their apartment building was nearby, she raced there, hoping to find one or the other at their condo unit. If nothing else, perhaps she'd find evidence indicating where they were. For the first time since they'd moved in together, she regretted the secrecy and distance between them. Each kept their own counsel, and until now, it'd worked perfectly for her. If she asked nothing of them, they'd ask nothing of her, and she wanted her privacy. She hadn't cared much what they did when they weren't with her.

She flashed back to the moment Philip burst into her store so long ago. She'd been human then and had never met a vampire before. His distress and concern over his missing daughter had touched her, but she hadn't intended to join the search until she discovered Josh was also missing. It'd been months since she'd felt any genuine concern for anyone. All the love she'd had for Philip vanished when she became a vampire, leaving nothing behind but lust, desire, and aching hunger for him whenever they encountered one another. But the thought that something might've happened to him, that he could've been harmed or even killed, revived those long-lost feelings of love and affection in a flood.

Was this emotional development? Growth? A return to humanity? Did other vampires experience this? It didn't matter. All that mattered was getting to Josh, who'd lead her to Philip.

She focused on the son who was her vampire father and identified his location as the forests in northern Skanadario.

With a sinking feeling, she realized he was at the faerie portal. She'd no sooner located him than all traces of him vanished.

Damn faeries. The last thing Kelsey wanted was to tangle with the damn faeries. Exactly how much did

Philip and Josh mean to her? Enough to risk an international incident? Too late now—Josh, and possibly Philip—had already risked that.

Guess it's up to me to pull their asses out of the fire. First, she'd continue on to their condo unit. She wasn't about to enter faerie country unarmed.

***

Josh hadn't sensed Philip in the faerie realm, but he'd guessed that was where his vampire father had disappeared to when his energy imprint was undetectable on the Earth plane. The logic behind his assumption had seemed sound at the time: Dakota was Philip's daughter, giving him a familial connection to the fae. Autumnland was the only off-earth land they'd dealt with before. If he wasn't on the Earth plane, this was as good a place as any to search for him. Finally, Dakota had risked her life leaving the faerie realm to confront her mother at Josh's urging. If fae security had caught her on her return trip, he blamed himself. If she was in trouble, he had to help her, whether Philip had beaten him there or not.

But Josh hadn't anticipated the heightened security.

He'd entered fae country without incident and made his way to the castle, then followed his usual path to Dakota's private room. He'd even slipped through the window without anyone stopping him. He should've known it was all too easy, the absence of any trace of Philip being another red flag. The final clue was the look on Dakota's face when she spotted him: a mix of fear, disappointment, and fury.

She rose from her seat on the couch, chains that bound her to the spot rattling as she cried out a warning. "It's a trap."

The moment he landed on the bedroom floor, a troupe of guards surrounded him, silver-tipped spears pointed at his most vital organs. At the head of the group stood a dhampir with pointed ears, clearly a half-faerie half-dhampir mixed breed. Josh's shock at the sight was great enough to drop his glamour, exposing him in all his vampire glory.

He snarled, the sight of Dakota in chains heightening his fury and hatred for the fae.

Culain stepped from whatever shadows he'd been lurking in and shoved one of the guards to the side. Sticking his face into Josh's, he said, "You son of a bitch, you're done trespassing into my home." He stepped back again and whirled around. Motioning to the guards, he added, "Take him to the dungeons."

Josh's gaze met Dakota's panicked one. Ignoring the burn of silver against his sensitive flesh as the guards wrapped chains around him, he shouted, "Let her go. Why is she chained? She had nothing to do with this. She didn't know I was coming here."

Dakota remained silent, her eyes pleading with him, but for what, he didn't know.

No one responded, the guards softly grunting while they shoved him toward the door.

Culain kept his back to Josh, whose gaze never left Dakota as he struggled against the chains. "Please. She's innocent."

She finally spoke, her voice barely above a whisper. "I told them."

"What? What did you tell them? You didn't do anything."

"You visited me here, and I let you in."

"So what? You never expected me. You told me

never to come." He fixed his gaze on Culain. "Listen to me, Your Goddamn Royal Highness. She did nothing wrong."

Culain continued to ignore him, but he drew closer to Dakota and spoke again to the guards. "Get that creature out of here. I don't want to see him until their trial."

"Their? What the hell do you mean 'their trial'? You mean Dakota, you smarmy jackass? She's your wife. She's carrying your child."

Culain spun around then and leaped in front of Josh. Before the vampire could react, the prince's arm shot out and Josh reeled backward from a blow to the face.

"Is it my child?" Culain shouted. "Is it, you son of a bitch?"

While Josh was physically incapable of gasping, Dakota wasn't, and she did so loud enough to catch everyone's attention. Until this point, she hadn't struggled against the chains—not silver—that held her, but at her husband's words, her arms flew from her sides. The shackles fell from her in a burst, links scattering around the room.

"I'll face any charge from you, Culain Shiels, contrived though some of them might be," she said, her voice harder than the coated steel that had held her, "but not an accusation of infidelity."

Pain skittered across his face, and he grimaced.

"We'll see" was all he said, but when she made a move toward Josh, Culain stepped between them. "Stay away from the prisoner, Dakota. I'll not tolerate your disrespect any longer."

"I respect you." Her voice lacked certainty.

He deflated, his expression turning distant, empty.

"Your actions, madam, belie your words."

"Culain, please." She wrung her hands. "My mother—"

"Screw your mother. We had a deal." The faerie prince spun on his heel. "Take them both to the dungeons."

When Dakota's head sank to her chest and she complied without a struggle, Josh too gave in.

His gaze followed Culain out the door.

This isn't over, Your Highness. But he kept the thought to himself. The prince would find out, eventually. As the guards grabbed his arms, ready to drag him from the room, Josh realized he couldn't sense Philip. After all that, the vampire wasn't even there. Josh had invaded the fae realm for no reason.

CHAPTER 49

Though Kelsey sniffed and searched with her full vampire abilities, she found no trace of the faerie ring. The portal, she finally had to admit after a fruitless hunt, was gone.

The fae had slammed it shut and trapped Josh inside—something she knew because she no longer felt him on the Earth plane.

What to do? Where to turn? Evans? She couldn't possibly go to him. They still owed him from the last favor, and that had trapped them into service she thought might last forever—at least for Evans's lifetime. The last thing she needed was to have his children inherit the use of her services.

Her fangs sprang out. *I'll kill them all first.*

She realized she was catastrophizing and forced herself to calm down. Philip, were he with her, would point out she was jumping to conclusions, making baseless assumptions.

Yeah, Mister Practical.

How she wished he were here. Of course, were he

with her, she wouldn't need to find the portal.

A sound behind her made Kelsey spin around, and she almost smashed into Philip.

She scanned him from head to toe to face, settling her gaze there. "You look like shit," she said.

He grinned.

***

Philip couldn't help smiling at Kelsey's reaction to his appearance. Something had changed in her eyes, something that told him she saw beyond the scraggly hair escaping the elastic holding his ponytail and the shredded clothing. He'd have to replace the leather jacket. While he liked to think he could force Dianeme to pay for it, that would be a futile vow.

"I came here right away. Josh—"

"Is trapped in Autumnland. What's he doing there?"

Philip raked a hand across his head, messing up his ponytail even further, and then scratched the back of it, more out of habit than to tame his locks or placate an itch. "I thought you'd tell me."

"Why? Searching for you, as far as I can tell. While you look as though you've been through the wringer, you seem fine, and Josh is the one missing. What happened?"

He frowned. "I don't know. I was ..." He didn't finish as a thought occurred to him. He cursed, loudly. "He felt my distress, and when he couldn't get a lock on me, he assumed I'd returned to the faerie realm. Something must've gone wrong there." He wanted to scream and rail at Josh's stupidity. Hadn't he told the boy repeatedly not to barrel headlong into danger? The

THE EMPRESS: A PROMISE OF RAIN

kid was always so "ready, fire, aim." Now he paid the price.

"Where were you?" She thrust her hands on her hips and stuck her face into his. "What happened?"

He gave a sigh devoid of breath, a simple movement of chest and lips. "A grizzly attacked me and tore me to pieces."

Her eyes widened, and she took a step backward as though he'd singed her. Confusion clouded her eyes. "What?"

"It's a long story, but I met my spirit animal."

"That clarifies nothing."

"My roots are Métis. My ancestors from Europe mingled with First Nation people, so I have First Nation blood. I never cared much about that part of my heritage—even less when I became a vampire." In his Native tradition, he'd experienced a rebirth, and Dianeme had called it such when she morphed back into her daemon form. He gazed into the distance, remembering the ordeal the daemon had put him through. He still didn't quite understand what had happened or how it was physically possible he'd survived. She'd torn him apart, eaten him, and then regurgitated him whole. In recalling the event, he re-experienced it, and his body trembled.

Kelsey drew close to him and draped an arm around his shoulders.

The whole experience had been surreal, and through the entire ordeal, he'd expected to die—which was probably why his blood had sung to Josh even from a different plane. But not enough to provide him with location coordinates to find his vampire father. The boy had thus started his search among the fae.

"What was the last thing you sensed from him?" He

met her gaze.

Kelsey closed her eyes and kept them closed as she spoke. "I picked up his distress, and I knew it had to do with you, that it wasn't his immediate danger. I fixed on his location here, where I thought the faerie portal was."

She opened her eyes and scanned the ground as if she expected it to reappear. "I got here, but it was all gone, including any sense of Josh's existence. He's not dead—I think I'd feel that no matter what realm he was in—but I can't feel him anymore."

She shook her head.

"He was here. I pick up his scent. It ends right here." She pointed to a spot on the ground before her. "This is where he entered the ring, but"—she snarled out her frustration—"no ring."

"We'll find another way." The words had no sooner left him than he caught the scent and sound of intruders.

A vampire appeared from the forest.

Her red hair was cut short and gelled back from her face, and her body-hugging pants and jacket were all leather. She trained her gun on Philip, who stood nearest her.

"Silver bullets," she warned. "You're to come with me." She flicked a glance at Kelsey. "Both of you." She nodded at the weapon in her hand. "Only a formality, so you wouldn't attack me on sight. Frank Evans sent me." She holstered the gun. "Your son seems to have stepped in it. The whole community is in an uproar. We need to prevent it from escalating."

Philip shifted from under Kelsey's arm and took her hand. "Fine," he said to the redhead. "You lead. We'll follow."

When Kelsey snapped her chin up and glared at him, he shrugged.

No choice, he mouthed.

Fire in her eyes, she said, "Fine."

The trio vanished into the forest.

CHAPTER 50

A clank and rattle signaled breakfast's arrival. Dakota rose from her cot and watched the guard open the door to her cage and carry in a tray containing an open bottle of blood, a bowl of oatmeal, and two pieces of toast. He set it on the small table standing against the wall across from the foot of her bed. No one spoke. When the pair left, she strode to the table. The bottle held about twelve ounces of ruby liquid, thick and warmed to body temperature. She'd grown accustomed to having her blood heated before drinking it—nothing straight from the fridge for her. She thought it a good sign that Culain maintained the courtesy even here. The oatmeal would be creamy, sweet, and heartily filling. A pat of butter softened atop the toast, and a small ceramic dish held glistening blueberry jam. She inhaled the scent of it all and salivated.

She sat in the chair at the table and picked up the bottle. Her fangs slid free in anticipation. After a moment's hesitation, she sipped from it. As the last few meals they'd provided had been, this one was excellent and catered to her human and vampire halves. The blood was real, probably sourced from the Earth plane. Someone had donated it—at least that was her assumption since laws existed preventing vampires from forcibly draining humans. Because few humans lived among the faeries anymore, the blood had to have come from outside the realm. For a species that claimed to eschew interaction with the Earth plane, they certainly traded with it when they wanted what it offered. They'd bought Dakota there.

Hypocrites! They refused to let her leave the faerie realm, but a privileged few were entitled to trade with the outer world.

The door to the cell next to hers creaked open, and Josh's voice floated through the walls and wooden doors.

"Hello, fellas. Come to feed the big bad vamp? Be a dear and loosen my chains a titch. It's a bit tight around the collar."

No reply came to that. He always tossed a quip to the guards, but they never responded.

The cell walls were stone, so Dakota couldn't see him, but the two talked when no one was around, which was most of the time. The chain around his neck prevented him from reaching the door but allowed him to move around the small cell. He'd told her they'd coated the metal with something so it didn't burn his skin, but to ensure he couldn't escape, the bars of his cell, including the ones making up the door, were all silver. At least her cell bars were wooden with only the lock on the door made of metal. She also wasn't chained. If she desired, she could escape, but to what end? No, she had to remain and help Josh as much as possible with her position as the future king's wife. She could probably thank Culain for the small favor that allowed her to roam her cell free of restraints and without the threat of silver burns.

Such compassion from my husband. Yet she still loved him and understood his position. Somehow, she had to convince him she hadn't betrayed him despite what it looked like and do it in a way that wouldn't make him believe she'd glamoured him.

Problem was, she *had* betrayed him. She'd promised to never return to the Earth plane, and she'd broken that promise. *They should've let me. Why can some and not others?* Yet shouldn't she have consulted with Culain instead of going behind his back? Too late for that now. She'd have to beg his forgiveness, and didn't that make asking permission the preferable choice after all?

Sometimes she wondered if the guards, or even Culain, listened to the prisoners' furtive conversations, but she concluded they must. Why not listen in on their conversations and let the captives implicate themselves? For this reason, she studiously avoided mentioning Annabelle, Haydon, or where Josh might've taken the boy. If they were lucky, the memory wipe they'd done on Annabelle would protect them. They'd planted in her brain a new history of what'd happened, and as far as Dakota's mother knew, Evans's lackey had bought, paid for, and taken the baby to an unknown purchaser. Dakota and Josh had deposited a hefty amount into Annabelle's bank account—enough that if she recovered her memories, she could still pay what she owed the mob for the kid and have money left over.

The only problem was that nothing would stop her from getting pregnant and selling another child. The woman was greedier than an alcoholic at a wine tasting. Dakota recalled her vow to gain power and stop the trafficking.

I'm off to a fabulous start. Another reason to have included Culain in the decision to visit Annabelle.

How had it all come to this?

The last time she'd drawn tarot cards, The Empress had popped out. It'd landed reversed, which foretold family problems, such as with a spouse, parents, or siblings. She'd known as soon as she saw it that it referred to a problem between herself and her husband, and it related to her mother. All her problems stemmed from her relationship with her mother.

Who's the empress in this scenario? Was the card literal? It represented the goddess Aphrodite, Mother Nature, Demeter, and other goddesses associated with fertility, family, and creativity. *The power of nature, but, reversed, it's showing me trouble—and I've certainly found that.*

The main door to the dungeons slammed shut. She and Josh were alone once again.

"You never should've admitted you'd talked to me," he said. "You should've told them you sent me away whenever I tried to talk to you."

This again. "I did, though. We've been over this. I don't want to lie to Culain or the fae."

"It's not lying if you simply keep it from them."

"Yes, it is. People say it's not so they can justify lies by omission, but that's exactly what it is. He asked me a direct question. Denying it would've been lying. I love my husband. I still want to be with him." She sipped again from the blood. She always took the blood first. Her vampire half demanded satisfaction before her human half was allowed to eat, no matter how much her stomach growled in protest or how delicious the human food smelled.

"You shouldn't be here. He turned on you. How can you still love him?"

Dakota hung her head. Josh had never asked her that before even during their most heated discussions. It'd been a line he hadn't crossed.

Until now.

Culain hadn't visited her in her cell since the guards brought her down here, but when she tried to feel him, to feel his emotions, she sensed his pain. He didn't visit her because he suffered and was afraid he'd release her if he saw her.

"He loves me. I know he does," she said.

She set the empty bottle back on the tray but didn't remember finishing the drink. Slowly, she picked up a piece of toast and nibbled.

A familiar sensation surged through her. *Culain.* He approached.

CHAPTER 51

His mouth dry, sweat beading his brow and dewing his neck, Culain approached the dungeon. Tempted to ask the guards to wait outside, he remained practical and cautious, as a fae prince should, and allowed one to lead him inside and the other to take up the rearguard.

Anger still ruled his emotions—he recognized that—but underneath, he held sorrow and, even now, love.

How could he get her back? How could he take her back? The two questions nagged him constantly, disturbing his sleep for the last two nights, ever since they'd arrested her and her ex-boyfriend. The vampire who'd destroyed their lives.

Because Josh's cell came first, and because Culain wanted to delay the confrontation with his wife, he stopped there before continuing to Dakota's.

The guards took their places a step behind Culain, ready to spring into action if needed. The prince kept three feet between himself and the cell's bars, not because he thought the vampire could reach him if he were any nearer but because he feared glamouring.

Josh rose with a swoosh of padded chains. His eyes held interest and curiosity. It made him look youthful and human.

Pain at the situation lanced Culain. Damn their laws. He didn't want to harm a boy.

Then the boy's fangs slid out and a snarl escaped his lips, and Culain's attitude shifted.

"Come for a visit, did you, Your Highness?" The vampire's body tensed as though ready to spring.

Culain ignored the comment and the aggressive stance, but he avoided gazing directly at Josh. "Your presence here has caused grief for many people, my wife most of all."

"She had nothing to do with this. I went to her. She never invited me."

"Yet she never alerted me to your comings and goings, and we know you were here multiple times." Culain's genuine desire to have an answer made him forget himself and stare directly into Josh's eyes. "Did you honestly think we wouldn't figure it out? Call in a vampire to question the guards you mesmerized? You erased their memories, but an experienced, older vampire can draw them out again."

He quickly shifted his gaze to the side again, but he noted the lad hadn't tried to take advantage of the slip.

"Honestly?" Josh closed his eyes. The silence stretched, and he opened them again. His gaze remained lowered, either out of consideration for Culain or because guilt made him unable to look the fae prince in the eyes. "No. I didn't think you'd get there. How would I know that people who insisted they wanted nothing to do with the Earth plane would have something to do with the Earth plane?"

"Your mistake, then, boy, and it's costing us all." Culain spun on his heel and stormed to Dakota's cell.

She already stood at the bars, her face almost pressed between the slats. "Culain." It came out a strangled cry, spearing grief through him.

Her blonde hair framed her face in a disheveled mess that somehow looked sexy even under the strained circumstances. She'd always look sexy to him. It was in her DNA. For him, she'd always be the perfect woman, the perfect mate. The perfect mother for his child.

The thought of their child had him glancing at her slightly rounded belly.

"How are you?" he asked, more out of concern for the baby than for the woman. She was dhampir. It would take a lot more than incarceration to impact her health.

"Fine." She pressed a hand to her pelvis and said again, "Fine."

"I trusted you." He didn't know how else to open the discussion even if it sounded accusatory. And why shouldn't he accuse her? She'd betrayed him.

The reminder of her disloyalty had the rage surging up again, and he scowled despite his vow before the visit that he'd remain detached and keep his expression neutral. It was just one more failure to add to his long list of failures.

He thought of his father then, who'd previously defended her but now demanded Dakota's execution, insisting she'd probably cheated physically as well and the babe was likely Josh's. It didn't matter that vampires and dhampirs couldn't conceive a child, as they'd learned from their vampire consultant, much to

Culain's vast relief.

That relief had prompted this visit to the dungeons. Somehow, he'd find a way out of this—at least for Dakota. Josh Davis was as good as dead.

King Killian refused to listen to reason.

"She had another man between her legs," he'd raged, making Culain recoil with revulsion.

He didn't believe it. Refused to believe it. He had to work this out with her.

An image of her standing in front of a firing squad, all aiming silver-tipped arrows at her breast, flashed through his mind. *No. Never.*

"Why, Dakota?" He didn't expand on what he meant—didn't need to.

She dropped her chin to her chest, but then drew in a soft breath and lifted her head to meet his gaze. "You refused to let me hear news of the outside, and when Josh brought it to me, I listened."

"As simple as that."

"Yes," she whispered. "My mother ..." Her voice broke then, but she soldiered on. "My mother got pregnant again. She shouldn't be permitted to sell another child."

"Do you resent your life here so much you'd throw it away to stop another child from living similarly?"

"You know that's not what I'm trying to stop." She threw her hands up and spun away from him to pace her cell. "I got lucky."

She stopped and stared into his eyes but not to glamour him. A connection formed between them, but it had no hint of manipulation or guile.

In a low voice, she said, "I was lucky. My kidnappers sold me to a man who loved me. To a family I could join and find happiness with."

She shook her head sadly. "But not all are so fortunate, and I can't stand idly by while they're sold into slavery or worse. I've felt the terror of sitting locked in a room, not knowing what'll happen next— or to what kind of monster they might sell me."

Her gaze traveled the cell, emphasizing that she found herself in a similar situation.

"This time, it's your doing." Because his conscience pricked him, he couldn't help reminding her.

"Yes, so it is." She strode to the bars and gripped them, sticking her face between the slats. "But it doesn't change the fact that when they first took me, it wasn't my choice, and I wasn't consulted. They stole my freedom, and you can justify it any way you like. You can tell me it's similar to being born into royalty and its obligations, but it's not. They could've sold me into slavery, Culain. It's just my luck they didn't, but my mother wouldn't have cared if they had."

She'd never disclosed all this before. She'd been strong, stoic, never revealing what simmered beneath the façade: rage and resentment, not at what had happened, but at what might have happened.

He recalled a folder Frank Evans's men had brought to the Shiels family to look through. Where were the women he hadn't chosen? The five other dhampirs, less lovely to his eyes, who hadn't suited him as perfectly? Were they sold to a brothel? To other fae? Where'd they go?

Shame that he'd never wondered, and a hatred for Evans, his organization, and even for fae society that encouraged this kind of thing by paying for it flushed his face. They called it tradition, but for every lucky woman who ended up wed to a faerie prince, four or five others had their lives destroyed. Oh, sure, maybe one or two ended up wedded to wealthy fae where they were treasured and pampered.

But what if they valued freedom more?

What paths would these women have taken if they hadn't been snatched from their homes? What would Dakota be doing right now? One thing was certain, she wouldn't be locked in a faerie dungeon, and neither would Josh.

With dawning shock and horror, Culain realized the young man probably wouldn't have become a vampire.

He raced to the bars and covered Dakota's hands with his, vaguely aware of a guard placing a restraining hand on his shoulder. Culain shrugged it away.

"My god, I'm so sorry. For everything you've gone through, for everything you aspired to do or be but couldn't, forgive me."

"I forgave you a long time ago, my husband," she whispered. "What I needed was for you to understand the great injustice, to see that it goes beyond me."

"Your Highness," the guard who'd tried to stop him from touching Dakota said, "she's dangerous. You shouldn't stand so close to her."

"Nonsense." He snapped a glare at the man and then returned his attention to his wife. "I'll get you out of here. I promise."

"And Josh?" she asked, her eyes shining with hope and relief.

Culain sucked in a breath. He might be able to rescue Dakota, but her ex's chances of getting out of here alive were slim.

"I can't promise," he said, "but I'll try." It wasn't a lie—he'd try—but the attempt would be futile. "I'll return soon."

Without thinking, he leaned in to kiss her, and she

automatically responded. Their lips pressed together between the wooden slats, and his tension eased at the touch, however brief, and despite the distracting guards, who both protested.

"Please hurry," she said when he released her.

He nodded, unable to speak. He strode away from her and, with eyes averted, started to walk silently past Josh's cell.

"Culain."

He halted. Had he ever heard Josh use his given name before? It sounded strange not only coming from the vampire but also in a tone laced with emotion. It loosened something constricting his heart, and the faerie prince approached the cell.

When the guards made a move to intercept him, he waved them away.

"Hold back, but stand ready," he said.

They obeyed reluctantly and with doubt and suspicion in their eyes.

"What is it?" He met the young vampire's gaze without fear. Somehow, he understood the boy wouldn't glamour him.

"You can save her." Josh whispered it, throwing a glance toward Dakota's cell. He motioned for Culain to meet him at the end of the cell farthest from hers.

Culain did as requested, his guards following as close as he allowed, but even so, he knew Dakota would hear any discussion no matter how softly spoken.

An idea spurring him on, he signaled he'd return and stepped into the hallway where another guard stood sentry. After obtaining a paper and pencil from the man, Culain returned. He handed the items to Josh, who quickly scribbled a note and handed it back.

Blame me. I wouldn't leave her alone. She loves you and never betrayed you. With me gone, she'll have peace.

The words stabbed at Culain's heart. Josh wanted to sacrifice himself for Dakota. He stared questioningly at the boy, and understanding passed silently between them. Culain offered his hand to Josh, who accepted it. They shook. The faerie prince acknowledged the vampire with a nod and then turned and walked away.

CHAPTER 52

The red-haired vampire led them swiftly through forests and highways to Frank Evans's office building in downtown Tkaronto. Instead of taking them to the main tower, though, she escorted them down the street to a warehouse on Lakeshore Boulevard. Kelsey glanced uneasily at Philip as they entered the seemingly deserted building. Somewhere inside, she sensed at least three heartbeats. All belonged to humans.

The large, empty building looked as if it'd stood that way for over a century. Their footsteps echoed off the walls, and a slight gasoline smell permeated the air. Perhaps it wasn't a warehouse after all—not for storage, anyway. Based on the oil stains on the concrete floor and the fluorescent lights dangling above, it was probably a manufacturing facility. The machines were long gone, but the aroma of grease and technology remained.

Red ushered them into a small office at the rear of the building. Evans sat at a small desk, and the two henchmen who always accompanied him stood on either side of his chair. His second-in-command was nowhere in evidence.

"What are we doing here?" Philip said.

The mob boss rose and thrust his face into the vampire's. "You three." He choked out the words as though he detested them. He probably did.

"You'll have to be more specific. And be quick. I have to find my son," Philip said casually.

"You have some nerve," Evans shouted in return. "That little bastard."

Kelsey had enough. "Careful. You're talking about my son." She shot a look at Philip. "Our son."

"He breached our agreement. He went to Autumnland without permission." Evans glared at Philip, then at Kelsey, returning his gaze to the former before continuing the tirade. "He interfered in Prince Culain's marriage. He visited the girl, who you all agreed to leave alone. The deal was done. His life is forfeit; the faeries will see to that."

Philip's voice turned menacing. "What the hell are you talking about? They have no right to kill him."

Evans spun on his heel and stalked back to his desk. Dropping into the chair, which groaned under his weight, he slammed a hand onto the desk. "They have every right. That imbecile. Not only has he incurred the death penalty, but they might demand a replacement for Dakota."

Philip's fangs slid free, and the vampire at the door cocked her gun. "Easy, slugger. Silver bullet, remember?"

"If they harm Dakota, they'll pay." He said it as a statement of fact, and Kelsey didn't doubt his seriousness. Without giving anyone a chance to respond, he retracted his fangs. "What the hell more do you want? We're already working for you, and we have no control over what Josh does. We had no clue about his involvement with the fae or Dakota. He certainly never told me if he did."

They all stared at Kelsey.

She shook her head. "He told me less than he told you. I lost him the moment he became a vampire, and when he turned me, everything we'd had before our rebirths vanished. We lived together, but we had separate lives." That last held a tinge of regret, and her expression turned sad as she realized all she'd lost. And now they wanted to execute him. Her boy. It popped into her head to wonder how Blair would take the news, but all thoughts of her ex-husband vanished at Evans's next words.

"Replace him."

"What?" Philip ran his hand across his head and patted the top of his ponytail.

Kelsey had an urge to grab his hands and hold them down, but she controlled it.

"I'm out one vamp. Replace him. I've got people you can turn. I'll pick one. We'll get the paperwork pushed through, and you'll turn him. Or her, as the case may be." He held up an index finger. "In fact, I know just the person."

Kelsey kept her gaze on Philip, suspecting whatever Evans said next would raise his ire even further. She spared a glance in Red's direction, verifying the vampire still held the gun on Philip.

"Annabelle Lawson has served her purpose as a human. I always turn my breeders when they're past their prime. She's not quite at that point yet, but she's proven more trouble than she's worth as a human breeder. She'll make a much more useful vampire."

A low growl started in Philip's throat and grew louder. His fangs broke free again, and Kelsey shifted so her body blocked his.

Red snickered. "I don't care which of you I shoot, sweetie."

Kelsey gave her a smug look. "He's stronger and faster than me. By the time the bullet hit me, you'd be dead."

The silent-until-now thugs snarled, drew themselves up, and pulled out weapons. Both trained them on Kelsey.

She snickered. "That won't help, fellas."

Philip had remained rooted to the spot during the entire exchange. What the hell was wrong with him? Why was he just standing there?

Hesitantly, she said, "Philip?"

"I'm not turning Annabelle Lawson." He stared at Evans. "Find someone else to do it."

Interesting. He didn't object to his ex getting turned, just to doing the deed himself.

"You're doing it. I want her under your, shall we say, tutelage? I want you as her sire. It would be fitting."

"No, it wouldn't." He retracted his fangs with obvious effort, and rage still distorted his face. "What makes you think Josh needs replacing? Have you heard something?"

The humans might have missed the grief in his voice, but Kelsey didn't. Likely, Red caught it also, but what that vampire heard, thought, or felt didn't matter.

"We'll find out shortly, which is why I wanted you here. Let's go."

Kelsey's stomach clenched. Something she hadn't

experienced since her human days. Her newfound conscience and compassion had sparked some other human traits. Part of her rejoiced; the other part of her despaired. Living as a narcissistic psychopath had its advantages. When you cared only about yourself, you worried less and experienced no emotional pain.

From outside the office came the sound of doors swinging open and footsteps entering the warehouse. Evans's expected guests had arrived, and there was a group of at least ten. Four were faeries. At least one was a vampire. Josh was with them.

CHAPTER 53

The new arrivals positioned Josh, restrained with silver manacles padded at the wrists and ankles, against the brick wall of the warehouse. When he spotted Kelsey and Philip, he gave them each a grim smile.

The leader of the faerie group dressed as royalty, but Philip didn't recognize him. It wasn't Culain, and Dakota wasn't with them either.

"What the hell is this?" Philip shouted. His fangs sprang out again, and beside him, Kelsey emitted a low growl and also bared her fangs. Both tensed, ready to spring when they noted three faerie archers lining up execution-style ten feet in front of Josh.

Frank Evans placed a hand on each of their shoulders. Both spun around to face him.

To his credit, the human didn't flinch.

"You're here to observe. Interfere, and you'll share his fate." To prove his point, he stepped aside.

Red stepped into the breach, her gun pointed once more at Philip. In a flash, another vampire joined her;

from where he'd come, Philip couldn't tell, but he dressed similarly to Red and held a duplicate weapon to hers, also likely holding silver bullets. This he trained on Kelsey. If either of them made a wrong move, they'd die. Neither Red nor her partner evidenced a hint of compassion. If anything, Red looked as if she dared him to try something.

He ignored her and turned his gaze back to Josh. His son—not by birth but by literal blood.

"Josh Davis," the fae leader said, "you stand convicted of high treason to your lands and the treaty shared between those on the Earth plane and those in the faerie realm. What say you?"

Kelsey interrupted. "He says nothing, you son of a bitch. What do you think you're doing?"

Evans cleared his throat and said, "One more word, and I'll have you physically restrained and gagged. Let the boy die with dignity."

Kelsey pressed her lips together. If a vampire could grow paler, she did so. Her eyes widened, and her hands fisted at her sides.

Just as Philip considered lunging at Red to give Kelsey the distraction she'd need to leap into the fray without getting shot, Josh spoke.

"I'm here of my own accord, Father." After meeting Philip's eyes, he turned to Kelsey. "Mom." His voice broke on the word. "I'm sorry. It's all my fault. I didn't let it go even though I understood the consequences. I must pay so you, Philip, and Dakota don't." He held his head up and turned to the fae leader. "Colin, I'm ready. Let's do this before I change my mind."

"No, please, he's just a boy." Kelsey's words, accompanied by the despairing tone, sounded incongruous coming from a vampire.

"Mom, it's okay. It's justice. I died once before. This time, I'll stay dead. Let me go."

She pressed a hand to her mouth but then dropped it. She looked over at Philip, who stepped closer to her and put his arm around her. No one tried to stop him, and he almost regretted it. Every move Evans's men or the fae group made tempted Philip to lash out at them. He turned his gaze to Josh, who met it with a steely, resolute one of his own.

"I'm not ready to let you go," Kelsey said.

Philip thought back to the day Josh had first faced death, how she'd refused to let him die—how the boy had resented her for it after Philip had turned him at her request.

"This time, we can't stop it," he whispered in her ear.

She straightened to her full height and thrust her chest and chin out. "I love you, Josh." No quiver marred the words, which came out clear and confident.

"I love you, Mom, Father." He held his head equally high. "I don't regret anything. I'd do it again."

Colin cut in then. "Archers, ready."

Josh's gaze met Kelsey's, then Philip's. "A son carries on the family legacy. Family is all."

Kelsey staggered forward, but Philip pulled her back. "No, he's not asking you to interfere. He can't be."

"Archers, aim."

Blood-tinged tears streaked down Kelsey's face, and she snarled, exposing her fangs.

"Steady." Philip pressed his lips to her ear. "We're not done here."

She trembled in his arms but stopped fighting him.

"Archers, fire!"

Three arrows twanged and hit their marks. Josh dropped to the ground.

Philip had witnessed a few vampire deaths over the years. None of them passed in an explosion of body parts and gore. They died as any other species died, and the swiftness or painfulness depended on the means.

At least one arrow hit Josh's heart because his departure was swift and probably pain free, but what did Philip know? He'd been shot once, true, and felt the scorch of silver on his skin, but he'd never experienced this kind of staking.

Kelsey tore from his embrace and raced to her son. She dropped to her knees beside him and pulled him into her arms, cradling him to her chest and covering his face with kisses.

No one stopped her or spoke until Colin said, "Archers, our work is here is done." He turned to Frank Evans. "As agreed, you keep the body." He gestured at Kelsey. "We aren't so cold as to deny a mother the chance to put her son to rest. I trust we won't see any further intrusions into the faerie realms."

The mob boss nodded. "Agreed."

As if they'd awaited that signal, the faerie group turned in unison and strode out the exit.

Philip watched them until the door slammed shut behind the last one.

Fangs out, he whirled on Evans. "You knew he'd returned to Autumnland, and you never told me?"

"Are you telling me you knew nothing of his visits there?"

"That's what I'm telling you." Which wasn't entirely true. Josh had snuck into Autumnland with Philip's knowledge and blessing once, the year before, to check on Dakota and verify she was content with her life there.

"I warned you what would happen if you interfered with the fae."

"You let them kill my son. I won't forgive you for that."

Evans shook his head. "What choice did I have? He brought it on himself. You all knew the consequences of trespassing. They had every right to judge and execute him. Interfering would've escalated this to international levels. You think the faeries wouldn't have exposed this? That they wouldn't have escalated to federal and World Alliance levels? All the species signed the Faerie Accord and agreed to strict noninterference in that realm."

Philip glanced over at Kelsey. She'd stopped crying but continued to hold and rock her son.

"You threatened that accord by selling my daughter to them." They'd hashed this out months ago, but he was in no mood to be reasonable.

"I'll give you two the rest of the week to bury him," Evans said. "Be back to work on Monday. Stay away from the fae. Your first task will be to replace Josh Davis with Annabelle Lawson. You're turning her, Belanger. That's not a request." He motioned to his entourage to follow him, and they disappeared back into the office, slamming the door on Philip, Kelsey, and the body of their son.

Philip raced to her side.

She stared up at him with bloody tearstained cheeks.

"I won't let this go," she whispered.

"No," he agreed, "we won't. But we'll have to bide our time."

"I want out."

For a moment, he feared she meant she wanted

away from him—after all, she'd lost not only her son but her sire. The ache of it must be all-consuming. He realized she meant she wanted out of their agreement with Evans. He agreed with her but ignored the comment. This wasn't the time or place to discuss betraying Frank Evans.

Her head dipped, and she kissed Josh's brow. She tilted her face up again. "I want to bury him."

He squatted beside her and stroked her hair. "Of course. Wherever you wish."

"They won't let me bury him on church ground."

The Catholic thing again. He couldn't understand her attraction to that religion. Most vampires despised God and the Church. Both had turned their backs on the whole species.

"Is it the soil that matters to you or that you want a priest involved in his burial?"

She frowned in thought. At last, she said, "I want to see Father Paul."

Philip regretted he couldn't sigh.

"All right." He patted her arm. "All right." After all, what harm could it do to ask?

CHAPTER 54

The dungeon doors swung open. Dakota rose from her cot and strode hopefully to the bars of her cell door. Three faeries approached, one of them Culain. A sob caught in her throat, but she refused to break down in front of them. She'd shed all the tears she planned to shed while they'd left her alone after they'd taken Josh away to execute him. They'd tried him without allowing her to observe the proceedings, which she considered a sham, but when they'd returned him to his cell after convicting him, he'd insisted the trial had been a fair one.

"I did what they said. I'm guilty," he'd told her.

It didn't ease her pain. She wanted everything to be different. For this to never have happened. To have refused to leave the faerie realm with him and visit Annabelle.

"I wouldn't change a thing except for returning that last time. I never should've come back," he'd insisted, and she realized she wouldn't have done anything differently either. They'd both known the consequences and committed the crimes anyway.

She was lucky she wasn't in front of a firing squad herself, but that added to her guilt. Without saying a word, Josh had demanded she keep her role in what they'd done a secret. Because she feared someone always listened in on their conversations, she never asked him what he'd done with Haydon. She could only assume he'd hidden his son somewhere safe.

When Culain and the two guards arrived, the guard in the lead approached her cell door. She took a step backward, afraid they were coming to take her to a trial that would see her convicted of treason. She swallowed past a lump in her throat and vowed they wouldn't see her anxiety. As the door swung open, she stood tall and defiant.

"You're free to return to our home, Dakota," Culain said.

She hesitated. Was he lying? Tricking her into stepping from the room so they could accuse her of trying to escape? She almost smiled at that. Culain needed no trickery. If he wanted her executed, he'd tell her to her face. She sensed no duplicity from him.

Even so.

"I don't understand," she whispered. She hadn't seen or heard from her husband in days. Guards had brought her meals, and a terror had grown in her with each passing night that he'd abandoned her.

"You're free to return to me, to our life. Do you want that?"

She couldn't believe the ordeal was over. Had Josh convinced them she was truly innocent in everything that'd happened? That she met with him against her wishes?

"Yes, very much," she said. "I love you. I've loved

you for a long time. I never wanted anyone else from the time we met." That, at least, was true. "This baby"—she pressed a hand to her belly—"our baby will bring us even closer together. We can be a family. Have more children." She hung her head but then raised it again because she wanted to see his eyes when she asked her question. "Do you want that?"

His icy expression scared her.

She gasped and took a step back.

"What I want is irrelevant. What I want—" He bit off the words, shaking his head. "The realm's needs come first. Our subjects don't know you're guilty of anything. After the vampire's trial, we've informed them you're *innocent*." He sneered as he said the word.

So he didn't believe her, didn't believe in her.

"The baby is ours."

"That much I know," he snapped. "It doesn't mean I forgive you for what happened."

With no reply to that, she turned practical. "Why are you releasing me? Why take me back? What's in it for the realm?"

"The realm needs a queen, and you're it."

"I'm not a queen yet," she whispered, afraid that admitting it would change his mind. He could divorce the princess, replace her, and the realm would have its queen.

Grief washed over Culain's face. "You will be soon. The day of our coronations approaches. My father is dead."

***

Agony crossed Dakota's face, and she gasped. Her hands fluttered as though she didn't know what to do with them, and she took a step toward Culain. The guard leaped to intercept her, but Culain put a restraining hand on his arm.

Dakota halted, clasping her hands together. "May I approach, my lord?"

Approach? Did she intend to touch him? He wanted that—yearned for it, in fact—but he feared her touch might make him forgive her, and he refused to indulge himself that much yet. His father's body still lay in state in the castle's main hall.

"You may," he said finally, "but don't touch me."

She flinched, but he didn't know how else to say it. If it hurt her feelings, so what? Did dhampirs have feelings? He immediately chastised himself for that thought. Maybe other dhampirs didn't, but Dakota sure as hell did. She was as sensitive as any woman, but she could be as stoic as any man. Even now, when he'd verbally wounded her, her eyes remained dry and showed only compassion.

She swept to his side, close but keeping a few inches between them. "I'm so sorry. What happened to King Killian? You and Colin—and your subjects—must be devastated."

He glanced at the two guards. "Wait at the doors."

One left immediately, but the other stayed to protest. "Your Highness, I'd feel more comfortable at your side."

"I'm fine. Do as I bid. If Dakota wanted to harm me, you wouldn't be able to stop her."

The guard nodded but remained in place and turned his gaze on the dhampir. He lifted his bow and slotted an arrow into it. "I'll watch from the door. Be warned, my aim is true and my arrows silver."

"I'd never hurt my husband," she replied.

The guard left, taking his place silently on one side of the door, his bow raised and the arrow pointed directly at Dakota.

Culain allowed it. Let her see they didn't trust her. She'd have to work hard to return to his good graces and harder still for those close to him to forgive her.

When they were alone—or as alone as they could be outside their bedchamber now that he was king—Culain met Dakota's eyes. He trusted her enough to believe she wouldn't glamour him, and that was something.

"They found my father dead in his bed yesterday morning."

"I don't understand. Faeries are immortal." She released her clasped hands, and they curled and uncurled and fluttered around her as though searching for somewhere to land. With obvious effort, she kept her promise not to touch him.

"As much as vampires are, yes." He buried his face in his palms for a moment, then returned his gaze to her. "He was murdered."

"How?"

Culain scanned the room, searching for evidence they were overheard. The two guards maintained their positions by the door. No other prisoners were held nearby. These dungeons held only high-level prisoners, which was why they were more comfortable. Any listening devices—magickally operated—were in the cells, not in the hallway where they stood. Still, he kept his voice low and conspiratorial, leaning slightly into her so she could catch his words.

"The coroner suspects poison."

"How? I thought your food was carefully prepared and tested."

"So did we. We haven't learned what type of poison was used, but whatever it was escaped our testing."

She paused, opened her mouth, and closed it again. "What is it?"

"Maybe nothing. I ... you've probably thought of it, anyway."

"That someone slipped it into his food during dinner?"

She nodded, her face betraying her distress. "I don't want to believe it. Was that meal served in the dining hall?"

"Yes." They'd had no feasts since Dakota's arrest.

"Did he eat anything after the meal, something no one else had? A bedtime snack or drink, perhaps?"

Culain almost smiled. She spoke like a true sleuth. A strong desire to sweep her into his arms and cover her in kisses washed over him, but he squelched it.

"We can't be sure. If he did, there's no evidence of it." He was grateful that, when his father had died, Josh was already on his way to his execution and Dakota was locked up. No one could lay suspicion on either of them. A small blessing, but a blessing nonetheless.

Touching her at last, he linked their arms. He ignored the startled yet relieved look she threw him and led her from the dungeons. They had far more to discuss, and he needed the privacy of their bedchamber.

CHAPTER 55

Josh's funeral was held in a remote corner of the church cemetery under the cover of darkness. It lacked a service and a coffin, and the only attendees were Kelsey and Philip, who dug the hole themselves. At least Father Paul agreed to say a few words. He spoke as if entranced—because he was. Kelsey had glamoured him. By morning, he'd remember nothing of what he did that night. After the priest finished speaking, Kelsey escorted him back to the rectory while Philip waited at the gravesite.

"Thank you, Father," she said before he climbed the stairs of the front porch. She stood in the shadows in case Father Michael looked outside. He knew nothing of what had transpired. He'd have opposed it, and if he found out after the fact, he'd probably dig up Josh's body and burn it.

"You're welcome, my dear." His voice came out dreamy.

She held his arms and positioned him so they stared into each other's eyes. "Go inside. If anyone asks, tell them you went for a walk. It was refreshing, but you're tired. Go straight to bed; sleep well. You'll wake up refreshed and happy." She released him. "Goodnight, Father."

He smiled. "Goodnight."

She watched him walk inside and sped back to Philip. She found him sitting cross-legged beside the disturbed earth of their son's final resting place.

"Father Paul okay?"

"Yes, he's home safe."

She dropped next to him and hugged her knees to her chest.

He put an arm around her. "Blair?"

She listened to the night sounds around them: crickets, an owl's hoot, the drone of cars in the distance. Earth scent filled her nostrils, but under it, she detected the rot of Josh's body.

Kelsey shook her head. "He wrote off Josh the moment he became a vampire. I invited him, but he refused to come." It didn't bother her. In fact, it simplified things. "Why didn't you ask me this before?"

He shrugged, jiggling her shoulders with the movement. "I figured I'd find out when we got here. Telling him was your business."

"And you're asking because?"

"I want to know where he stands, darling. If you kept this secret from him, I need to know—to help you keep it hidden."

"Thank you." She appreciated his thoughtfulness. He was always considerate of her needs. Hearing him call her darling, the endearment she'd resented when they'd first met, increased the affection that had developed once more for him. She'd missed that sensation and welcomed it back. "I'm glad he didn't come. If he cared, he'd ask questions." As it was, they owed Evans even more now. He'd taken care of the legal paperwork related to Josh's death. An electronic copy of the death certificate already sat in Kelsey's inbox.

Clouds scudded across the sky, blocking out the crescent moon and the stars. The air was probably cold. If she were human, she'd shiver.

"We should leave." She said it reluctantly and made no move to rise. Here, under Philip's protective arm, she felt safe and at ease. The moment they walked away, reality would strip it all away.

"Evans will pay; I'll make certain of it." His fangs snicked out with a soft click.

She angled her head so she could see his expression, and as soon as their eyes locked, he dropped his lips to hers. They kissed, long and deep, and part of her wanted to screw right there beside her son's freshly filled grave.

Their location must've dawned on him because he pulled abruptly away. His lips remained slightly parted, and if he hadn't been a vampire, she was sure he'd be panting.

"Sorry," he said. "I didn't intend that. Completely inappropriate, under the circumstances."

"You're forgiven," she replied. "When were we ever appropriate?"

They rose then and went home to their condo at vampire speed.

When they arrived, Kelsey rushed straight into Josh's room. She hadn't entered it since his death, but she wanted to know if he'd left behind clues about his activities these last few days or weeks. He'd visited the faerie realm without her knowledge. What had driven him there?

A son carries on the family legacy. Family is all. What had he meant? He'd said it even though he knew he was about to die.

She strode to his desk and searched through drawers and papers. Nothing of interest there. Some artwork. He'd made a lot of sketches of various lakes and of shipwrecks lying on the bottom. She had no idea he could draw. There was so much he'd kept hidden from her.

A sound behind her told her Philip had entered the room. "I'll help you clean out his things."

"Later. First, I want answers."

She shifted to his bookcases. He had two tall ones, both filled with books; mostly horror, science fiction, and fantasy, but also plenty of non-fiction about history and archaeology. Some shelves displayed knickknacks, most looking as though he'd salvaged them from shipwrecks. Wasn't there a law that mandated reporting such finds to the authorities?

She picked up a sextant, examined it without seeing it, and set it down again. "He spent a lot of time scouring sunken ships. He frequently went out. When I questioned him about it once, he mentioned visiting the lake." She put a hand on Philip's arm. "He went there a lot, based on what's here, but he clearly also entered the faerie realm during some of those outings, or he wouldn't be dead."

"What are you hoping to find?"

"I don't know. I guess I'll know it when I see it." She returned to searching the bookcase while Philip wandered over to the dresser. She listened with half an ear as he opened drawers, rooted around in them, and then shoved them closed.

"Kelsey," he said.

She raced to his side, reacting to the urgency in his voice.

"Dakota's hairpin. Barrette. Whatever you women call them."

She examined it. Pretty. Simple style. It looked familiar, but she'd probably seen Dakota wearing it when she came to the store. "She could've given it to him any time."

"No. He took it from her after she went to the fae. She was wearing it in that video Evans gave us when we were hunting for her."

Kelsey held it up. Philip was right. It'd seemed familiar to her because the girl had indeed been wearing it in the video—which meant Josh had to have entered Autumnland to get it from her. "They didn't lie to us. He didn't lie to us. He went multiple times." Anger at him had crept into her voice.

How could they justify getting revenge on Frank Evans when Josh had done exactly what they'd convicted him of doing? Even though he'd admitted it, she'd hoped he'd lied, perhaps to save Philip, Dakota, and herself. She sank to his bed and pressed her face into her palms. The silence dragged on, and she finally lifted her head to meet Philip's gaze.

"We can't do a damn thing about his death. They didn't murder him. They were in the right."

Philip sat next to her and took her hands in his. "Yes, he did it." He frowned. "Doesn't mean I agree with the punishment they meted out. He caused no harm to them other than trespassing. Why should that be punishable by death? Lock him up, sure. For years, if they felt justified, but execute him?"

"He knew the risks, and he did it anyway. We all

knew the risks. That's why we forbade him to return."

They sat in silence for a moment.

The night outside the window lit up suddenly as distant lightning flashed. Thunder followed seconds after. She strode to the window, keeping a safe distance from the glass. Vampires attracted lightning, and unwary ones caught out in such storms often died from a sudden strike. It always made the vampire newspapers. Sometimes, he human media reported the story though with much less sympathy than contained in the vampire media reports.

They'd returned home just in time.

The rain hadn't broken yet, but the gray clouds scudding overhead promised it. The wind picked up, swaying tall plants on neighboring balconies.

"Yes, Josh knew the risks," Philip finally admitted. "I guess, for now, we're stuck with Evans, but I swear to you, we won't be his slaves for much longer."

"A storm is coming," she said and left the room.

CHAPTER 56

Their bedchamber hadn't changed since she'd been locked up. Dakota wasn't sure what she'd expected—perhaps she'd assumed Culain would remove every bit of her presence—but it remained the same as when she'd left it. She took that as a sign he'd expected her eventual return. As it happened, he'd been prudent to leave her things alone.

The bedroom door thudded shut behind them, and they were alone at last. The guards remained on sentry duty, but at least they stood outside of the room. She'd feared they'd insist on accompanying them inside. As it was, they'd searched the room thoroughly, closets and under the bed included, before allowing Dakota and Culain to do more than wait inside the entrance.

Unsure what he wanted now that she was no longer a prisoner but still distrusted, she strode to the couch and sat. She gazed up at him questioningly. When he frowned and she sensed he wanted to escape her presence, her hand fluttered to her breast, and she stifled a gasp.

"Talk to me. Please," she said.

He remained standing, but at least he responded. "It'll take you a long time to regain my trust even with Josh ... gone."

She flinched but remained silent, afraid that interrupting him would make him fall silent.

"Oh, I have a lot to say to you. I'm not about to clam up now." He could always guess what she was thinking. She loved that about him. Their past closeness had felt reassuring, like a favorite throw you curled up on the couch with. While she no longer felt close to him and she'd do anything to recover that, at least he could still read her as if he were her best friend.

"I want to hear it." She rose, because he continued to keep his distance, standing across the room in front of the closed door. She longed to feel his arms around her, to make love to him. How long before they recovered what she'd thrown away so thoughtlessly?

Maybe never. The thought terrified her.

"We're to stay married." Hesitancy laced his voice. Did he wish he could divorce her?

"Okay," she said, simply to prevent another silence from descending on them.

"My advisers insist on it. They maintain it'll keep the peace in the realm if we create a united front."

"I don't have to pretend. I'm with you. All the way." She stood and involuntarily took a few steps toward him, but he waved her away.

"Not yet. I ... I can't." He glanced at the bed as if seeing it for the first time. "I'll sleep on the couch."

He didn't want to touch her. But when he'd escorted her to the bedchamber, he'd held her arm. *For appearances. For the sake of the guards.*

An ache grew in her heart, and tears sprang to her

eyes. She refused to let them fall. She deserved this. After all, she'd betrayed him and now must deal with the fallout.

Dakota bowed her head. "Yes, my lord. As you wish."

"We'll eat meals together, and for all intents and purposes, we'll play the happy couple."

Her silence meant her agreement, but inside, she vowed to get him back. He loved her still; she was certain. They'd become the happy couple they once were, and then they wouldn't have to playact. For her part, she wouldn't be acting, anyway. They were already halfway there!

"The child matters the most—more than any relationship between us. We'll need a spare, of course." His vague tone implied he spoke more to himself than to her. "It'll mean having sexual relations again, but we won't have to worry about that until after this baby is born."

That struck her to the core, and she averted her face so he wouldn't see the tears welling in her eyes. She deserved this, she reminded herself. Her betrayal had wounded him probably more than he was wounding her right now. His hurt had been so deep he'd believed she'd cheated on him with Josh. How would she have felt if she believed he'd cheated on her?

"Shall I go to my quarters, Your Highness?" If he didn't want her around, she'd stay out of his way. Perhaps missing her would help him return to her.

He frowned. "The servants are packing up your private quarters. You'll move in here completely."

She gasped. He was taking away her sanctuary. Her place to sit and read or get away from the entire family, her husband included—not that she'd used the space to escape his company in the time she'd had it. "Culain, please, you don't have to do that. Why do that when you don't want me around you anyway?"

"Appearances. I indulged you with separate quarters, hoping you'd eventually give them up on your own. Look what it got me. Talk among our subjects is that you used it to meet your lover."

Tears of rage flowed then. "That's a lie. I never slept with Josh. You're the only man I've ever been with."

"I'll say it again: appearances, Dakota. We live in a castle. It has plenty of rooms, including multiple libraries, you can retire to for privacy. You'll never get another opportunity to make me look the fool. This is one way to prevent that. I can't control you, not completely, but I can control your environment and what you have access to." He checked the time on his pocket watch. "I have business to attend to. Whenever I'm not with you, the guards or a female servant will keep you company. You'll not be alone again." He strode to the door. "If you plan to stay here, I'll have one of the guards summon Lysandra. Otherwise, they'll escort you wherever you want to go."

He tilted his head and waited for a response.

She had nowhere to go. "Send for Lysandra."

He nodded and left without another word to her.

When the door shut behind him, she indulged in a few tears but not for long. Lysandra would appear soon. The girl shouldn't see her mistress crying.

Dakota went to the dresser where she kept a spare deck of tarot cards. Time to do another reading.

She carried the deck to the sofa, shuffling the cards after first settling her emotions. She placed three cards, face up, on the coffee table: The Three of Swords; The Empress, not reversed this time, thank the gods; and

The Emperor, reversed, which elicited a gasp of despair from her.

Her eyebrows rose at that last one. The Empress and The Emperor were cards III and IV of the Major Arcana. In their current position, they represented the present and the future, respectively. The Three of Swords signified the past.

How appropriate. The Three of Swords showed a bright red heart, three swords jammed through it, representing betrayal. In the background, storm clouds and rain signified tears, quarrels, and separation. On a larger scale, it could signify political upheaval.

Dakota scrubbed her face with her palms, tired of it all. She and Culain hadn't discussed his father. She'd forgotten, during their distressing discussion, that her father-in-law was dead. *Murdered.* How would this affect the realm? How would this affect the Shiels family? Colin would face more pressure to marry. Perhaps now that his father was dead, he could get permission to marry Alina. They clearly loved each other, but King Killian had desired a more suitable match for the prince.

Uneasiness crept through her. Colin had something to gain from the king's death. *You don't know that for sure. Culain might also forbid the marriage.* Nevertheless, she stored the information for later retrieval. She'd ask him about it. At least he was still speaking to her even in private.

I'll win him back, she vowed once more.

Still, the card represented the past's influence and accurately reflected what had transpired between her and Culain and certainly the betrayal that ended King Killian's life.

The Empress card was obvious. She'd drawn it

before, and the empress, seated on her golden throne and representing the goddess Demeter, continued to influence the present situation. It was yet another card that symbolized rain though not the storm the previous card heralded. It obviously didn't represent infertility for her, as she'd feared the last time it'd appeared in her reading. The last time, it'd landed reversed, which might've indicated material loss and, on a larger scale, famine or war. She and Josh had risked an international incident with their recent actions. It was only by Culain's grace the faeries hadn't made a public show of Josh's trespasses. Dakota herself would have shared his fate had her husband accused her of leaving Autumnland or having an affair with the vampire. That she was guilty of one crime but not the other didn't matter. What mattered was the accusation made public.

Unease again radiated through her. Culain had something to gain from his father's death. Had King Killian's death allowed the prince to release Dakota from prison? What if the king had demanded her execution?

No. Culain never hinted at anything like that—and he loved his father. She was letting her imagination take control, but she filed the thoughts away for later anyway. After all, someone had betrayed the royal caravan to the kobolds when they were on their honeymoon tour. Someone might be plotting against the whole family, and the king's death was a part of it.

Dakota rubbed her temples. Power came with a lot of paranoia. Now that she and Culain were the realm's rulers, they held the power and attracted the enemies that came with it. *It's not paranoia if they're really after you.*

She moved on to the next card. The Emperor represented future events. It signified male dominion, a complement rather than an opposition to the empress. The emperor, like the empress, sat on a golden throne. In her deck, both thrones had red cushions. This card represented power and war. Were the fae and the Earth plane moving inexorably toward war? Was it her fault?

Stop it. You're catastrophizing again. She mentally took a step back from the large-scale ramifications and focused on her situation. It was all about masculinity and leadership. Culain certainly fit that description in her life, the emperor incarnate. He headed not only their little family, but he'd become the entire family's patriarch and the kingdom's ruler. Her whole life had changed in a heartbeat. Their honeymoon tour seemed so long ago.

The card spoke of protection, not just of war, but it had landed reversed. That upended all its positive qualities. What would the future hold for them? Issues with an inheritance. War could result in injury. She shook her head. What difference could one person make in a world going to hell?

She collected the cards and shoved the deck back into her dresser drawer. She'd always believed she had autonomy, control over her own life. Then her mother had sold her to the fae. Ever since then, her belief in her power to control her destiny had vanished. She refused to accept that. Refused to stop fighting for her rights, fighting for what was right. She was married to the realm's most powerful man. She'd overcome the negative future outlined by a reversed Empress card. She'd do the same for The Emperor. Whatever fate had in store for them, Dakota vowed to have a hand in the outcome—after all, wasn't that what free will was for?

CHAPTER 57

"Come," Culain said tersely in response to the knock on his office door. He sat behind the desk that used to belong to his father, feeling both intimidated and incapable. How was he to rule the entire realm? His father had raised him for it, but they hadn't expected him to assume the role this quickly. King Killian should've ruled for many more years.

Colin entered the room and strode to stand in front of the desk.

"The deed is done, Your Highness," he said, bowing to his older brother.

Though Culain had expected the formal verification of Josh's execution, it still shocked and numbed him. Grief pushed the numbness away. He'd never wanted that boy to die. He'd only wanted Josh to leave Dakota alone and never enter Autumnland again without invitation. An invitation he'd never have gotten, but that was incidental. The kid had trespassed. The penalty for that was death.

"Thank you. I appreciate everything you've done to get a speedy resolution to this, brother." He closed the report he was working on and rose from his seat. "Any news on Father's murder?" The words felt strange on his tongue. *Father's murder. Mother's murder.* Was his family getting picked off one at a time? Was he next? Or Dakota, since of his parents, his mother had been killed first.

"The suspicion is a guard turned traitor."

Culain frowned. "One of your guards?"

"I'm afraid so."

"What makes you think that?" *Dakota was right.* He stifled the "told you so" that threatened to burst out.

"Godric Wagar, the guard captain, vanished around the time Father died. He's not anywhere in the castle."

"He accompanied us on the honeymoon tour." Culain frowned, recalling the kobold attack. He tried to remember where Godric had been in the fracas and couldn't. "You might be right. What would he gain from this?"

"For now, that's his secret to keep, but we'll find him, my lord, and he'll answer for everything he's done."

"Thank you. Double the guard on myself and Dakota. Make sure all our food is tested thoroughly before serving."

Colin gave a head bow. "As you wish." He turned to leave, but Culain gripped his arm.

"Be careful, brother. They may not stop with me. If I die without an heir, they'll come after you."

Colin nodded, but his expression was unconcerned. "No worries there. I've already taken steps to improve security and surveillance. Believe it or not, Josh Davis helped us shore up the holes we'd left that allowed him to enter the portal."

"I believe it." Damn the boy for committing the crime and forcing Culain to punish him so lethally. But if he'd ignored their laws and excused Josh, what kind of leader would he be? He'd begin his ruling term weak and pliable in the eyes of his subjects. "Sometimes good men die when they commit serious crimes."

Colin grinned. "He wasn't a man, but I get your point." He stared his brother in the eyes and then clapped him on the back. "We'll forge ahead. You'll make a great ruler. Don't doubt yourself."

How did he know? "Am I that transparent?"

"Only to me, but it'll be our little secret."

For the first time in days, Culain cracked an inadvertent smile and felt his tension ease. "Thank you—again."

They parted, and as the office door closed on his brother, Culain returned to the desk, ready to rule.

***

Days had passed since Josh Davis deposited baby Haydon with Patrick, and the lycan wondered if the vampire kid would ever return. The baby had grown, as Josh had predicted. Initially appearing six months old, he now seemed about a year. He toddled around, chasing Fool, Patrick's West Highland White Terrier, around the cabin. The dog rarely minded, but the dhampir boy always got too rough, and Patrick had to watch the pair closely to make sure the dog didn't become baby chow.

All in all, his stress levels had increased and, while he wanted to keep Josh's secret, he also didn't want to keep Josh's kid. As it was, he'd already had to steal clothing to keep the child from bursting out of his baby clothes.

Imagine me raising a kid! He chuckled at the idea, the first good laugh he'd had since the little dhampir had entered his life. *Laura would get a kick out of it.*

Thinking of his sister sobered him up. He hadn't seen her in months and not because she hadn't tried to visit. Before Haydon had arrived, he'd put her off because he didn't want to listen to her unasked-for advice. Now, he wanted to prevent her from learning of the child's presence, never mind that it belonged to Josh. The last time Laura had encountered the vampire youth, Philip had erased her memory of the event. It wouldn't do to risk triggering remembrance by bringing up Josh, Philip, or Kelsey. Laura and Kelsey had met around the time Philip's daughter disappeared and the vampire ruined Kelsey's life.

As if she'd sensed her brother's thoughts on her, his phone sounded with Laura's ringtone. He yanked his cell from his shorts, verifying her name and number displayed on the screen.

Great. Like I don't have enough problems. He considered letting it go to voicemail but answered it on the last ring. With a glance at the baby, who currently napped at one end of the couch, Patrick said, "Hello," keeping his voice soft.

"Patrick?" Laura sounded puzzled. "Is that you?"

"Yes." He growled low in his throat, the desire to speak quietly battling with the desire to be heard.

"You'll have to speak up. I think we have a poor connection."

Patrick's jaw clenched, and his lips peeled back from his teeth. With another glance at Haydon, he strode into his bedroom and closed the door.

"This better?" He sat down at the bistro table he used as a desk.

"Yes."

"What can I do for you?" His fingers drummed on the tabletop. *Make your point and hang up.* He oozed impatience and hoped she picked up on it.

"We haven't met for one of our lunches in ages. You promised me when you moved out there that I could meet with you at least once a month. I don't even expect to visit the cabin. The least you could do is meet me at a pub in Bancroft." Her tone was a mix of hurt and anger, making him feel guilty.

"I know. I'm sorry." He had no excuse—at least, he'd had no excuse before Haydon. He couldn't exactly bring the kid along to a lunch with Laura. "I've been ... busy," he finished lamely.

"Busy!? With what? You don't work."

He brushed a hand across his curly brown hair in exasperation. *Butt out, Laura.*

"I have responsibilities," he said. *Patrol, keep the local druids in line so they don't sacrifice anyone or anything they shouldn't.*

The species of druid that appeared during the unmasquing was a different breed from the peace- and nature-loving human druid that had evolved over the centuries on the Earth plane. This hypernatural version had magickal powers and medieval beliefs and superstitions. Laws kept them reined in when they lived among the regular populations, but those who'd hidden themselves in the isolated hypernatural communities fell into their old ways. Somehow, Patrick had become the forest's law enforcement, and what he enforced didn't fall under the rubric of human law.

Hypernaturals had separate laws, and the humans

allowed them to police themselves to a degree. In turn, the hypernatural community permitted humans to police their own at the local level. From there, state laws came into effect and then federal laws, followed by international laws. The law and government had grown more complicated following the species wars— not that they'd been simple before.

The residents here accepted and appreciated Patrick's leadership, many of them referring to him as "Sheriff." Some paid him a tribute, but he never asked for or expected it.

Laura needn't know any of this, though, and telling her would likely end in an argument. She was his younger sister, but ever since the pack had banished him, she insisted on nurturing him—which was more than his own mother had ever done. Male lycans got tossed from the family den to fend for themselves at a young age. Every mother hoped her son would be the next alpha, and that meant showing off his strength and independence. Patrick had moved out on his own at sixteen. Less than ten years after that, the pack had banished him when he killed the alpha's mate. Except the killing was only an excuse. They'd really banished him for his telepathic and precognitive abilities. Most of them feared him after they learned he could read their minds or predict their futures. They considered him a pariah after that, afraid he'd intrude on their privacy or learn their dirtiest secrets. He'd accepted the punishment willingly. If anyone preferred the lone-wolf lifestyle, it was Patrick Growley.

That thought reminded him of the boy sleeping in the next room.

"I can't have lunch with you. Give me a week." Surely, Josh would return by then.

"Why?"

"I told you, I'm busy." His voice held a low growl. He considered hanging up on her, but knowing her, she'd interpret that as an admission of trouble and show up at his door, ready to help.

To stave that off, he said, "What's happening with you? You still seeing that human?"

It bothered him whenever she showed signs of falling for a human. Long ago, his intuition had told him she'd become involved with a human who'd bring trouble into her life. When she'd appeared at Patrick's door with Blair Davis in tow, searching for Kelsey, Patrick had treated the human with suspicion and contempt. So far, things had remained casual between Laura and Blair, who just happened to be none other than Josh's father and Kelsey's ex-husband.

"Yes, but we're not serious." Her voice held a tinge of regret, raising Patrick's ire. "These last few days have been tough for him. His son is dead."

Patrick sucked in a breath, and chills shivered his body. "What son?" *Please have more than one son. Please, not Josh.* But he didn't need psychic powers to figure out she meant Josh.

"Well, he has only the one. Josh. Remember him? Everyone thought he was dead, and then one day, he and his missing mother reappeared. He'd been turned into a vampire." She said that last with distaste. Lycans and vamps weren't exactly enemies, but they weren't best pals either. Both preferred to maintain a distance from one another. Laura had confessed to Patrick once that she was glad Blair had disowned his son, but his death might raise some guilt over that.

"Yes," he said tightly. "What happened?"

She told him as much as she knew: Josh had tangled

with the fae, and they'd executed him for breaking their laws. It was all legal. So far, it'd been kept from the media to prevent blowback from the vampire or human community. The faeries governed themselves and lived apart from the Earth plane, but not everyone believed they deserved such autonomy when all others had to adhere to international laws and participate in world politics.

Patrick allowed the growl to escape this time, and it'd barely faded when he heard the thud of tiny feet hitting the floor.

Damn. He'd awakened the kid. He brusquely told Laura he had to go and disconnected while she was in mid-sentence. *I'll deal with her later.*

He left the bedroom to face his charge. He scooped Haydon up and carried him to the kitchen to find something to eat and figure out a course of action, which soon became obvious.

Patrick set Haydon at the table on top of a stack of books on one of the kitchen chairs and patted the lad's head. "Time to meet your grandparents, kid," he said.

CHAPTER 58

A week had passed since Josh's burial. For Kelsey, nothing had yet returned to normal and, vampire though she was, she grieved over the loss of her son. She pretended to Philip and anyone else she interacted with, especially Frank Evans and his associates, that she'd accepted what'd happened, but inside, she seethed. The more she dwelled on it, the greater grew her desire for the faeries to pay for what they'd done. The only problem was, how could she blame them when Josh was guilty?

The impasse worked away at her nerves, and she'd been moody and miserable for days.

This day found her cleaning the apartment, despite the housekeeper having done so the previous day.

They'd boxed up Josh's possessions, keeping only those things Kelsey felt, while not sentimental about, attached to because they were mementos of their lives together. Most of his possessions they'd donated to charity. His bedroom became a spare bedroom though who might stay with them remained a mystery.

Philip suggested they turn it into a library. She wasn't opposed to having a room dedicated to books and reading, but she wasn't quite ready to release all traces of her son's presence.

She was deep in the middle of scrubbing the kitchen floor when she froze, her senses picking up a sound and a scent from the hallway outside the apartment door. Was that a child's laugh? The smell of lycan?

Kelsey whizzed to the door and threw it open.

No lycan in sight, but his overpowering scent still lingered. He'd been out there, all right.

Before her stood a toddler, about a year old. Chronologically, he was probably younger, since he was a dhampir. Not only did her vampire senses tell her that, but he bore a lapel pin on his sweatshirt. She saw no bag or possessions around him. Nothing indicated who he was or why he'd been left at her door. While Kelsey had always denied having any intuitive abilities, something told her that this related to Josh.

She noticed then a piece of paper sticking out of the boy's sweatpants and yanked it out. The boy goggled at her in silence, as though sensing something momentous.

She opened the paper and read.

Kid belongs to Josh. Name's Haydon. Can't keep him. Sorry.

"Well," she told the boy. "Short and sweet." Now that she knew he was Josh's, she could see the slight resemblance, which was probably why she'd suspected the connection. Her throat constricted, and her eyes welled up.

She scooped up the child, a rush of nostalgia making her want to sob. She stifled the urge and carried him inside.

Philip wasn't home—off doing something illegal for Frank Evans, probably. Each continued to keep their errands for the mob private. It was safer that way and allowed them to avoid discussing a situation both found distasteful and unbearable.

She carried the boy into the apartment to await her partner's return.

***

Night had fallen two hours before. Philip strode to the door of Annabelle's house and rang the bell. In his other hand, he held papers Evans had procured, stating Annabelle desired of her own free will to become a vampire. Who'd actually filled them out and signed them Philip didn't know and didn't care. His job now was to break the news to his ex and turn her—whether she wanted it or not.

The door opened silently, and Annabelle stood before him.

She looked good. Sexy, yes, but despite how hard she desired to appear classy, she always came across as trashy. She wore a formfitting minidress, her dark hair loose and flowing. As always, she wore a multitude of rings, bracelets, and a necklace. Her earrings dangled almost to her shoulders.

"What are you doing here?"

"Annabelle." He bowed sarcastically. "Always a treat."

"Even so. Did Evans send you?" Her eyes grew wide with fear, and she made a move to push the door shut.

Philip shoved it open wide and brushed her aside. "None of that." The door slammed behind him, and he locked it.

"Get out." Her voice trembled, but she daringly pressed her hands to his chest and shoved.

He remained rooted to the spot.

Giving her a nasty smile, he said, "Nice try."

When he pressed the papers into her hands, she automatically accepted them. She looked down at the completed forms in a daze.

"What the hell is this? Are you suing me?"

He gave a despairing laugh. She thought he was serving her legal papers. In a way, he was.

"I wish."

Her hands still trembling, she read the first page. As realization dawned, her eyes grew even wider, and her olive skin blanched. Tears sprang to her eyes.

"What? No! Why? Why?"

"You think I want this?" He'd have to live in her house. He hadn't told Kelsey. Somehow, he thought he could juggle living in two places at once until Annabelle could live alone. The prospect of raising another baby vamp exhausted him, though, and shortened his temper. He'd come to get this over with.

Philip leaped onto Annabelle and bit into her throat.

***

Dawn found Kelsey putting Haydon to bed in Josh's old room. The boy seemed to accept her as his caregiver, and while he'd been energetic and rambunctious through the night, he'd remained cheerful. He wound down as dawn approached and allowed her to settle him into the bed.

Philip hadn't called, which wasn't unusual, but it irritated her this time because she craved to tell him about their grandson. It'd crossed her mind to tell Blair, but she'd decided against it. She wanted to tell Philip first. He'd take it better than Blair would.

Not sure if she should leave the child unattended while they slept, she lay down beside him and went to sleep.

It felt as though she'd barely slept when a hand on her shoulder woke her. Her eyelids flew open, and she grabbed the arm attached to it, ready to fling the interloper across the room. At the last moment, she recognized Philip. He stared down at her with such intensity she almost laughed. The sight of the sleeping child had likely confused him. She didn't blame him for waking her.

She carefully extricated herself from Haydon's embrace—he'd somehow wrapped around her—and slipped from the bed. They left the bedroom, shutting the door, and strode into the living room.

Philip wasted no time.

"Who's the boy?" He kept his voice a whisper. Dhampirs didn't possess vampire-level hearing, but it was still better than a human's.

"Our grandson. Josh's child. Someone left him at our door." She didn't know how else to tell him, so she blurted it out.

"Are you sure it's his?"

"I see the resemblance, but we can certainly verify with a DNA test. Either way, I couldn't leave him standing in our hallway." Did that sound defensive? She hadn't meant it to, but it wasn't as if she didn't plan to verify the kid's identity.

"A son carries on the family legacy. Family is all," he said. "Christ on a tortilla, he was trying to tell us he had a son."

She pressed a hand to her mouth, her eyes widening. Of course. He couldn't say it outright, or Evans would've jumped all over it. Josh had probably hoped his vampire parents would track the boy down and take care of him. Luckily, whoever had sheltered him hadn't bothered to wait for them to figure it out.

"We can't let Evans know," she said.

"Agreed. He'd want to sell the boy."

"We don't know who the mother is."

"Everyone's DNA is on file. I can get that information, but I'll have to do it on the sly. We don't want anyone figuring out we have him here." Philip placed a hand on Kelsey's shoulder. "I've got a lot to deal with right now, and the less you know, the better."

She nodded reluctantly. She understood, but that didn't mean she liked it. Yet she always kept her jobs a secret from Philip, too.

"God, I hate this life."

He tucked a finger under her chin and tilted her face up so their eyes met. "I still love you, Kelsey, even if you don't feel the same about me. I promise to take care of you and help you escape this prison. We'll be free one day. Do you trust me?"

Affection for him filled her, and she recognized the stirrings of love. "I do trust you," she whispered. *I love you.* She didn't know why she kept that unsaid except that she wanted to avoid raising his hopes. What if this wasn't really love? What if it was just the circumstances? Some kind of Stockholm syndrome that made her believe she loved him?

"It'll get better; I promise." He stroked her hair, and she drew closer to him, allowing him to embrace her.

She swept her arms around him and hugged him tight. "I believe it will."

Philip had brought her into and out of hell, had taken accountability and responsibility for everything that had happened since they met so long ago in her store. He'd made mistakes along the way—they both had—but he always tried his best to keep her safe and make things better.

She drew back and met his gaze again. "I'll help you do whatever it takes."

Somehow, simply saying the words made the world feel brighter. They'd had the storms. Now it was time for the skies to clear, and as long as Philip was by her side, they could handle anything.

"I love you," he said again, and their lips met in a passionate kiss filled with hope and promise.

Can't wait to dive into more tales from the unmasqued world? Watch for the next exciting installment, *The Emperor: The Cross of Life*, coming soon.

If you enjoyed *The Empress: A Promise of Rain*, won't you please take a moment to leave me a review?

ABOUT THE AUTHOR

Val Tobin lives in Newmarket, Ontario, with her husband. After ten years in the computer industry programming web and software apps, she now spends her days writing, reading, and searching for the perfect butter tart. Her educational background includes a diploma in Computer Information Systems from DeVry Toronto, a B.Sc. in Parapsychic Science from the American Institute of Holistic Theology, a M.Sc. in Parapsychology from AIHT, Reiki Master/Teacher certifications, and Angel Therapy Practitioner® certifications.

I really appreciate you reading my book!
Visit my website for contact information and to sign up to receive my newsletter: www.valtobin.com

OTHER BOOKS BY VAL TOBIN

Fiction

Paranormal Sci-Fi Thrillers

The Valiant Chronicles Series

Earthbound (prequel): A spirit becomes earthbound after refusing to cross over in order to solve her murder and prevent more deaths, some of which might be predestined.

The Experiencers (book one): A black-ops assassin atones for his brutal past by helping an alien abductee escape capture.

A Ring of Truth (Book Two): A rogue assassin triggers an apocalypse when he attempts to rescue a group of alien abductees.

The Valiant Chronicles books are also available as a complete set in e-book and paperback.

Romantic Suspense

Injury: A young actress at the height of her career has her personal life turned upside down when a horrifying family secret makes front-page news.

Gillian's Island: A socially anxious divorcée confronts her greatest fears when she's forced to sell her island home and falls for the dashing new owner.

About Three Authors: Poison Pen: Three wannabe authors suffering from various mental disorders find love in unexpected places when they interfere in the investigation of a colleague's murder.

Forever Young: You Again: Complications arise when an accounting tech is assigned her former lover as a client and his company's previous financial controller is found dead.

Paranormal Romance

Walk-In: A young psychic woman fights an attraction to a handsome but skeptical novelist while she battles a power-hungry sorcerer determined to make her his next conquest.

Horror Suspense

The Hunted: A Storm Lake Story: A monster hunter revisits her terrifying past while helping a reporter uncover the origins of Storm Lake's creatures. A stand-alone sequel to the short story "Storm Lake," *The Hunted* takes place twelve years later.

Urban Fantasy

Tales from the Unmasqued World Series

The Fool: New Beginnings (book one): A newly divorced woman suffering a midlife crisis gets involved in the search for a missing half-vampire teen.

The Magician: Infinity's End (book two): After getting expelled for setting a demon loose on campus, a student mage searches for the real culprit and finds his troubles have only just begun.

The High Priestess: Persephone's Return (book three): Stuck in the spirit world, Jaycie struggles to find a way out. But others want to keep her there forever. Will she make it out of Hades alive?

The Empress: A Promise of Rain: Dakota Lawson seems to have it all: beauty, intelligence, wealth, and a prince of a husband. But her past just won't let her live happily ever after, and when it comes calling, she risks losing it all.

Nonfiction

Angel Words by Doreen Virtue and Grant Virtue
Val contributed a story to Doreen and Grant Virtue's *Angel Words: Visual Evidence of How Words Can Be Angels in Your Life*